Praise for Anne Louise Bannon and Fascinating Rhythm

Fascinating Rhythm is reminiscent of Agatha Christie or Dorothy Sayers' novels of the time period. A very nice story to cozy up to a fire with and imbibe. Legally, of course.

Literary R&R

Those who love a great (who-done-it) mystery will enjoy Fascinating Rhythm.

Sheri Wilkinson

JuniperGrove.net

Praise for Tyger, Tyger

I like Bannon's main character, Brenda, enough to follow her anywhere. Her boyfriend (no! wait! they're "just friends") trains animals for the movies, and between Brenda, the BF and his tiger, "Sweetness," they are a fun, crime-solving trio. I enjoyed this book.

Petrea Burchard
Author of Camelot and Vine

THAT OLD CLOAK AND DAGGER ROUTINE

ANNE LOUISE BANNON

Healcroft House, Publishers

Published by Healcroft House, Publishers, a subsidiary
of Robing Goodfellow Enterprises.
2591 N. Fair Oaks Ave., #408
Altadena, CA 9001
626-502-7416

ISBN # 978-0-9980838-0-3

Cover by Tatiana Vila

DEDICATION

When I first wrote That Old Cloak and Dagger Routine and the books that follow, I was, like Lisa Wycherly, a young woman trying to figure out my values in a rapidly changing world. Thankfully, I had walking with me some truly wonderful priests and sisters who taught me to love first and ditch the judgmentalism. Sadly, religious like them are few and far between these days. So this one is for them – may you always preach love.

PROLOGUE

'Twas Glasnost what done us in. That and a CIA mucky-muck with a chip on his shoulder. All those years of guarding our secret, and now we're on overt status. Quickline has folded, a victim of the thawing cold war.

At least my journals can see the light of day. I started them shortly after I was first adopted by Quickline. It was a dangerous and perhaps even stupid thing to do. But my life had suddenly and profoundly changed. I needed some way to understand it and the person I was becoming. The things I was doing were so unlike the person I'd always thought I was and the values I'd spent so much time working out. As it turned out, my values weren't challenged. Just me.

Anyway, all the names have been changed, and some of the places. Secrecy remains a habit with us. Still, as I look over the pile of tattered notebooks and binders stuffed with pages scrawled over with cipher, I'm glad I wrote it all down. [Dear Lisa, so am I – SEH]

September 10-13, 1982

My name is Lisa Wycherly.
     I live with my boss.
     I'm not sleeping with him. He's got enough women in and out of his bedroom. He doesn't need me.

Oh, Lord, that sounds so defensive.

It's just that, thanks to my boss, my life has radically changed, and I still don't know how to make sense of it all. Things got just plain scary last weekend, not to mention that horrible fight, and I'm still more freaked out because I'm sharing a house with a man. Okay, maybe not that I'm living with a man, but this man, a guy whose values are so totally opposed to my own when it comes to sex and relationships.

Maybe I should just start at the beginning.

Neither of us knew what we were getting into that night. [And let's be thankful we didn't. -SEH] We were in a bar, the absolute last place you'd find me under normal circumstances. He sat down across from me.

"Ditched your date?" he asked, pleasantly casual.

He was very nice for someone so obviously on the make, and good looking with dark wavy hair, a cleft chin, and very bright blue eyes. He wore a light-colored silk shirt with a sweater neatly tossed over his shoulders. Later, I found he was on the small side of average, about three inches taller than me, but just barely.

"Yes," I replied, as coolly and politely as possible. "And thank you, but I don't care to be picked up by anyone else."

He glanced into the restaurant of which the bar was a part.

"Well, I suppose getting grabbed while starting your salad is enough to sour an evening." He started to get up. "My apologies for presuming, Lisa."

"Wait."

He sat. "Yes?"

"How did you know my name?"

"You're wearing it around your neck."

My hand flew to the necklace as I let out a sniff.

He gazed at me softly. "Are you in trouble?"

"I'm alright!" I snapped, then blushed. "I'm sorry. I don't mean to be rude."

"But you are in trouble."

"It's nothing life-threatening."

I felt the tears well up again. And I'd thought I was past crying about it. I blinked them back and looked at the man across from me. There was something about him...

"I've been out of work for a year," I heard myself say. "My unemployment's run out, and things are getting tight." I touched my necklace. "This is the only thing I haven't pawned."

He nodded. "No money for a taxi, I presume."

"I'll be alright. I can call my sister."

"Who is not currently home, at least I assume that's who you called earlier."

"They won't be home 'til eleven, and they're in Fullerton."

"And we are in Hollywood." He checked his watch. "Which means you've got a long wait. Why don't I buy you dinner and take you home?"

I sighed. It was certainly my night to fend off aspiring Don Juans. Except the current one was anything but sleazy. In fact, he was the first genuine threat to my honor that I'd ever known. Wouldn't you know, that's the moment my date decided to show up.

"Wo, there you are, Lisa." Larry was not wearing a leisure suit, but he might as well have been. "You were taking so long. I thought I'd better make sure you didn't fall in."

"I survived the restroom, Larry," I said.

Even though I wanted to fend off the man across

from me, I still felt embarrassed by Larry.

"It's a pleasure to meet you, Larry," said my nameless friend. He got up smoothly and shook Larry's hand. "Lisa and I go way back. We haven't seen each other in a while, and I just had to have a chat with her."

"Well, the waiter brought dinner," Larry said to me.

"Oh, that's too bad," said the nameless one. "Lisa's coming to dinner with me." He signaled the maitre d.' "In fact, our table's ready now."

"Now, wait a minute!" protested Larry. "Lisa—"

Larry made a grab at me. My benefactor stepped between us and put his arm around Larry's shoulders. They spoke together quietly for a minute. I couldn't hear over the music. [I told him blind dates were a drag, and that I'd take you off his hands, and put him onto Sue Wilkins if I remember correctly. - SEH]

"Happy hunting," my new friend said. He slapped Larry on the back, then slid around and took my hand. "Come on, Lisa. He won't hold that table forever."

I went with him. I don't know why I did, but I went with him. Larry gaped at me, then at some redhead. I didn't see what happened next. The maitre d' seated us in a nice, secluded booth, and my friend slipped him something.

The maitre d' grinned. "Thank you, sir."

"You're welcome."

I put my face in my hand. "You didn't have to do that."

"It's my pleasure." My friend smiled, and there was something utterly sincere about it.

"What about Larry?" I asked.

Mischief lit up in those incredible eyes of his. "That desperate little dork is getting the fate he so richly deserves."

"What do you mean?"

"The redhead at the end of the bar." He nodded in that direction.

I peeked around the booth. I couldn't see the bar.

I turned back to him. "She isn't going to dump him, is she?"

My friend laughed. "Hardly. In the first place, she's so easy he won't know what to do with her, and in the second, should he figure it out, she's into S and M."

"That's... Oh no!" I started to get up.

"Let him be." His hand landed gently on my forearm.

"But—" I sat down.

He sat back and folded his arms. "The jackass drove you from a salad you desperately wanted, felt you up in a public place, he's crude and he thinks he's God's gift to women."

"Just because he's a jerk doesn't mean he deserves to get hurt."

He looked at me. "Are you serious?"

"Of course, I'm serious."

He shook his head. "Well, relax. She won't hurt him. Unless he asks, and that's a different matter, isn't it?"

I slumped back into my seat. "I guess it is. I don't know. I'd always heard pleasure was the idea."

"It's not how I get my kicks, but who are we to judge?"

"True." My face felt fever hot. "Do you know if he's left yet?"

"They left just as we were sitting down."

"Good. I'd better be getting back to the bar." I almost got up again.

"Why? Don't you want dinner?"

I swallowed. "Yes. But I don't want to get any deeper in."

"It's nothing." His smile was, again, genuine and warm.

"A maitre d' at a place like this does not grin at nothing."

"You're hungry." He looked puzzled. "I saw you attack that salad with the ferocity of a starving child."

"How do you know that's not the way I always

eat?" Which, in truth, it is.

"I also saw you slide two dinner rolls into your purse."

I blushed again. "Alright. I'm hungry. Like I said, things are tight. But I'm not hungry enough to compromise my standards."

He shrugged. "This is merely a philanthropic gesture."

"I've heard that before."

"I don't doubt it. Well, I'll confess to ulterior motives."

His manner was relaxed, his grin casual. But his eyes had an intensity that made me catch my breath. I could see he would not trespass without my permission, but he would be happy to convince me to give it.

"Look, it's not you," I stammered. "You seem really nice, and I really appreciate your being honest about it, and the way you got rid of Larry, and it's very sweet of you to offer, but I just don't believe in sex outside of marriage."

"Don't you want dinner?" He seemed genuinely surprised.

"Yes, but... Well, I just can't. Larry was a blind date, and the friend who set me up knows how I feel, and I told him how I feel, and he ignored it, I guess. Anyway, I don't have any money, and I can't give you my body, so..."

"I can accept that." He looked at me again. He was considering something, unrelated to the messing around, for once. "Can you accept dinner and a ride? I promise I won't touch you."

"Sure, if you really want to." I shrugged and he nodded at the waiter.

"What's your name?" he asked after I'd ordered. "I mean, your full name."

"Lisa Wycherly. Yours?"

"Sid Hackbirn."

"Oh. What do you do for a living?"

"As little as possible."

I grimaced. "Not funny."

It was almost imperceptible, but he winced. "I suppose not. Apologies. I do some occasional freelance writing and dabble in the stock market. Just enough work to maintain a comfortably high standard of living. And you?"

"Well, I was a teacher."

"Was, huh? Hmm." He considered again.

I don't why, but it made me nervous. After I'd eaten, he put me in a taxi, gave the driver my address, and I thought that was the last I would ever see of him.

I was wrong. Still, I didn't regret it when Mr. Hackbirn showed up on my doorstep three days later.

"What are you doing here?" I asked, with the door opened only as far as the chain would let it.

I wasn't particularly surprised that he was there. I'd thought I'd seen heads of dark wavy hair following me in the previous days. I wrote it off to my imagination, but it did make his appearance less of a shock. Besides, I had other problems just then.

"I'd like to talk to you," he said.

"Right."

"I'm serious. I have a business proposition for you, and nothing more."

"Alright." I shut the door, removed the chain, and let him in. "The worst you can do is kill me."

He chuckled. "I like that attitude."

"The place is a mess," I said, sighing over the boxes and stuff all around.

"You're packing." He shifted the vest of the discreet three-piece suit he was wearing.

"I'm being evicted." I choked and grabbed for a tissue.

"Going to your sister's?"

"For a couple days. Then, Neil, he's my brother-in-law, he's going to help me move to Tahoe. I'm fleeing to the security of the womb."

"Not your preferred option."

I fought back the tears. "Well, Mae and Neil don't

have the room. They've got five kids. It won't be so bad. I'll be working. My dad has a business up there."

"A resort and a souvenir store, I believe."

"You've been there?" I was a little more surprised at that, but I'd met people who'd been to my parents' place before.

"Not really. I stay on the Nevada side when I'm there."

I turned on him. "You've been poking into my private affairs!"

"I prefer to call it research."

"I call it nosy."

"I reserve the right to gather basic background information on a prospective employee."

That caught me. "Mr. Hackbirn, are you offering me a job?"

"Yes. I need a personal secretary to take over the mundane trivialities of life." He smiled. "You impressed me last Friday with your backbone."

"I don't understand."

"You are a person who sticks to her convictions even when there's strong temptation not to. That's a very difficult quality to find in people."

"I don't type very well."

His eyebrow lifted. "A master's degree and you don't type?"

"Not very fast. I stayed up late a lot of nights." I looked him over again. "Just how much do you know about me?"

He shrugged. "Basic facts. Your college background, your year of community college teaching, things like that. You got excellent references from your former employer, by the way."

"Let's hear it for budget cuts." I sighed. "What makes you think I'm going to take a chance working for you?"

"I'm offering an excellent salary and a place to live, neither of which you have at the moment."

"I do so."

"Independent of your parents?" He shook his head. "That is what you find most galling about going back there, and don't think I don't know it."

I looked away. "So where is this place to live?"

"My house. I will need you to live in."

"Sure." I snorted. "Now, I get it."

"Miss Wycherly, I assure you, I have no time to waste on virgins with standards. This is a business proposition, nothing more."

"I still feel like it's an elaborate plan to seduce me."

"If you really want to think so."

He smiled a truly sensual smile. I blushed and swallowed and tried to control the way my heart was racing. He was mulling over the possibilities of bedding me by sundown. He could have done it. But he wouldn't unless I said yes, and I knew that I could trust him not to. In fact, his job offer seemed to be the answer to all the prayers I'd been offering. A really strange answer, to be sure, but my gut said that it was the right one.

I smiled. "Alright, it's not. Why don't we talk some terms?"

They were attractive, to say the least, and included my own rooms and guaranteed time off to go to church on Sundays. We dickered for an hour. Finally, I shook his hand.

"I guess I can take my chances with you," I said, happily.

Mr. Hackbirn sighed. "Miss Wycherly, before we call this final, I'd better tell you. I wanted you specifically because I need someone with guts. I can be a dangerous person to know."

"Mr. Hackbirn, I'm not a thrill-seeker. But danger beats stifling hands down. Don't get me wrong. I love my parents, and they wouldn't hold me back intentionally, and I'll probably end up running their businesses when they retire, or whatever. But with them... Well, you get the idea."

He got it. I was the one who didn't have a clue. I called my sister and told her about the eleventh hour save.

"What are you going to do about your landlord?" Mae asked.

"Well, I'm moving." I looked over at Mr. Hackbirn. "I found a new place right away."

"What about first and last months' rent?"

"Um. My new boss said he'd loan me the money. He's taking it out of my check."

Mr. Hackbirn smirked. Maybe he had a right to. All I knew was that I didn't want Mae talking me out of it. I told her I'd phone her with the address and phone number as soon as I was settled in and hung up.

"Mae's a nice person," I explained awkwardly. "But she gets judgmental sometimes, and you never know when."

"I see. Well. Why don't I call the moving company? We'll get them straightened out, and then you can come over to my place and start today."

I took a deep breath. "Okay."

There really wasn't much left in the apartment except my clothes, my books and other odds and ends. Anything of value I'd pawned or sold, even my trusty old sewing machine. The movers arrived a half hour after Mr. Hackbirn called them from the pay phone down the street. While we waited, I tried to find out about my new employer. He was pleasant but evasive. I didn't realize it until some days later when it dawned on me that he hadn't answered one question I'd asked him about himself.

His car is a dark slate blue Mercedes Benz 450SL, one of the first ones they ever built. I had expected something a little newer, although not necessarily flashier. One thing that was obvious about Mr. Hackbirn, he had excellent taste.

He also has plenty of money to spend. His house is in Beverly Hills. I was in awe as we rolled up the steep driveway to the gray ranch-style house at the top of an ice plant covered slope. The place had been built in the early sixties and looked like it.

We went in through the bare garage. There's a small utility room to the right of the garage door, with the kitchen and breakfast room just beyond that. The breakfast room is a sunny yellow with a white French provincial breakfront, table, and chairs with light green upholstery on the seats. The kitchen door was closed.

"We don't go in there unless Conchetta is gone for the day," Mr. Hackbirn said.

"Conchetta?"

"My housekeeper and cook. She prefers to be left alone."

Mr. Hackbirn then led me to the small suite of rooms on the other side of the breakfast room.

"This will be your space," he said, opening the door. "Feel free to decorate it in any way you like. In fact, I can have my decorator come in and confer with you."

The outer sitting room was a large open space with a writing table on one wall and a huge sofa upholstered in an ugly shade of eggplant. There was a small oak coffee table that didn't match the sofa, and a small waist-high bookshelf, as well. I went on through the door to the bedroom and bath.

The bedroom was very nice. I really liked the comforter decorated with small red and blue flowers on nice green stems. The bed was brass, too. My bedside tables and dresser were white French Provincial, and the walls had been painted a soft light blue. The bathroom matched, with fluffy blue towels. My closet, which had mirrored sliding doors, was huge.

I put my box down on the dresser and set my lone suitcase next to the bench at the foot of the bed.

Then it was time to see most of the rest of the place. It looked like a model home or something out of a magazine. Mr. Hackbirn, or his decorator, really liked period furnishings. The formal dining room was Eighteenth Century, the rest of the place tended towards Victorian and lots of oak.

The library was sheer heaven. Books lined all

four walls, and there were two burgundy velvet wing-backed chairs, each with a good reading lamp next to it. There was also an ebony baby grand piano.

"Do you play?" I asked Mr. Hackbirn.

"Sometimes," he said.

The offices were also oak paneled. I think they must have been one room in the past because to get to Mr. Hackbirn's, you must go through mine. My desk was modern, and it had a computer to one side, with two printers next to it. There was also a green leather couch on the opposite wall, sliding glass doors to the front yard on the side, and four oak filing cabinets with five drawers each.

The phone rang. Without hesitation, I went over and picked it up.

"Mr. Hackbirn's residence, Miss Wycherly speaking," I told the caller.

"Already?" answered the man on the other end. "Is Sid in?"

"I'll see. May I tell him who's calling?"

"Mr. Henry James."

There was a hold button, and I pressed it. It was a multi-line phone, and it looked like Mr. Hackbirn had three lines hooked up.

"It's a Mr. Henry James," I told him.

He sighed in relief. "Miss Wycherly, I appreciate the way you screened that call, but in the future, under no circumstances are you to identify yourself, or this place as my residence."

"Should I call it your business?"

"Don't identify it at all. A simple hello will do. I'll take the call in my office. Why don't you start getting the files in order, then I'll show you how to work the computer."

The file cabinets were empty except for the first one. That was loaded with papers randomly tossed in. Almost all of them were clippings of articles from magazines and newspapers. Mr. Hackbirn was certainly well read, and given the number of different newspapers I found, got around. Traveled a lot, I mean. He gets around a lot the other way, too. But that has nothing to do with the clippings.

After his call, it was lunch time. Mr. Hackbirn explained that we would eat the majority of our meals in the breakfast room and that he generally avoided work talk at the table. The plates were set out on the table when we came into the room.

Lunch was chicken salad with butter lettuce, whole wheat toast made from homemade bread and a fruit compote. The portions were on the small side, but I was in no position to complain. I was done quickly. Mr. Hackbirn told me to leave the dirty dishes on the table. Then it was back to the office where Mr. Hackbirn showed me how to boot up the computer and the different programs on it.

I played around for the next few hours until it was five-thirty and time for dinner. Again, the plates had been set on the table when we got into the breakfast room. There was grilled mahi-mahi, salad with vinaigrette, fresh steamed zucchini, brown rice, and small portions. Mr. Hackbirn, it seemed, was on a diet.

Not that he said so. Nor did he comment on the fact that I was done eating in a few short minutes. It's not obvious because my mother did pound good manners into me, but I tend to wolf my food down.

"You should feel free to watch television in the rumpus room if you like," said Mr. Hackbirn, trying not to notice how fast my food was disappearing. "Or if you prefer, I can arrange to have a television put in your room."

"I don't watch much TV," I said between bites. "I was wondering about the library, though."

"Help yourself. To any of the common areas. I'd just as soon consider you a housemate outside of business hours." He paused. "Although, you might be more comfortable if you make a habit of knocking first before opening any closed doors."

"Well, of course. I—" I stopped. "Oh. Yeah, you

might be right."

Mr. Hackbirn chuckled, then looked at me. "One more thing. I would appreciate if you'd not leave the house for a week or two. Just until we're settled in with the arrangement and all."

"Oh." I frowned. "I was going to go shopping on payday. All I have is one suit, and you did say business wear during office hours."

"That's right. I did. I think I can arrange that. Why don't you go Friday afternoon? We can put together a more detailed plan that morning."

I nodded. It seemed a little weird. So, the guy was kind of eccentric. I didn't have any place to go, anyway. I agreed to stick around.

Once Mr. Hackbirn had finished eating, he got up and collected our plates and silverware.

"Come on," he said, nodding at the kitchen door. "I'd better show you how to load the dishwasher."

"Okay, but I have loaded dishwashers before." I followed him into the beautiful tan and black kitchen with gorgeous almond-colored appliances.

Mr. Hackbirn chuckled. "No. It's how Conchetta wants it loaded."

I looked at him, puzzled. "Aren't you her boss?"

"Yes, and she makes that perfectly clear. That being said, she puts up with surprise guests and other small messes. I give her full rights to the kitchen when she's here."

Conchetta's system wasn't that hard to learn and actually made a lot of sense. As soon as we were done, I went to my rooms. I have no idea what Mr. Hackbirn did.

Later that night, while unpacking some of the several boxes of my stuff that had been delivered that afternoon, I found a Complete Works of Shakespeare and thumbed through just for the heck of it. In the second scene of Julius Caesar, a line jumped out at me. It was Cassius': "Therefore it is meet that noble minds keep ever with their likes, for who so firm that cannot be seduced?"

Well, me, for one. Then I thought back to that morning and that really hot little smile of Mr. Hackbirn's. Alright. Maybe it was possible. But I wouldn't go down without a fight. And what the heck was I doing there in the first place?

For the rest of that week, I was pretty busy. Tuesday morning, I didn't have anything specific to work on, so I played some more. Mr. Hackbirn had a database program he wasn't even using. Just for the fun of it, I indexed his clippings on it, then cross referenced it all to the file folders. Mr. Hackbirn can't find a thing without me. Talk about making yourself indispensable.

Tuesday afternoon I got my first article to word process, a piece on the F.B.I. The sheets of binder paper were a mess. Not only was the handwriting cramped and angled funny, any crossed out words were completely blacked out. At least there weren't any arrows. When I finally deciphered it, I saw why he didn't do a lot of writing. The points were logical and flowed well, but his grammar and spelling stank. I knocked on his office door and entered.

"Uh, Mr. Hackbirn, would you mind terribly if I cleaned this up a little?" I asked.

"What do you mean?" he asked back.

"Just little things like spelling corrections."

He let out a rueful chuckle. "It's not so good, is it?"

I winced. "Your grammar's pretty bad, too. It's mostly just sentence structure. You state your case well, and it flows together beautifully."

"That's right. You got your degrees in English."

"Well, literature. But... Yeah."

The phone rang. There was something funny about the way the line on his phone lit up.

"Miss Wycherly, would you please excuse me?" Mr. Hackbirn put his hand on the phone but waited to pick it up. "And make sure the door is shut on the way out."

I left, shutting the door. Sitting back down at my desk, I looked at my phone. None of the lines were lit.

And there were only three hooked up. I picked up the fourth line. Nothing. Yet a fourth line had lit up on Mr. Hackbirn's phone.

Mr. Hackbirn came out of his office in a hurry.

"I don't know how long I'll be gone," he told me as he rushed past. "Go ahead and eat dinner without me."

"Where are you going?" I asked.

"Out." And he was gone.

I shouldn't have. It was his office, and how he chose to live wasn't really my business. On the other hand, I was dying to know. I told myself that it could affect me. I went into his office and picked up the phone and pressed the button for that fourth line. I got a dial tone.

That was as far as my nerve got me. The next day I noticed something else that was funny about the phones. It was Wednesday night, really. Mr. Hackbirn has the same three-line phone that I have on my desk in every room in the house. I was in my sitting room and picked up to call my sister without noticing which button I'd pushed. The conversation I heard was intimate. I slammed the phone down, then fretted because he had to have heard me slam it, and then had to explain, and...

The next morning at breakfast, I apologized.

"For what?" Mr. Hackbirn asked.

"Well, I accidentally picked up your line, and you were talking. I didn't listen very long."

He chuckled. "I can imagine. Don't worry about it. I had no idea you were on."

"You must have heard me slam the phone down."

"No." He went back to his paper.

"You mean you can't tell if an extension is picked up?"

"Can't hear a thing. Unless you speak, of course."

I mused. "Makes it real easy to spy on someone. Hey, you're not listening in on my calls, are you?"

He flipped down a corner of his paper to look at me.

"What do you think?" he asked in a bored, but amused tone, and went back to reading.

It was odd, but, hey, the guy was an eccentric. I let it pass. That morning, I stumbled onto all his personal papers, like his birth certificate. He was born in New York City to Sheila Hackbirn and an unknown father. A death certificate had been filed for his mother when he was two. She'd died of massive cranial injuries. There were papers giving Stella Hackbirn, aunt and only living relative, custody of him. Those all had been filed in New York.

There was a report card from a public school kindergarten in San Francisco. Mr. Hackbirn was a bright little kid, and had a mind of his own, much to his teacher's chagrin. I found a few notes from what I guessed were schools. They were all called Free-something-or-other and were not too interested in structure. Well, that accounted for the lousy grammar and spelling. Then there were four years' worth of report cards from San Francisco High School. His grade point average was none too shabby. The comments, for the most part, decried his inappropriate behavior. [Gee, I wonder what that could have been – SEH]

Then I found his draft notice and army papers. He served two years in Vietnam, which surprised me. He made corporal and was honorably discharged. There were some more grade reports, this time from Stanford, with a diploma. He graduated summa cum laude with a B.A. in business and a minor in journalism. I don't know how he did it with his grammar and spelling. [There were several girls who didn't mind helping me. – SEH] And finally, the deed to the house in Beverly Hills.

Was it nosy? I figured it was my right to gather basic information on my employer. Not that it told me much about the man, himself. He kept me at arm's length, responding to my questions without answering them.

Friday morning, Mr. Hackbirn asked me for a

detailed list of my plans for my shopping trip.

"Why?" I asked.

"I might be able to drop you and meet you some places," he said. "It'll be faster than taking the bus."

"Okay."

We set out at about twelve thirty, right after a fabulous gazpacho, with wheat toast and melon for lunch. Good food, just not enough of it. We stopped first at his bank so I could open my accounts since I'd closed mine when I no longer had money to put in them. Then we went to a discount office supply store. Mr. Hackbirn was appalled until we went to the regular price place to get the things that we couldn't get at the first place. He remained appalled but admitted it was kind of silly to pay full price for the same items offered at the discount store.

Then we went to a huge appliance store on Wilshire, where I bought a sewing machine. Mr. Hackbirn offered to buy it for me, which I refused. I did let him co-sign for the payment plan, though, threatening dire consequences if he even tried to pay it off.

Next stop was the Beverly Center. It was Mr. Hackbirn's idea to go there. He groaned when I went straight to the Broadway sale racks.

"You don't have to stick around," I told him. "I'd just as soon shop by myself."

"I can stay," he said, then saw something. "On second thought, I think I will take off."

I looked in the direction he had but didn't see anyone, male or female. He went in the opposite direction, anyway, so he wasn't chasing someone. I couldn't figure out what he'd seen that had changed his mind.

The man was unobtrusive, with sandy hair, glasses, sport shirt and jeans. In fact, I couldn't be sure he was the same guy I'd seen at the food court. I left the mall and went across the street to the fabric store. I was so absorbed there, I didn't notice him. But I did as I paid.

I walked up the block to the bus stop. He watched the shop windows. I changed my mind and walked down Beverly Boulevard. He just happened to be coming my way. I did an about face and went back to La Cienega. Out of the corner of my eye, I saw him scramble into a doorway. At the corner, I put on a sudden burst of speed and just barely caught the bus. Through the window, I saw my shadow running up, looking for me.

I changed buses twice. I had planned to visit some shops I knew of in Westwood but changed my mind. Instead, I ended up at a strip center in Brentwood, and there was no way I was going to pay those prices. That left only one more errand. I got on a bus headed east on Sunset.

It was a nice, conventional little church, with a school and a hall. The sort of church your parents grew up at. It was also almost a mile away from Mr. Hackbirn's house, but I still figured I could walk. So, I registered there and got the mass schedule.

I didn't see him that time. Just an odd glimpse or two, but someone was again following me as I left. I could have cried. I had that big, heavy bag from the fabric store, and a couple others from the mall, too. I all but ran up to Sunset.

I had to wait for the bus. No one approached me. I still couldn't shake the feeling that I was being watched. Mr. Hackbirn's house is a good hike in from Sunset, also, with really steep hills. I was so tired, I didn't care if I was being followed. I promised to save my next paycheck for a car.

Mr. Hackbirn was in the front hall, waiting for me as I entered.

"Where have you been?" he demanded.

"I gave you a list this morning," I gasped. I dropped my bag and stumbled into the living room. I could see the street from the window. It was empty.

"What are you looking for?"

I flopped onto the couch. "It's weird. Ever since I met you, people have been following me. All last

Saturday and Sunday, I kept seeing someone that looked like you. Then today, at the Beverly Center, someone else starts in. I ditched him, go to register at church, and then someone else is following me again. Either I'm getting paranoid, or something strange is going on."

"You seem awful short of breath." Mr. Hackbirn looked me over thoughtfully.

"It's a hike up that hill."

"What kind of exercise program do you have?"

I looked at him. "Me? I attribute my excellent health to a complete avoidance of physical exercise and a steady diet of junk food."

Mr. Hackbirn winced. "I was afraid of that. Well, Miss Wycherly, that changes tomorrow morning. After breakfast, I will drive you over to my health club and sign you up. Monday, you will start martial arts training."

"What? Don't I get any say in this?"

"No. It's a condition of your employment. I need you in top shape."

"Why?"

He paused. "So you can keep up with me. Dinner is ready. Let's eat."

True to his words, Saturday morning found us first at the sporting goods store for workout clothes and shoes, then at the health club. I was in pretty bad shape. I used to hike a lot, and camp, and ride horses when I lived in Tahoe. While I was in college, I worked up there during the summer and did all that stuff then. I hadn't done much of anything since my first year of teaching. I was so stiff Sunday morning.

I made it to mass on time. Walking home, I got that creepy shadowed feeling again. I turned a corner, then hid. Sure enough, around the corner came Mr. Hackbirn. I whirled around and almost smashed into him.

"Alright. This is too much," I shouted. "What are you doing, following me?"

"Uh..." He fumbled for an answer. "You said you were followed Friday. I was just seeing if you had reason to be concerned."

"You are so lucky that the last thing I want to do is go back to Tahoe." I stalked off towards his house. "What is going on with you? I mean eccentric is one thing, but this is ridiculous." He walked next to me and didn't answer. "Don't you trust me? What am I going to do to you? Am I supposed to be setting you up for a robbery?" He still didn't answer. "Well?"

"It seems to me that is a rhetorical question."

"Hmmph."

"Perhaps it would be better if you just remained at the house. I appreciate the inconvenience. But in the first place, you won't have to worry about being followed, and in the second, I won't have to worry about you being followed."

"For how long?"

He sighed. "I wish I knew, Miss Wycherly, but it shouldn't be too much longer."

Monday morning, I started running with him. Mr. Hackbirn runs for an hour every morning. I walked. He shook his head, and walked with me, pushing me to a run every so often.

After breakfast, we visited Mr. Fukaro at his dojo on Melrose. That seemed ridiculous, too. So did getting a mace can for my key ring, including the certification. Mr. Hackbirn insisted. It beat stifling in Tahoe, and it was nice to know I could fend Mr. Hackbirn off, should he try anything. He wasn't about to.

That afternoon, he hovered over me at the UCLA research library. Wonder of wonders, someone wanted to look at an article he'd offered them. He told me a friend of his had typed the query letter and cleaned it up.

Wednesday morning Mr. Hackbirn showed up for our run very stiff and with a nasty bruise on his left cheekbone.

"What happened to you?" I asked, swallowing.

"Never mind," he grumbled.

"Are you alright?"

"I'm fine."

"What did you do? Run into a door or something?"

"No," he replied curtly.

"It wasn't one of your girlfriends, was it?"

"No such luck." He stopped as he saw my shocked look. "I told you, I'm not into S and M."

"I wasn't thinking that. I just figured you must have been mugged. Did you call the police?"

"Miss Wycherly, enough. I do not care to discuss it."

"But..."

"No more." He took off.

And he meant no more. I'd learned that much. Right after lunch, we were working on the article he'd written the day before.

"I've never heard it before," I told him. We had the article laid out on his desk, and I leaned over him. "And I can't tell what it means from the context unless there's a word missing in there. Either your pen leaked, or you didn't write in the word you decided to use instead."

"Mont Blanc makes the finest writing instruments and inks in the world," he said. "Nor is there a word missing. It's a basic concept when it comes to funds."

"Yeah, but would your audience know it?"

He thought. "Good point. How to define it..."

He leaned back in his chair. The phone rang. It was that fourth line. I dove for it. His hand got there first.

"Miss Wycherly, you are not to answer that line, under any circumstances, even if I am not here."

"What is it?"

"A private line. Now, leave, and shut the door."

I left. He didn't seem angry, but there was something deadly serious in his voice. It scared me. I wanted to know, and I didn't want to ask.

I did my best not to think about it. I had a job. It paid well. The food was good, if sparse. And it was a nice place to live. The rumpus room had a large screen TV, and a VCR, and a superlative stereo system that could be piped throughout the house, thanks to the intercom system. There was a full wet bar in there, too, which I didn't mess with. My rooms were lovely. The library was great. The living room had a fireplace and cozy overstuffed furniture.

I did spend a lot of time sewing. Patterns and pieces of fabric don't get you much cash, so I'd hung onto those. Friday night, it was getting late. I stopped sewing, and got into my nightgown, then poked around in one of the boxes I had yet to unpack. I found several cassette tapes and an old Panasonic cassette recorder. Laughing, I put in the tape I'd made of the Sergeant Pepper's album way back when I was in high school. It was my best friend's record, and we'd taped it on her dad's hi-fi set.

I danced as the guitars twanged and beat on pretend drums. I took the tape recorder with me into the bedroom, only to find that the Nero Wolfe novel I was reading was not on my bedside table. I'd left it in the living room. I didn't want to stop my tape. I was having too much fun regressing. I found the ear plug, and plugged it in, so I wouldn't disturb Mr. Hackbirn if he were hanging around somewhere.

It wasn't likely. He was out most evenings. I assumed he was off chasing women. I didn't expect to find him in the living room, and I really didn't expect to find him naked as a jay bird with his hands all over an equally naked woman with full brown hair. See, the living room is open, with a really wide doorway and no door.

I yelped and scrambled into the hallway. Mr. Hackbirn's date also screamed.

"What the hell?" yelped Mr. Hackbirn. "What are you doing up?"

"What are you doing in there?"

The woman laughed.

"What does it look like?" asked Mr. Hackbirn.

"I meant why are you there? There's no door."

"I thought you were asleep. Why the hell aren't you? It's after ten."

"I came to get my book."

"It's no wonder you're so dead in the mornings."

"Can I have my book? It's on the coffee table."

"Come on in. We're not doing anything."

"You're in your birthday suit!"

"You're a grown woman. Haven't you ever seen a naked man before?"

"No. And I don't want to." I put my hand in the doorway. "Will you just hand it out, please?"

I didn't look. The book ended up in my hand.

"I'm sorry I surprised you. I hope I didn't stop anything."

Mr. Hackbirn snickered. "You wouldn't have."

My face flushed fire hot as I fled.

I spent most of Saturday afternoon trying to convince Mr. Hackbirn to let me go to Fullerton to visit my sister and her family. He wouldn't budge.

"Miss Wycherly, please," he said finally. "It's just for a little while longer. Why would you want to go to your sister's, anyway?"

"To relax."

"How can you relax around five small children?"

He had a point, but I wasn't going to let on. Besides, I enjoy my nieces and nephews.

"I manage," I replied. "I get the feeling you don't like children."

"Not really."

I sent him a snide glare. "Surprise. You spend so much time starting them. I can't believe you haven't produced a few by now."

He didn't seem in the least perturbed. "I had that fixed a long time ago."

"Fixed?"

"A vasectomy, Miss Wycherly."

My face went red. Mr. Hackbirn just chuckled and sauntered off to his room.

Sunday, instead of following me, he drove me to and from church. Monday morning, he threw (figuratively) his household accounts at me. The stocks and stuff that made his money were all handled by his broker and accountant. Getting it into his bank account and keeping track of what happened to it from there was my job. I'd been wondering where his money came from, i.e., was it legal? Everything in the shoe box he handed me seemed legit. Did it all make sense?

The checks from Amalgamated Paper Company didn't. All the other check stubs were quarterly, and the amounts varied. The APC stubs were all monthly, and payroll checks at that. Admittedly, that wasn't much to worry about, except for all the other stuff.

At lunch, I told Mr. Hackbirn there wasn't any way I could get the information he wanted over the phone, so he insisted on driving me to the library at UCLA. He hovered over me, claiming he was interested in how I did my research. He wasn't. I finally sent him to get some microfilm reels.

The moment he was gone, I slipped out of the viewing room, and downstairs to the reference floors. I checked all the business abstracts. No Amalgamated Paper Company. I checked through the Yellow Pages for the city in which it was supposedly located. It wasn't listed, nor was it in the Business-to-Business supplement. I thumbed through Dun and Bradstreet once more.

"Why the hell did you sneak off like that?" Mr. Hackbirn's voice snapped behind me.

I slammed the book shut. "I, uh, wanted to double check something."

"Dun and Bradstreet has nothing to do with drug smuggling."

"Well, not that. I'm sorry, Mr. Hackbirn. I've just been noticing things, and you've got a whole bunch of check stubs from a company that, as far as I can tell, doesn't exist."

"Oh." Mr. Hackbirn pressed his lips together and

thought. "Miss Wycherly, there is a logical explanation for that. Give me a few more days."

"It's not only those check stubs. There're all sorts of other things."

"I know. Now is not the time to discuss it. Please, Miss Wycherly, in a few more days you will have a full explanation."

"Are you involved in something criminal? Because if you are..."

"Miss Wycherly," he interrupted, "now is not the time. You will know in a few days."

When we got home, he went straight to his office and shut the door. The line on my phone lit up a second later. I went to the door and put my ear against it. I couldn't hear a thing. It's a sliding door, too, on a track, so nothing could escape through a crack at the bottom. For all intents and purposes, that office was soundproof.

I went to my desk and picked up the phone and pressed the lit-up line.

"Sid, what can I do for you?" Henry James' voice asked. He was the public information officer for the local F.B.I. office and he called fairly often.

"Hasn't that paperwork come through yet?" Mr. Hackbirn complained.

"Have patience," replied Mr. James. "The adoption has been approved. The clearance should be through any day now. We're dealing with a bureaucracy, remember?"

"I know. But Wycherly is showing her aptitude and she's asking questions. Not to mention that business is booming. I need the help and she's sitting there completely impotent."

"I'll try to redirect a little of your business."

"I'd rather have that clearance. What's taking so long?"

"Who knows? Can you just hang tight?"

"I'm hanging fine. It's Wycherly I'm worried about."

"Well, worry about Lipplinger, too."

"Aw, hell. What now?" Okay. He didn't say hell. Mr. Hackbirn's language is frequently the kind that strips paint off walls.

"Someone's putting the feelers out. We're pretty sure it's Gannett."

"Only pretty sure." Mr. Hackbirn cursed again. "I don't know, Henry. Something's off about this."

"Everything's off about this one. That's why I need you on top of it."

"When aren't I? I'll talk to you later. Call me the second that clearance comes through."

"I will. Bye, Sid."

"Bye, Henry."

I put the phone down quickly and spread my notes out over my desk. Not that it mattered. Mr. Hackbirn didn't leave his office until dinner. I decided not to say anything about what I'd heard. He was definitely up to something. Still, it could have been related to his writing. Mr. Hackbirn did do a regular feature on the F.B.I. for a newsweekly magazine. That could be why I needed a clearance. Which really didn't make sense, but I was too worried about going back to Tahoe to question it until it was obvious Mr. Hackbirn was doing something illegal.

I was surprised the next morning when Mr. Hackbirn sent me by myself on an errand. That mysterious fourth line had rung again, and he'd kicked me out of his office. Five minutes later, I was called in.

Mr. Hackbirn wanted me to pick up a package for him at an address on Highland Avenue.

"Tell them you want the package for Big Red," he told me.

"Big Red?" I asked, trying not to laugh.

"It's an old joke," he replied without any sign of humor.

I made the hike down to Sunset and picked up an eastbound bus, connecting to a southbound one at Highland. I got off at Santa Monica and went half a block south.

As I approached the building where the package was, I noticed a man leaning up against the building watching the door. He was the sort you see every now and then. He had longish stringy light brown hair and a half-grown beard with patches of gray in it. His denim pants and bomber jacket had both faded but not at the same rate. Something about him bothered me. By that point, I was convinced I was paranoid, so I ignored the feeling and went into the building.

It was a pretty non-descript office with an empty glass display case separating the desks from the waiting area. A young Black man came to his side of the case as I walked up.

I swallowed. "I'm here for the package for Big Red."

I could have sworn I saw someone further in look up suddenly.

The young man smiled and handed me a ream of eight and a half by eleven paper in a brown wrapper without any markings. At least that's what it looked like. I assumed the paper inside had some information on it. It seemed rather unlikely even for Mr. Hackbirn to go to so much trouble just for plain paper.

I left the building carrying the package and headed south again for a different bus stop. I wanted to go to the bank to deposit my check, which I hadn't done Friday because Mr. Hackbirn hadn't let me out of the house. I stopped at a window to look at something and noticed the man in denim about half a block away staring at the traffic. I wasn't paranoid. I was being followed again.

I ducked in front of a stopped bus, then dashed across the street to a northbound bus, and got on board. I'm not sure which was the greater miracle, that I didn't get hit or that there was a bus available right then. My guardian angel must have been working overtime. I changed buses three times, then stood for an hour at the bank. Well, it seemed like it. I didn't see anyone in denim, let alone potential vagrants, although I kept looking. I was exhausted by the time I got back to the house.

"What took so long?" Mr. Hackbirn asked as I handed him the ream.

"Call me paranoid. I was followed again."

Mr. Hackbirn became deadly serious.

"When?" he asked quickly.

"After I picked up the package."

"Terrific!" He took off for the living room. "Did he follow you all the way here?"

"No. I grabbed a bus and it left before he could get on." I followed him. He glared out the bay window to the street below. "I didn't see him after that."

"Tell me exactly what you did."

So, I told him. I even described the man.

"Who was he?" I asked when I was finished.

Mr. Hackbirn turned from the window and shrugged.

"I don't know," he said.

"Why would he be following me?"

"He was probably just some weirdo."

"Then why are you so bugged about it?"

"Miss Wycherly, why don't we just forget it happened?"

"No," I snapped. "Something pretty darned strange is going on around here, and if you don't tell me what it is, I'm leaving."

"Miss Wycherly, please. I promise. Just a few more days."

"Not good enough. See you." I started for my rooms.

He grabbed my shoulders and turned me to face him.

"I can't tell you now. Please. Trust me. I will tell you the very second I can."

Man, his eyes were gorgeous. Dumb, I know. For all I knew, this guy could be signing me up for the Mafia, and there I was getting hot and bothered over his eyes. Definitely hot and bothered. I pulled away quickly, my face blazing.

"The very second you get that clearance?" I blurted out and regretted it. "Yeah, I can listen, too." Terrified, I burst into tears. "I'm sorry. I shouldn't have. But there's too much weird stuff going on. But if it's something criminal, you'll kill me before you let me go, so I don't testify against you, and I gotta find a chance to escape before I know too much, 'cause you know too much about me."

"It's nothing criminal," he said softly. He was upset, also, but not angry at me. If anything, he looked guilty. "If you want to escape, go now. You already know more than you should, but if you want out, trust me, get out now, and forget you ever knew me."

All of a sudden, I felt... I don't know, like, I was totally blowing it.

"I didn't mean to do anything wrong," I said, hoping he still wanted me, which I know was strange, given how worried I was about Mafia. But I also really wanted to keep the job, and it wasn't just about having to work for my parents if I didn't stay. My gut just knew that I was where I was supposed to be.

"Oh, hell." His laugh was short and cost him. "Lisa, you've done more right than you could possibly know. That's why you're so confused, damn it. But I can't clear it up without locking you in. I'm sorry I got you into this."

"Do you really want me to leave?"

He turned away. "No. I want you. You're good." He looked at me sadly. "But in some ways, I want to warn you off, and I can't tell you why."

I bit my lip. "You're not like into murder or something?"

"I promise you, it's nothing criminal. I don't give my word lightly."

I could tell he didn't. There was only one other thing worrying me.

"I won't find myself undressed, or... You know."

He laughed. "No. I don't go around trespassing

upon the virtue of innocents unless they ask me to."

"But you'd like to talk me into it."

"I can't say the thought hasn't crossed my mind." He came over and laid his hand on my cheek. "However, I do respect the word no."

His touch was so light, so gentle and caring. My breath was coming shorter than after running. I pulled away and started for the office.

"Mr. Hackbirn, I—"

"Call me Sid."

"Mr. Hackbirn, I think... I don't know what to think."

"Lunch is ready."

I made up my mind and turned to him. "You say I'll be locked in. I have to admit that's pretty scary."

"Then why don't you think about it? You can take off any time tonight. Assuming you want to."

I shook my head. "Thinking about it isn't going to change anything. This might sound pretty crazy to you, but I'm not afraid of taking risks. You've given me your word. That's good enough for me. I'll stay, that is, if you really want to put up with me."

He smiled. "I think I can take my chances."

October 4, 1982

It took six more days for me to get my explanation. Mae wanted to know why I couldn't come out that Sunday. Something told me that telling her what was going on was not a good idea. I made a vague excuse and said I'd try to get out on the following Sunday.

Monday was D-Day. I knew it as soon as Mr. James showed up on the front doorstep. He's a tall man, somewhere in his late forties, balding and much of the dark hair that is left has gray streaks in it. His shoulders are broad, and he has a definite middle age spread. He also has the reddest face I've ever seen in my life.

I ushered him into Mr. Hackbirn's office and didn't quite shut the door. I stayed near the crack, too.

"Is this what I think this is?" Mr. Hackbirn asked, pleased.

"What the doctor ordered," said Mr. James. "By the way, I got an interesting report from Highland when they closed down."

"Yeah." Mr. Hackbirn sounded caught. "Well. I didn't have much choice. They sent it there, and Gannett's been seen watching the place. I didn't want to chance it. He knows me too well. She's obviously clean. No harm done, right?"

"You're just lucky it didn't blow up. Shall we bring her in?"

Mr. Hackbirn chuckled. "Come on in, Miss Wycherly."

Flushing, I slid open the door.

"She's been...?" Mr. James looked at Mr. Hackbirn.

"I told you, she's got the aptitude and then some." He grinned at me, then turned serious. "Please sit down, Miss Wycherly."

Puzzled, I sat down on the edge of one of the chairs in front of the desk. Mr. James stood next to it.

"Miss Wycherly," he said, pleasantly. "Sid has informed me that you have noticed a few oddities about his household."

I glanced at Mr. Hackbirn. His face was passive and unreadable.

"I have," I answered slowly.

"And has it occurred to you that Sid might be a little bit more than just eccentric?"

"Well, I have thought that certain of his little oddities seemed a little too planned to be mere idiosyncrasy."

"I see," replied Mr. James. He looked at Mr. Hackbirn.

"She's bright," said Mr. Hackbirn.

I decided to be bold. "Am I bright enough to be let in on whatever it is that's going on around here?"

Mr. James smiled and so did Mr. Hackbirn.

"That's why you're here, Miss Wycherly," Mr. Hackbirn said, becoming serious once more.

"Miss Wycherly, you picked up a package for Sid last Tuesday," said Mr. James. "Do you know what was in it?"

"As far as I could tell, paper," I replied. "I assumed that it was some sort of report."

"The paper was a blind," said Mr. Hackbirn. "What really made that ream important was a microdot containing top secret information."

"It's beginning to make sense," I said. "That clearance."

"Miss Wycherly," said Mr. James. "Within the structures of the FBI and CIA are several smaller organizations. Organizations so secret that mostly only their members know they exist. Mr. Hackbirn is a member of one called Operation Quickline."

"He's a spy." I swallowed back my fear. "For the US?"

Mr. Hackbirn smiled and nodded. "Yes. I work

secretly through the FBI, and now so do you."

"Me?" The news hit me like a punch to the breadbasket. Locked in. He'd warned me off. Something inside me snapped, and it was if I was watching everything that went on from another corner of the room.

"Your security clearance and adoption came through this morning," said Mr. James.

"You mean you guys want me to be a spy, too." My voice sounded distant as if another person were speaking.

"No," said Mr. Hackbirn. "You are a spy."

"What if I don't want to?"

Mr. Hackbirn sighed. "You will just have to live with that. I've had to do the same. All I can do is offer my sympathies."

Mr. James stepped forward. "You have to understand, Miss Wycherly, that the only reason Quickline is effective is because it is so secret. Therefore, when we must recruit new members, we cannot ask them without endangering the system, so we draft likely candidates."

"I can't believe this," I gasped.

"It will take a day or two," said Mr. Hackbirn.

I got up as well as I could. "I gotta get out of here. I've got to think."

"As you wish," Mr. Hackbirn replied. "But, Miss Wycherly, please keep in mind that my life, and now yours depends on your secrecy. It is that critical. I told you I am a dangerous person to know. This is why. I'm afraid you'll be risking your life right along with me. I wanted to tell you what you were risking, but I couldn't. I'm sorry."

"I understand. Sort of." I looked at him helplessly, then turned. "I'll see you later."

I grabbed my purse, left the house, and ran down the streets to the bus stop. I was confused. I was a spy. They hadn't even asked me, and, oh, that made me mad. But I was also excited. They had chosen me. But for what? Yes, I would be risking my life, but how did I know these guys were telling the truth? I only had Mr. Hackbirn's word for it that Mr. James was from the FBI. The bus arrived, and I found myself making my way to UCLA, then south to Wilshire and FBI headquarters.

I was scared as I paced the foyer, and I realized the thing that scared me the most was that I had no way of knowing if Quickline truly existed and if it really did work for the US. What if it was really an enemy operation?

Oh, I was so naive. That should have been the least of my fears. Of course, I had never laid my life on the line before and risking my neck didn't sound that bad in theory. I never really believed that I had no choice in the matter either. I'm not sure I do even now.

I don't know how I got past the security at the front desk, but I did. I told the guard that I was a reporter for the newsweekly that Mr. Hackbirn wrote for and had stumbled across something potentially dangerous. The guard sent me upstairs to an office labeled Programs Coordinator, Public Information Office.

I waited in the outer office until a buzzer sounded above the rattle of the young woman typing. She looked up at me.

"Go on back."

The office was well appointed and comfortable. A woman about my mother's age sat behind the desk and smiled professionally. [That had to have been Helene. She retired sometime later that fall, I think. Well, as close to retiring as any of us get. – SEH]

"May I help you?"

I took a deep breath and began the story I'd rehearsed on the bus.

"I'm a writer, doing a story on espionage in the US, and I've stumbled across something. I can't reveal my sources. Is there a spy operation working for our government called Operation Quickline?"

She blinked. "Not necessarily."

"Look. I need to know."

"You don't necessarily have the right to know. Can you tell me why this is so important?"

"If I could tell you that, I wouldn't be needing to ask you!" I felt my voice go shrill and took a deep breath to steady myself.

I don't know if the woman guessed what was on my mind, or if God merely intervened and made her do something she wouldn't have normally. I didn't care then, and I don't now.

"I can't really say yes or no," she said softly. "You should forget you ever heard the name. But I wouldn't worry about Quickline being a threat to national security."

"Thank you."

I left the office feeling somewhat reassured. On a lark, I went to find Henry James' office. It was just down the hall and labeled with his name and Chief Public Information Officer. The secretary seemed vaguely familiar, with brown hair, clipped into a barrette. She must have been expecting me because she sent me right into the inner office.

Henry James was there, too.

"Quite a shock, isn't it?" he said smiling with paternal warmth.

"Yeah. I don't know what to say."

"Well, you're probably feeling angry, and a little mixed up. Don't worry. We all do. Any questions?"

"Not right now, Mr. James."

"Please, call me Henry. We're going to be seeing a lot of each other. I'd like to be friends."

I smiled rather weakly at him.

"Sure." Fumbling for something to say, I looked at him. There was something reassuring about him. "Uh, you can call me Lisa."

"Thank you, Lisa."

There was another awkward pause.

"I'd better get back," I said finally.

"Before you go, Lisa, I need to say something."

"Yes, sir?"

"Operation Quickline is one of the most successful spying operations that the U.S. has. It is successful because it is so secret. Even my secretary doesn't know it exists. Its continued success depends on your ability to maintain its secrecy. Lisa, absolutely no one can know about it except you, Sid and myself."

"Not even my family?"

"Not even your family."

"I've never held anything back from my family before. Well, I haven't told them where I'm living right now. I haven't gotten around to it. But I will."

"That doesn't matter. Quickline does, for their safety as well as yours."

"I suppose. Is it really as deadly as Mr. Hackbirn says?"

"The risk is always there. That's why you can't tell your family, Lisa. No one must know about this but you and Sid."

I winced. "Are there any restrictions on friends? I'm meeting some nice people at church."

"That's fine. Just be careful, and don't let them get too close. If you need support, I'm always here, and you've got Sid."

I had to chuckle. "I don't know if I'd trust him that way."

Henry chuckled, too. "Maybe, maybe not. Lisa, he's a very lonely man. He uses Quickline as an excuse not to reach out. Your life may have been turned upside down today, but so has his. The sad part is, he doesn't even know it yet."

"I guess." I got up. "I'd better get back to the house."

"Fine. See you around."

"Sure, Henry."

I left his office deep in thought.

"Excuse me," said the secretary. "Have we met before?"

I looked at her again and flushed pure vermillion.

"Oh, my god," I groaned. "The clothes."

"What? Oh!" She recognized me and laughed. "You're Sid Hackbirn's secretary. You didn't recognize me with my clothes on, did you?"

"I'm sorry."

"Boy, you sure put Sid off his paces."

I turned to her. "I did?"

"Yeah. He couldn't believe you'd never seen a naked man before. He kept saying you were a genuine innocent."

"Oh." I paused. "I hope I didn't mess things up too much."

She purred. "You can't mess up Sid that badly."

"Oh."

She held out her hand. "I'm Angelique Carter."

"Lisa Wycherly." We shook. "It's nice meeting you... Uh, again."

She laughed. "Yeah. Again. To many more meetings. With our clothes on."

I laughed also. "Right."

I hurried out. Once on the street, I paused. No one seemed to be following me. I decided to test it. I walked up to Westwood and went into the first burger place I found. I knew lunch would be waiting for me at the house, but I'd had one heck of a morning. I deserved a real meal for a change. I got a double chili burger with fries, cole slaw, onion rings, a chocolate milkshake, and a piece of cheesecake for dessert.

I suppose I should have been more upset. Mr. Hackbirn had radically changed my life without doing me the courtesy of asking me. Well, he had tried to warn me, and he had given me a chance to back out.

At first, I was too numb from the shock to protest. As the shock wore off, I became caught up in the romance of being a spy. The danger seemed very unreal to me. Later, when I realized just how real the risks were, I was too caught up in other problems to feel much outrage at my fate, and I'm not the type to spend much time brooding about things I can't change, anyway.

It was almost two when I got back to the house. Mr. Hackbirn was waiting for me in the living room.

"Well?" he asked.

"I guess I'm in," I replied, brightly.

"That goes without saying. Any questions?"

I thought. "Why me? Why even have a secretary?"

"As I said before, you are a woman who sticks to her standards, even when it's hard not to. That takes a lot of strength. When I told you I needed someone with guts, I meant it."

"That's not very reassuring." I sank onto the couch.

"No, it isn't." He sighed as he sat in the easy chair. "Ours is a dangerous business, I'm afraid. Anyway, as to why a secretary..." He looked away then shrugged. [Okay. I should have anticipated that question, and, yes, I was trying to come up with something plausible because the truth about why it took me two years to find you was more embarrassing than I was up to admitting at that point. It was Henry's idea to hire you as my secretary and insist that you live-in so that I could keep you under surveillance. – SEH] "That was, uh, my idea. I've always wanted someone who could handle those mundane little trivialities of life that are so time-consuming and dull yet must be done. Because of the nature of my business, any secretary I'd hire had to have a security clearance. The people upline didn't want any more people involved than necessary, so they put the krabbatz on that."

"What made them give in?"

He smiled. "Business got good. I'm not physically capable of making all the drops and pickups they want made. So, when they said they were going to give me an associate, I said I wanted a secretary. I did need to recruit somebody, and I'd have to keep that person under twenty-four-hour surveillance, which is why you're living here."

"And why you followed me to church that Sunday. And why you wouldn't let me out of the house."

"That was because you ditched your tail that Friday you went shopping."

"You mean he was part of the surveillance?"

"Yes. They caught up with you at the church because of the list I had you give me. However, since you kept ditching them, I couldn't keep you under surveillance, that's why I kept you in."

"Except for last Tuesday. Was that also surveillance?"

Mr. Hackbirn winced. "No. I was glad you ditched him. I wasn't supposed to send you. You weren't cleared yet, nor did you have any training."

"You mean he really was a bad guy."

"Yep. You handled it well, though." His smile was rather proud.

"Thanks." Something else occurred to me. "I wasn't followed to the FBI offices. Does this mean no more surveillance?"

"You're on your own."

"So, I suppose I could move now if I wanted to."

He made a face. "You could. I'd rather you stayed. It is convenient."

"There's that. I'll have to think about it." I leaned forward. "Tell me about Quickline."

"We're a courier group, hence the name."

"We don't do any of the actual spying?" Believe it or not, I felt a little disappointed.

He smiled and chuckled. "It depends on what you call actual spying. We do sometimes have to break into places to get things, and sometimes we handle investigations. But we are a domestic operation. Only under exceedingly rare circumstances will we do any foreign work. In any case, you and I are what is called a hub team. Couriers coming in from overseas and elsewhere frequently get tailed, and they don't always want to ditch the tails because that exposes them as operatives. So we play a little shell game once the package gets to our operation. Floaters pick up the packages from the overseas couriers, process, address, and route them, then pass them onto the nearest hub team, which passes the package to the first mover on the route."

"That sounds pretty straightforward." I smiled at him. "How long have you been a spy?"

"I started in the army when I got drafted. Intelligence first got me in boot camp and kept me undercover. After my discharge, I was transferred to Quickline."

"So, what now? I assume you've got me in the self-defense class because of this."

"Right." His smile turned ominous. "Tomorrow your real training starts."

I swallowed. "Oh dear."

"By the way, Amalgamated Paper Company will be augmenting your salary from now on."

"So that's what those checks were."

"Precisely. And you'll be getting them, too."

"You mean I get a raise?"

"It's a promotion. You are now my associate."

I grinned. "Not bad for two weeks work."

"To all outward appearances, you are still my secretary, and you'll still be performing all the same functions."

"I was afraid of that."

Mr. Hackbirn laughed. "Don't worry. I'm still paying for the mundane trivialities."

"You don't have to."

"That is my decision, and I will continue to pay."

"Thanks. I appreciate it."

We looked at each other. I was filled with that warm cozy after the storm feeling, the kind when you know everything is going to work out just fine. The kind when you know you've just found a very good friend.

October 5-15, 1982

As Mr. Hackbirn drove us to Mr. Fukaro's dojo the next morning, he seemed perplexed. He didn't say anything about it until we were headed for our next stop.

"You seem very up," he said. "Are you sure you're not in denial?"

"About what?" I asked.

"About being drafted. Don't you have any feelings of anger? Outrage? Anything like that?"

I thought. "Maybe a little. I suppose I should be angrier, but I'm really kind of excited. I've always felt like I had such a boring life, and now I'm a spy. It's pretty neat, really."

"I might have known," Mr. Hackbirn grumbled. "Miss Wycherly, you had better get those happy, romantic little notions out of your head right now. This business isn't James Bond, and it isn't a neat, painless undertaking. Most of it is deathly dull, and when it isn't, it's ugly."

"Well, it can't be totally awful. You don't seem like you're that miserable."

"I'm not, and I can't say that there are no fringe benefits. However, I don't want you lulled into a false sense of security. You and I are in perpetual mortal danger and will be for the rest of our lives."

"I know. I just refuse to let it get me down is all."

He didn't say anything to that. I think he knew that the danger part hadn't sunk in for me. What I found at the deserted warehouse in Long Beach that he took me to after the dojo helped make his point. It was a shooting range for a variety of operatives, all of whom needed a place to practice without being seen. The shooting range itself didn't faze me. The target did. It was a police silhouette of a man. I made a face.

"I don't like shooting at them either," said Mr. Hackbirn. "But that's what you're facing."

"Right." I reached for the revolver he had.

He pulled it back. "Miss Wycherly, this is not a toy."

"I know."

"It's a Smith and Wesson Model Thirteen, three fifty-seven magnum revolver. I know it's a big gun, but believe me, you don't want a peashooter. Now, you've got to stand and brace your arm so that you can absorb the recoil. I'm warning you, this baby packs a wallop."

I let him show me the proper position.

"Do you want me to stand behind you?" he asked. "It's got quite a kick. And maybe I'd better move that target closer."

"Don't waste your time." I slipped on the ear guards and put a shot into the target's left shoulder.

Mr. Hackbirn squinted. "Not bad for a first try. Just remember to aim for the chest. It's the easiest to hit."

"You can kill someone that way." I squeezed off four more shots to the left shoulder.

Mr. Hackbirn pushed a button, and the target floated towards us. He looked at the five holes, then at me. I smiled weakly.

"I got fourth place in the Tahoe Region Skeet Championship," I told him. "The first three went on to international competition."

"That's pretty good." He looked me over again. "I guess I owe you an apology. You just don't seem the type."

"Well, sewing and knitting are about as domesticated as I get. Daddy and I nailed a lot of ducks and pigeons together."

"Ah. Well. We'll go right into shooting on the run. Now, remember, aim for the chest. You won't have time to finesse a shot."

We worked for an hour. I must admit, I didn't put

everything into a shoulder, but I hit the target every time. Mr. Hackbirn was impressed.

"I just put it between Donna Reed's eyes," I said, as I reloaded.

"You what?"

"Oh." I blushed. "It's an old joke. My best friend always said that. She's a hardcore feminist, and there was this TV show."

"I'm familiar with it."

"I've never seen it. Anyway, neither of us were big on traditional housewiving. I mean, it's alright if that's what a woman really wants to do. I just don't think a woman should have to."

"I'm liberated myself," said Mr. Hackbirn with a bemused chuckle. He shook his head. "I just didn't expect it from a church-going type like you."

"Look, I believe in God, and I try to live my life in a way that's consistent with what I know about Him." I tried not to glare at him and failed. "But that doesn't mean I turn my brain off just because some Bible thumping conservative thinks women belong in the kitchen. I've spent a lot of time thinking about my values, and I know what I believe and why I believe it. Okay?"

He backed off. "Okay. I'm sorry I assumed."

"I don't mean to get so defensive," I sighed. "I just get so tired of people treating me like a mutant because I believe sex belongs in marriage."

"Actually, I know how you feel."

"What do you mean?"

"I get tired of people assuming I'm some depraved monster because I'm sexually active."

"Oh. I guess you would."

I hadn't really thought he was a monster. But I considered him depraved. He was pretty busy most evenings.

We were just as busy during the days. Getting his office together was put on hold. In the meantime, I had to learn how to administer certain drugs, how to locate hidden microphones, how to install hidden microphones, how to ditch a tail (well, how to do it even better), how to tail someone, how to make microdots and how to read them, and codes.

There was a new code every day to break, and I also had to learn how to encode things. It was miserable. I spent so much time working on those codes I wondered if I'd start mumbling keywords in my sleep.

The only thing worse than the codes was Mr. Hackbirn's safe. What few records we had on the business were stored there and they were relatively innocent at that. The safe was in Mr. Hackbirn's office under the floor next to his desk. His waste can covered the almost imperceptible cut in the carpet. The dial was behind a false back in a drawer of one of the file cabinets.

Getting to the dial and to the safe was easy compared to opening it. Each number of the combination had to be dialed exactly, having been passed a specific number of times. If you didn't do everything just so, the safe wouldn't open. To make matters worse, the safe was finicky and I often suspected that it sometimes wouldn't open out of plain orneriness. Mr. Hackbirn took it all in stride and pointed out that it was better that the safe was so hard to open. I think he was just glad he didn't have to do it anymore.

Then there was all the technical equipment, including listening devices, surveillance devices, tracking devices. Most of the stuff you see in spy movies is out and out ridiculous, but we do get to use some pretty sophisticated stuff. It's all very small, too, to make it easier to hide.

And speaking of hiding, Friday was spent on all the different places and things I could hide on myself to get me out of a tight situation.

"You can always hide something," said Mr. Hackbirn. "In fact, I think you ought to get your hair permed. It's long enough, with a little extra body, you'll be able to hide all sorts of things in there."

"Like what?" I asked.

"Like one of these." Mr. Hackbirn pulled something small and dark out of his hair. It was a quarter inch wide and about two inches long. "Spring steel. You'd be amazed at all the things this little goodie will unlock, and it can cut strapping tape, too."

"Strapping tape?"

"Used to bind hands instead of handcuffs. It and duct tape are carried because handcuffs can arouse suspicion."

"Oh." I shuddered. "I don't know if I want to carry a piece of metal in my hair all the time."

Mr. Hackbirn shrugged. "I don't, except when I'm working. But even then, it probably wouldn't be a bad idea. You could be attacked or captured at any time. Anything you can keep on you to help you just might save your life. In fact, I would be surprised if you're not carrying a bit of spring steel on you right now that no one will ever think to look for."

"Really?" I looked over my jacket and clothes, then flushed when I noticed Mr. Hackbirn studying my breasts. He was perfectly clinical about it, but I was still embarrassed and closed my jacket over my chest.

"You're wearing an underwire bra, aren't you?"

"Mr. Hackbirn, isn't that my business?"

"Spring steel, Miss Wycherly, that's the wire. You could get out of a pair of handcuffs with it."

"Well, maybe." I put my hands behind my back and tried to reach my bra strap. "Except I'd never be able to get the bra off my arms if I was cuffed."

"True." Mr. Hackbirn studied me a moment longer, mulling over the problem instead of my breasts. "Ah. The solution is simple. Wear bras with detachable straps."

"I wonder where I'd get one."

"The lingerie department might be a start. In any case, I know they exist. I've seen them."

I smirked. "Oh, really."

"I've seen a lot of bras in my time. But don't just

get one. Wear them all the time."

I snorted. "This is getting a little ridiculous. It's bad enough you're telling me how to wear my hair, now you're dictating the style of my underwear?"

"Miss Wycherly, I understand your irritation." Mr. Hackbirn glared at me. "But you need to understand just how deadly serious this is. You are entering a new way of life. You are a spy, and everything you are as a person is affected by it. How you act, make friends, what you eat, even your damned underwear. Secrecy is the word you live by now and being prepared is how you'll stay alive. I'm giving you every trick, hint, whatever that I know to keep you that way."

I hung my head. "I'm sorry."

"It's alright." He smiled softly. "I know what you're going through. I went through it, too. But I'm alive because I accepted it."

"Well, I guess I'd better make that appointment for my perm."

"Good. But first, I want you to try these on."

He pulled a box off the file cabinets. He had brought it in that morning when he returned from making a pickup. The box held a pair of black running shoes. Mr. Hackbirn gave me a pair of tube socks, which I put on over my nylons.

"They feel great," I said after lacing the shoes up. I walked around. "Sheesh. I've never had shoes this comfortable before. Are these why you did that plaster cast of my feet the other day?"

"Mm-hm. I have a pair just like them. They've saved my butt more than once."

I giggled. "Don't tell me. I click my heels and a knife will pop out."

"Not quite. Sit down and slide your fingernail between the sole and the shoe on the inside."

I did. "Hey, there's a groove. Oh, my god."

The sole popped open. Inside was a stiletto, a flat handle, two screwdrivers, and more spring steel.

"There's wire, a wire cutter, a transmitter and

batteries in the other," said Mr. Hackbirn. "It's a pity platform dress shoes aren't in style anymore. You'd be surprised at all the stuff I could stick in those. We won't be able to hide much beyond some spring steel in your dress shoes, and there's always the last. That can be sharpened and makes a very effective weapon."

I looked at him. "What about your dress shoes?"

"I have a similar set up in all my heels. Most of the time, I have no need for it, but you never know."

I put the sole back on and tested the shoe again.

"Armored running shoes." I tried to smile. "What will they think of next?"

Saturday, I asked Mr. Hackbirn to let me go out to Mae's the next day.

"You did say I was on my own," I said at breakfast that morning.

"Of course." He put his paper down. "Isn't she in Fullerton?"

"Yeah. I get there on the train. I can take a bus to Union Station."

"That's fine. Fullerton, though."

"So?"

"There's a lot of covert activity going on there. Well, in most of northern Orange County. That's why we have a contact in Santa Ana."

I snorted. "That's no surprise. There are a bunch of defense plants out that way."

"We've got a contact in Fullerton, too."

"Oh. Well, it's not my sister."

Mr. Hackbirn laughed. "Nobody with five kids would have the time. I was merely bemused by the coincidence. Are you planning on taking the bus back tomorrow night?"

"Yes."

Mr. Hackbirn shook his head. "Why don't you come back Monday morning instead? I'd rather not worry about you on the bus after dark."

"I can always wear my armored shoes."

"It's better to avoid trouble. Come back Monday

morning."

"If you insist." I didn't like the worrying nonsense, but coming back on Monday meant no running, so I wasn't about to argue.

Mae's whole family picked me up at the train station in Fullerton. I could see that Mae was dying to give me the third degree about my new job, and why I hadn't been able to visit the previous Sundays. Even though she's six years older than me, people sometimes think I'm older because I'm taller than she is. She's got more padding than I do, too, with brown hair, which she keeps short and permed to stay out of her way.

Neil was calm, as usual. It takes a lot to flap him, although he can be a real smart aleck at times. He's tall and skinny, with bright red hair and glasses. His son, Darby, looks a lot like him. Darby was nine at the time and had just gotten his glasses. He manfully picked up my overnight case. Janey, age seven, and Ellen, age four, both attached themselves to me. They have their mother's coloring, only Janey has big hazel cow eyes, and Ellen's eyes are blue, like her father's. The twins, Marty and Mitch, were whooping up their greeting noises from their stroller. They were two and looked more like Darby and their dad.

"Is there surprise?" asked Ellen shyly.

"Of course," I told her with a squeeze.

There always was. Mae's a health nut and Neil's a dentist, so the only time those kids see candy is when I or the grandparents bring it. It's one of the advantages of being an aunt, and one of the few times I press it.

Mae didn't get to her interrogation right away. She and Neil had to go to some Marriage Encounter shindig, and they didn't get home until nine that night. While I usually visited on Sundays, one of the reasons Mae had gotten so fussed that Mr. Hackbirn had kept me at home was that I was needed to babysit. Mae and Neil have a little problem that way. Janey won't stay quietly with just anyone.

When Mae and Neil got home that night, Mae only

waited long enough to check on the kids.

"So?"

"So... What?" I asked.

Neil sat back in the kitchen chair with his arms folded and chuckled.

"Tell me about your job," Mae pressed.

I swallowed. I wasn't used to lying to my family. Still, Mr. Hackbirn had been right, and, strangely enough, I didn't want to tell Mae what he had gotten me into.

"He just takes some getting used to," I explained slowly.

"But you sounded so worried before," said Mae. "And you said something strange was going on."

I forced a laugh. "Oh, that. It was nothing. My boss, he just... you know, gets around."

"You already told us that," said Neil.

"Well, he really gets around," I replied. "And he was trying to cover it up. Only I kept catching little things, and he finally came clean with it."

Mae snorted. "Are you sure?"

"I accidently walked in on him in his living room, and he was buck naked with a naked woman."

Neil laughed.

"In the middle of the day?" shrieked Mae.

I was puzzled, at first, then remembered that Mae didn't know I was living there, so daytime would have been the only time I'd have seen such a thing.

I shrugged. "He wasn't asking me to."

"I don't know, Lisa," said Mae. "Something's not right about all of this."

"Leave her be, Mae," said Neil. "Lisa's a big girl. She can take care of herself."

Mae didn't believe that for a second, but she did let up. The next morning, everything went as smooth as silk, except that Mr. Hackbirn drove me to the gym that night to make sure I worked out, seeing as though I had missed running that morning.

The training went on, and between that and

sewing enough business wear, I didn't think much about finding my own place. Mr. Hackbirn was right. It was convenient being there, and I was starting to settle into my little suite of rooms.

I'd filled the bookshelf in the sitting room, which also had the same light blue walls as the bedroom, and still had to pile more books on the light oak coffee table. I'd set my sewing machine on the writing table, and was able to drag in a small dresser from one of the two guest rooms to store my fabric and patterns in. I laid out my patterns on the tan carpeting that ran through most of the house. It was feeling more and more like home, although I did spend a fair amount of time praying and debating with myself about whether I should stay.

There was one major advantage to living in Mr. Hackbirn's house: Conchetta Ramirez. She doesn't live in. She works from ten to five-thirty, Monday through Friday, and that's it.

Those first few weeks I was there, I never saw her. I couldn't figure out why. Still, I could tell that my rooms were regularly vacuumed and dusted, the bathroom cleaned, and my towels and sheets changed. Admittedly, the only time my bed got made was when the sheets were changed, and my clothes did tend to land on the bench at the foot of my bed until they were laundered and put away.

The big thing was, I wasn't doing any of it. I hate housework. With a passion. On my own, I only cleaned when I had to because a dirty place can get pretty gross. In fact, the longer I stayed at Mr. Hackbirn's house, the more I came to appreciate that I had cleaning service, and I didn't have to pay for it.

It was near the end of my two weeks of training, on a Friday, when I finally met Conchetta. She's got black hair with gray, some padding on her figure and wears all these concert t-shirts from hard rock bands or with revolutionary figures like Pancho Villa and Che Guevara over her jeans. I had needed to check a quote from some poet or another for one of Mr. Hackbirn's articles and went to my room to find the book the poem was in. Conchetta was in there, dusting. She had on a Black Sabbath t-shirt, and looked at me a little strangely.

"I'm Lisa Wycherly, Mr. Hackbirn's new secretary," I told her. "You must be Ms. Ramirez."

"I'm Conchetta," she growled after another odd look. "You're still here."

"Yeah. I work here," I said, puzzled.

"I've never seen a woman move in here and stay longer than two weeks," Conchetta said. "And I've seen plenty of women move in."

"Oh. Well, I just work for him. That probably helps."

"Probably." She shrugged. "I'm not your friend, though. We both just work here, right?"

"Right."

"Good. I just want to do my job and be left alone."

"Okay. Um. I'll get my book and leave."

I hurried back to the office. She hadn't seemed mean or anything. Just very clear about what she expected and wanted. It was very odd, but that night, as I prayed, I decided that I was happy to let Conchetta do her job, which meant that I was going to stay right where I was.

October 18-20, 1982

That Monday, I finally got my hair permed. I got home from the beauty parlor late that afternoon. As I walked in the front door, I heard piano music coming from the library. I didn't know the piece, but it was something classical and complicated. [It was the rondo allegro from Beethoven's Pathetique Sonata, number 8, opus 13. – SEH] My interest was aroused. I'd been trying to play the piano for years, despite lessons. Whoever was playing that afternoon was certainly accomplished. [Accomplished? I hadn't played in two years, and I made a mess of it! – SEH]

It was Mr. Hackbirn. He stopped when he saw me.

"I thought you said you only played sometimes," I said coming over to him. "That sounds like pretty often to me."

He just shrugged.

"Where in your unstructured background did you pick up something as structured as playing like that?" I asked.

"It was the only disciplined thing my aunt had me do. Although, strangely enough, I practiced pretty much by my own choice. When you're in a private school, your friends don't live near you."

"And the parents who lived near you didn't want their kids playing with a commie."

"In a couple of cases." He stopped and looked at me. "How'd you know about that?"

"Observation and research." I smiled, glad that my guess was accurate. "So, you had a lonely childhood."

"Yes and no. I was a loner. I didn't have many friends because I didn't want them. And it was my aunt who was the commie, by the way."

"Why didn't you take up music? In college I mean."

"Didn't want to."

"And what motivated you to play now? Something bothering you?"

"Not really. Why do you ask?"

"You kind of hinted that you hit the music when you were lonely."

He looked at me intently for a moment.

"That is often the case," he replied slowly as if he wasn't sure that he could trust me. "Not this time, though. I just felt like it."

Something told me he wasn't hiding anything. He shifted, quirked his eyebrow up, and smiled at me.

"Your hair looks good," he said.

"Thanks."

He stood up. "You might want to get ready for tonight."

"What's going on tonight?" I swallowed.

"You're going to make a pickup."

"A pickup!" I was shocked. "I'm not going out with any strange guy."

"No," groaned Mr. Hackbirn. "You're picking up a piece of information to be sent up the line."

"Oh. That's almost as bad."

"It'll go as smooth as silk. It's a code three, which means minimal to no contact. All you have to do is sit at the end of the bar and put your purse on the back of the bar stool."

"What if the bar stool doesn't have a back?" I swallowed again. "And what if I can't get a seat at the end of the bar?"

"It's Monday night. The crowd should be pretty light, and the bar stools have backs. I've used the place any number of times before."

I shook my head. "I'm going to really botch this one up."

"What could you possibly botch?"

"I don't know, but something will present itself."

"Don't worry. I'll be there just in case the Soviet army shows up. Just don't come near me unless there's a genuine catastrophe."

"That's so reassuring."

He smiled. "You'll be fine. You probably won't even know it's happened. All you have to do is sit there between seven and eight and enjoy a margarita. They make the best in the city. You can even dress down if you like. It's a casual place."

I had little choice but to do it. Mr. Hackbirn gave me a medium-sized red leather purse with a zipper on the top and said to leave the top open. After dinner, I put on a black linen trumpet skirt I'd just finished with a red polyester blouse and red heels.

The place turned out to be a rather comfortable bar, attached to a traditional Mexican restaurant on Sunset. The lighting was muted and there was a television at the other end of the bar from me. I walked in and found a seat at the bar on the side nearest the door. It wasn't exactly at the end of the bar, but that seat had been taken by a blonde woman whose eyes darted everywhere. After ordering a margarita and chips and guacamole with extra jalapeno, I looked around the bar. It wasn't quite seven o'clock, yet I couldn't help wondering who among the several people milling about was my contact. My eyes fell on a tall man with medium brown hair, and he grinned at me and made his way over to where I sat.

"Hey," he asked. "You looking for company?"

"Not really," I said. "I'm just killing time before meeting my boyfriend."

He sighed and moved on. He wasn't my contact. Mr. Hackbirn had been very clear that this mysterious person wouldn't even speak to me. I sighed in relief as the bartender slapped a cocktail napkin next to me and placed the margarita on top. The chips and guacamole arrived a second later. The guacamole was good, even if someone had laid off the jalapenos. Of course, I don't really look like someone who enjoys eating fire, but I do. The slushy margarita was as advertised, though, even if I got a bit of a brain freeze from it.

I'm not sure when Mr. Hackbirn wandered into the place. He was wearing a yellow silk shirt with a coordinated cotton sweater tossed over his shoulders and was sitting in a booth at the back. I turned back to my chips for a minute, then scanned the room again.

I saw Mr. Hackbirn smile and raise his glass to me. I was certain something had gone wrong, and he needed to talk to me. I left my purse on the chair and hurried over to the booth.

"What's wrong?" I whispered as I sat down next to him.

"What are you doing here?" he hissed back.

"You meant me, didn't you?"

"No, I was signaling to the blonde behind you!"

"Well, I never!" I said loudly, getting up.

I all but stomped back to my place at the bar.

"He wanted you," I growled to the blonde.

"He did?" She smiled at Mr. Hackbirn, who smiled back.

"You're nuts if you do," I told her as she left the bar.

I checked my watch for what seemed like the millionth time, but it was only twenty 'til eight. My chips were already gone, but a minute later, the bartender replaced the basket with a full one. At least, I still had some guacamole and half of my margarita. Several guys went past me and a couple women. [I'm trying to remember if Elena Montoya had been promoted to floater yet. She was still in Santa Ana at that time, although her dad, Eduardo, had already been moved up to Seattle as the Blue Line floater. Not that I knew their names then. But I'd seen her plenty of times before and that night, saw her walk right past you and make the drop. – SEH]

I tried to eat the chips slowly. After all, a third basket of chips might have made me more noticeable than I should have been. So, while it wasn't quite eight o'clock when I finished the basket, the guacamole was gone and there was only a sip left in my glass. I looked in my purse and there was a white legal-sized envelope that hadn't been there before. I paid my tab and it took all the control I had to not run out of the bar.

When I got home, I dropped the envelope on Mr. Hackbirn's desk and headed for the kitchen. There I found everything ready to make a mug of peppermint herb tea, a particular favorite. I knew Conchetta had some idea something was going on but didn't know about Quickline itself. I wondered what Mr. Hackbirn had told her when he asked her to set out the tea. I was pretty sure he hadn't set it out himself. That's not like him and even if it had been, I doubted he would have set out the peppermint, which he loathes. Conchetta had set out the tea, no doubt about that. [No. I'd set it out – SEH]

As I cleaned up what little mess there was in the kitchen, I debated waiting up for Mr. Hackbirn, but only briefly. Considering the blonde, if he were to return home at a decent hour, he would probably not be alone. Sighing, I took my tea with me to my room and went to bed.

The next morning at breakfast, Mr. Hackbirn congratulated me on a job well done, then asked me where the pickup was.

"I put it on your desk."

He smiled. "Great."

He sent me to the office first. Well, it was his turn to take the breakfast dishes into the kitchen. A minute later, he hurried through my office and into his, but left the door between us open. I got up and watched as he opened the envelope on his desk. He read what was inside, then cursed and picked up the phone. He did not sound happy as he rattled off some code, then listened.

"Why did they set it up that way?" he asked the person on the other end. Okay, he added a few extra curse words. "Are you sure there's no one else?" There was a pause while the other party answered. "Yeah, but Gannett is not going to come anywhere near me...

In a couple months, no problem... She's great, but she's only made the one pickup. You can't send someone with no experience on something like this... There's got to be someone else..." He sighed. "Alright. Set it up... Gee, thanks. Talk to you later."

I walked the rest of the way into the office as he hung up.

"What's that all about?" I asked.

"Your pickup last night," Mr. Hackbirn grumbled. "You're going on another tonight and it's a major one."

"You don't sound as if you have a lot of confidence in me."

"In you, yes. You're doing very well, but you need experience. This assignment..." He sadly shook his head. "I don't know."

I bit my lip. "What is it?"

"A certain gentleman has let it be known that he has some very important top secret U.S. information that he's willing to sell."

"Gannett."

"Right." He smiled. "He's technically one of ours, with the CIA. However, he's been working as a double agent for several years. We call it walking the fence."

"That sounds bad."

Mr. Hackbirn shrugged. "It is and it isn't. Most doubles start out posing as people selling out in order to get inside the enemy's operation. It's a necessary part of what we do, and trust me, it's the scariest work out there."

I gulped. "You've done it?"

He nodded. "Yeah. The problem is it's very easy to slide from simply trying to get inside to working both sides for fun and profit."

"And you know that because..."

"That, I didn't do." He sighed and chuckled. "I like keeping myself in one piece. But I did see it happen a few times. And the fence walkers are often our best sources of information. The problem is, at some point, you're going to have to favor one side or the other.

Gannett has very probably toppled over onto the other side. So, The Company has been setting up a couple stings here and there, hoping to catch him."

"The Company?"

"It's a nickname for the CIA." He rolled his eyes and let out an obscene variation on the acronym. "There's a very unfriendly rivalry between them and those of us on the domestic side. They're complete jerks." [I did not say jerks. – SEH] "Anyway, tonight Gannett is supposed to turn over the goods. They want somebody he hasn't seen before to pose as a potential buyer and pick him up."

"I don't like the sound of that, but it doesn't sound terribly complicated." I sounded more confident than I was.

"Except that you won't be the only buyer Gannett has been entertaining. You might have some competition tonight."

"Terrific." All pretense of confidence fled. I flopped into the chair in front of the desk.

"That's not the worst of it."

"Gannett's seen you, so I'm going solo."

"I'm afraid so."

But Mr. Hackbirn wasn't going to let me out of it. We discussed every possible thing that could happen, then exactly what our plan of action would be. At 3:30, he gave me an article to enter into the computer and left to run an errand or two.

He didn't get back until five-thirty, just as dinner was ready. As we sat down to eat, he pulled something out of his pocket and tossed it on the table. It was a round gold brooch about two inches in diameter made of a ring of gold wires twisted together.

"That's how Gannett will spot you," said Mr. Hackbirn. "He'll be asking for a one-way ticket to the zoo. Just say you have one."

I had to laugh. "Where did you come up with that crazy line?"

Mr. Hackbirn just smiled and shrugged. "A vivid

imagination, I guess."

"I guess."

I felt rather better about the whole affair as I drove Mr. Hackbirn's Mercedes to the bar where I was to meet Gannett, wearing a double-breasted jacket I'd bought the week before, with the brooch pinned on the lapel, over nice jeans, and a shiny green blouse. My armored running shoes were on my feet. During dinner, Mr. Hackbirn had drilled me on what I was going to do. By the end of the meal, he seemed relieved and told me he thought I was going to be fine and that he'd underestimated me. I looked at him closely and saw that he meant it.

After dinner and before I left, Mae called. The kids were getting to her. Somehow the conversation got around to our own childhoods.

"Do you remember how we used to tell each other stories?" Mae said wistfully. "Especially you."

"You told some pretty good ones yourself."

"Yeah, but you told the best. You should have written them down. You could have made a fortune in adventure stories."

I laughed. If only she had known about the adventure I was living. As a child, I had longed for adventure. In kindergarten I'd wanted to be a smoke jumper – someone who parachutes into a wildfire to put it out. Later, I'd play the knight slaying the dragon or pretend I was a superhero flying to save the day while jumping out of the hay loft in Daddy's horse barn. Cloak and dagger stories had always enthralled me. Now I was living one.

I thought about that as I walked into the meeting place, yet another meat market (I mean, singles bar), this time on Santa Monica Boulevard near where it went through the West Hollywood neighborhood. I walked up to the bar and ordered a glass of white wine. Though I didn't need to be told, Mr. Hackbirn had drilled it into me that one drink a night was plenty for a person whose livelihood depended on absolute secrecy.

I wasn't there half an hour before I was asked for a one-way ticket to the zoo.

"I've got it," I replied to the man who had addressed me. "Let's go get a table and talk about it."

Gannett was about average height. As far as I could tell, he had light brown hair and was basically as nondescript as they come, wearing a nice shirt and sport coat.

"Have you got the money?" he asked anxiously.

"What have you got that's so good?" I said a lot more coolly than I felt.

"Not so fast. Money first."

"I have it at my place."

"Then go get it."

"Not so fast yourself. I hear there are other bidders." My voice still sounded cool, but my heart was pounding.

"So?"

"So, you can come to my place, and we'll see what you've got."

My left hand rested casually on the table in front of us. My right hand was on my lap. Trembling, I reached into my purse and pulled out the 9 mm automatic Mr. Hackbirn had insisted I carry.

"What if I choose not to go to your place?" my guest asked.

Underneath the table, I pressed the gun's barrel into the guest's side. I watched him stiffen at the contact.

"Do you feel that?" I asked. He nodded. "You no longer have a choice. Now we're going to get up and leave here. You'll do as I say and just because you don't see my gun, doesn't mean that it's not pointed at you or that I don't have friends with me. Is that clear?" He nodded again. "Alright, let's go."

I held onto his arm and kept him close to me to cover my gun as we walked out of the bar. When we got to the parking lot, I thanked heaven it was empty of people. At the car I blindfolded Gannett and after putting on the seat belt, taped his hands. It had been my own idea about my "friends," and I was glad he'd believed me. [Although you did have one "friend" there. You just didn't know about him. – SEH] After seeing that Gannett was secure, I ran around to the driver's side of the car, stashed the gun under the front seat, and for some reason my brooch also. As I turned to get in, two men came up to me.

"Yes?" I asked.

"We're interested in that guy you just picked up," said the man closest to me. He tried to sound casual, but the threat was there. The other remained in the background.

"Who I pick up is my business." I tried to sound sophisticated. I think I just sounded hard.

"That's an interesting way to treat a date." He glared at Gannett.

"So, I'm kinky," I shot back.

"I want that man and now!" The man reached for me.

At that moment, something clicked, and it seemed like what I was doing, I wasn't doing, instead I was standing outside myself and watching a stranger do it. The man grabbed me and started pulling me away. Instead of resisting, I fell into him, throwing him off balance. He let go and I landed two good punches in his belly. He fell backward into his companion.

I jumped into the car and backed out of the parking space. I almost hit a large car. I could see the two men getting into it.

I stepped on the accelerator and shot out onto the street. It was a miracle I didn't hit anyone. I turned right on some side street after La Brea, then right again. The car following me all but kissed my bumper. I took another right and ran several stop signs, then turned right onto Highland. Another right and I landed on Hollywood Boulevard.

I knew the only way I could lose them was to make

a lot of quick turns. But that was almost impossible with the way traffic is in on Hollywood. A residential neighborhood would have been ideal, except that I didn't know the streets in L.A. once I was off the main bus routes. Losing my tail wouldn't have done much good if I lost myself in the process.

I saw a sign for U.S. 101, south to Santa Ana. I knew the streets in Fullerton, so if I couldn't lose them on the freeway... I nearly creamed a car trying to get in the right lane for the onramp. Once on the freeway, I checked my mirror. My tail was still there.

They say stress can help us perform in a heightened manner. Well, the stress I was feeling, and the grace of God are all that got me through that night. I believe I already mentioned that I was working on automatic pilot. I had to. I hate freeway driving. It scares me. When I can't avoid using the freeway, I stay in one lane and drive fifty-five.

That night I rarely drove under seventy. I changed lanes constantly, dodging around cars. My tail stayed tight on me. I hardly dared breathe. My guest remained silent. I thanked God. I found myself caught behind a slow car and the lane beside me blocked. I hit the brakes and checked the mirror. The tail was still there. If Gannett heard my litany of Our Fathers and Hail Marys, he didn't say anything. I pulled around the slow car. I made it to Orange County in less than thirty minutes. I turned off the freeway at the last second from the middle lane. My tail hung on.

I swallowed and headed for the housing tract where my sister lived. I knew the area, although it had been two years since I had lived with Mae while going to college. The tract was a veritable labyrinth.

I suddenly turned off the main street. The tires squealed in protest. I remembered that Mae had told me something recently about cops cracking down on reckless drivers. I made another rapid turn. Cops were the last thing I needed. I turned again and accelerated. Even if they didn't pull me over, they'd send somebody after me. The tires screamed as I turned again.

I drove like that for about half an hour. Somewhere in the last five minutes of that time, I lost the tail. I drove on, relieved but afraid it was too good to be true.

For once it was true. I stopped at a stop sign. Around the corner to my left, a large car was parked by the corner. Behind it I could see the flashing lights of a police car and the silhouette of a policeman talking to the driver. I drove on, half watching my rear-view mirror. I had lost them. I smiled and breathed a thank you to God.

Three minutes later, I was going north on the 57 freeway, headed back to L.A. via the 60 freeway (we tend to refer to them by numbers here). No one tailed me, though I had one eye in the rear-view mirror all the way. I didn't even slow down until I hit the big interchange between Interstate 10, Interstate 5, and the start of U.S. 101, and from there (on I-10), home.

I sighed as I pressed the button for the garage door opener back at the house. I drove in, braked, and turned off the ignition. Then I summoned everything I had left for one last surge of energy.

"End of the line," I said, reaching under the seat for the gun.

I got Gannett loose from the seatbelt and out of the car. Mr. Hackbirn was at the garage door and held it open as I led Gannett into the house. Silently, Mr. Hackbirn took the lead. He guided us to the room where we were going to put our guest for the night. At the door to the room, I removed the tape and shoved the guest in. Mr. Hackbirn shut the door and locked it. Numb, I headed for the office.

It's at this point things get fuzzy. I do remember hearing Mr. Hackbirn ask what took so long. I remember dropping the gun on the desk and I remember sinking into the chair. But that's all I remember until I woke up the next day.

The sun was shining. It seemed exceptionally bright. I was in my bed. My jacket had been neatly hung up and my shoes were in the closet, but otherwise I was still fully dressed. My tongue felt like it had swollen three times its original size and there was a dry taste in my mouth.

Foggy, I groped my way to the mirror over the dresser. I still don't know what I was looking for, but I stood there a long time. The phone rang. I stumbled my way to the bedside table where it was, picked up the receiver and grunted into it.

"I figured you'd wake up about now," said Mr. Hackbirn's voice.

"Yeah."

"How do you feel?"

I thought a moment. "Nauseous."

"That's to be expected. You'll probably feel a little groggy for a while. Why don't you take a shower? It'll wake you up some. Then I need you in the office promptly."

"Breakfast?"

"My dear, it's past lunchtime."

As I hung up, I looked at my clock. It was 12:30. Groaning, I realized that if I thought any more about food, my nausea would come to fruition.

It took over an hour for me to shower and dress. I was still drowsy as I headed for the office but awake enough to wonder what had hit me. I was also trying to remember going to bed and couldn't. I didn't have a headache, so I doubted I'd been drinking.

"I don't understand it," I replied when Mr. Hackbirn asked if I was still feeling groggy. "I know I'm not that swift in the mornings, but I've never been this bad. I feel awful. I wonder if I'm coming down with something."

"I doubt it," said Mr. Hackbirn.

I sank into the chair in front of his desk. He sat on the edge closest to me, looking at me intently.

"The funny thing is," I continued, "I don't remember anything after we locked up Gannett."

"Anything?" Mr. Hackbirn lifted an eyebrow.

I thought for a moment. "I think I remember coming in here. I wanted to get rid of that gun. And I think I remember crying."

"You were hysterical."

"Hysterical? That's ridiculous. I've never been hysterical in my life."

"You were last night."

"I was?"

"It took two barbiturate tablets to calm you down. By that time, you were knocked out."

"You fed me dope?" I was halfway out of my chair.

"A sedative, Miss Wycherly." Mr. Hackbirn remained infuriatingly calm. "Which you sorely needed."

"So that's why I feel like a wrung-out wash rag," I grumbled, sinking back into the chair.

"That's an interesting image. I'll have to write that down." He paused as I glared at him. "Well, maybe later. In any case, the side effect should be gone by tonight. What I need to know now is what happened to cause your reaction."

"I was scared."

"That is obvious. What scared you?"

So, I told him in detail what had happened. Mr. Hackbirn listened without interruption.

"I have two questions," he said when I had finished. "First, did you see the license plate of the car tailing you?"

I shook my head. "It was too dark, and the lights were shining."

"Perhaps it's just as well. Secondly, did they shoot at you at all?"

"No," I replied. "I guess it was too crowded."

"Then what frightened you so badly?"

"Wasn't that enough? Good heavens! Haven't you ever been scared?"

"Well, of course..."

"Then try to think of me. I'm new at this. I come from a basically sheltered background. Nobody's ever even wanted to physically hurt me and now I've got to deal with two men who want to kill me just for some jerk I've never seen before, and they're willing to chase me all over to do it. Wouldn't that have put you a little off track at one time? You might also consider the fact that I'm basically an optimist. I'm used to trusting people. I find it hard to believe that anyone could willingly want to hurt someone else. Oh, I know intellectually, it happens, but deep down it doesn't make sense and, therefore, it's hard to believe. At least it was 'til last night. You want to talk about a shock to the system? Mine got a major jolt. Okay, maybe I did overreact. I don't know, I wasn't really there. All I know is that man was utterly malicious and that frightened me like nothing has ever frightened me before."

Mr. Hackbirn sighed. "Miss Wycherly, I don't want you to take this as a rebuke. It isn't. You are to be commended for keeping your head and waiting until you did to break down. I might add it was probably waiting that caused the hysteria. However, that reaction could get you into big trouble if you panic at the wrong time. As a result, I am very concerned. What's going to happen to you when real violence occurs? I can't have you becoming a basket case every time you find yourself endangered."

"I know," I groaned.

"Miss Wycherly, you are going to have to get used to the fact that A- there is a great deal of evil in this world and there are quite a few people in this world that have no qualms about taking a human life; and B- this is a very dangerous business. Most of it is rather dull. But the US is, in effect, involved in an underground war with the Soviets and a few other countries. We are part of that war so that the vast majority of our country can lead peaceful, productive lives."

"You make it sound as if we're on the brink of disaster."

"We are." Mr. Hackbirn removed a piece of paper from the inside breast pocket of his suit coat. "This is the information Gannett wanted to sell."

On the paper was a written mathematical equation, only there were no numbers except exponents, and it contained a symbol I'd never seen before.

"Looks fairly innocuous." I shrugged. "Of course, I only got as far as precalculus in college."

"It's called the Lipplinger Formula. It was developed by Doctor Miles Lipplinger. He teaches physics at Georgetown University. That formula is probably the most dangerous piece of information in the world."

"Why?"

"It makes possible limited nuclear war."

"Oh, my god. Surely, the Soviet Union wouldn't..."

"The only reason we are at peace now is because a nuclear war would destroy the world. If that formula were made possible, we would be plunged into the worst war humankind has ever known. As it stands now, I'd say only fifty people know of its existence. Fortunately, they're on our side, and out of that fifty less than ten, including our guest, have actually seen it."

I swallowed. "How could it stay so secret?"

"According to the scuttlebut, Professor Lipplinger discovered it by accident. He thought it could be used for peaceful purposes, specifically clean energy generation. I'm not sure who he contacted when he realized the other potential of the formula, but it somehow got to The Company. They also felt that destroying the formula would only endanger the U.S. in the likely event that the Soviets also developed something similar and did not hesitate to use it. Professor Lipplinger agreed to monitor information provided by the CIA to see if he could detect the formula in the development and so cue the CIA, who would arrange to sabotage the work."

"So how did Gannett get a hold of it?"

"We're not sure. He was supposedly working with Professor Lipplinger on the project."

"So now what do we do?"

"I doubt anything. There is a cause for concern

because of Gannett's disloyalty, but he's already been sent upline and will soon be dealt with."

"I don't like the sound of that."

"I understand. But like I said, Miss Wycherly, we are at war and betrayal is a crime."

It had taken some doing, but I had finally convinced Mae that my earlier qualms about Mr. Hackbirn and my new job were resolved. However, that opened up a whole new line of speculation regarding his nocturnal prowling. We pretty much concluded that while Mr. Hackbirn was a nice guy, he was no candidate for sainthood either.

This is important because Mae and I wondered what would happen if he ever met my niece Janey. To most people, Janey is a normal kid, and in most respects, she is. But she is also an incredible judge of character. She has two basic categories: good or bad, and people are either one or the other. Janey has yet to be wrong.

She started when she was about three-and-a-half or four. About the only people then that Janey had any real contact with, apart from her family, were babysitters. Finding someone to sit with three kids, one a toddler, as Ellen was at the time, was hard enough. But then, all of a sudden, it seemed, Janey wouldn't stay quietly with anyone she'd decided was bad. There was one girl, in particular, (I can't remember her name) that Janey would not tolerate at all. Mae found out later that the girl was caught stealing from someone who had hired her.

Janey's perception increased with age. Unfortunately, her tact didn't, at least not for a while. By the time she was six, she had gotten into the habit of telling anyone what she thought of them, in spite of Mae's efforts to teach her discretion. Worse still, every time the doorbell rang there was a race to beat Janey to the door. If Janey opened it, whoever was on the other side got Janey's own peculiar brand of the third degree and was only admitted upon her approval.

Mae and I both wondered what her reaction to Mr. Hackbirn would be. Neither of us really thought she would be able to label him good. But how exactly would she react to him? And I had to wonder how he would react to her. While Mr. Hackbirn admitted he didn't particularly dislike children, he didn't really like them, either. He was bemused by my weekly visits to my sister's and couldn't imagine how I could find it relaxing to spend time with five children under the age of ten.

The Sunday after my little escapade with Gannett, Neil picked me up at the train station by himself. We didn't say much, but that wasn't all that unusual. Neither, really, was the tension inside the house.

"They're fighting again, huh?" I said to Darby, after a few minutes.

"Yeah," he mumbled miserably.

"It won't last long," I said reassuringly. "They'll resolve it soon."

"I guess," said Darby. "The Finsters down the street are getting a divorce."

"They are? Well, they probably never fought with each other."

"They were always fighting."

"Then they never resolved their fights. And you know your parents always do."

I put my arm around him. Neil popped his head in the front door (he'd been waiting in the car).

"Mae?" he bellowed. "Are you coming or not?"

"It would have been nice if you'd have let me know you were here," Mae's voice came down from upstairs. "I'm saying goodbye to the children!"

Neil slammed the door. A few minutes later Mae came running down the stairs.

"Oh, there you are, Darby," she said breathlessly. She came over and hugged him. "I'll see you later, honey. And don't worry. Daddy and I will have it settled by tonight, okay?"

His reply was lost in another squeeze. Mae let go of her son and tackled me next.

"Thanks for coming." She let go. "We'll talk tonight."

"Sure. See you later."

"Okay. Bye-bye." Mae scurried out.

It was about three-thirty when Neil called.

"Yeah, Neil, what's up?" I asked into the phone.

"I'm at the hospital," he replied.

"Oh no!"

"It's not that serious."

"What happened?"

"Well, we'd just patched things up between us and were taking a walk, when Mae tripped on a sidewalk crack."

"Oh my god, is she alright?"

"She, uh, messed up her knee pretty badly."

"Oh no! The poor thing."

"They've got her all doped up right now. But she'll be having surgery tomorrow or the next day."

I rolled my eyes. "I thought you said it wasn't serious."

"Well, it's not life and death." That was typical Neil.

I gulped. "Oh my god, you guys are going to need a sitter!"

"Yeah, I know. Is the phone book right there?"

"Neil, who can you call?"

He sighed. "I haven't the foggiest."

"Look, let me make a phone call first."

"I hate to ask you, Lisa, but with Janey..."

"I know. Give me the number where you're at."

"Never mind. Mae's asleep, so I'll head home."

"Okay, see you in a bit."

I hung up, took a deep breath, and dialed again. Fortunately, the boss was home and answered after one ring.

"Yes?" said the familiar voice.

"It's Miss Wycherly, Mr. Hackbirn. I'm afraid

there's been an emergency."

"Are you alright?"

"I'm fine. But my sister has to have surgery and will be in the hospital for a while."

"And...?"

"They need someone to stay with the kids while Neil's at work or the hospital."

"I assume you're the poor unfortunate."

"I'm afraid so."

"What about your work here?"

"Well, if there's anything that really needs getting out, there's a typewriter here I can use."

"This is very awkward. Can't they get someone else?"

"Mr. Hackbirn, they're not rich and when you come right down to it, do you know anybody else in their right mind who'd look after five kids under ten years of age besides a relative?" In truth, I did but I knew he wouldn't.

"I'd question the sanity of the relative."

"Ever hear of family duty?"

"On occasion." He let out a sigh. "I suppose I'll have to let you take care of them. How long will you be gone?"

"I don't know. As soon as my brother-in-law gets back, I'll borrow their car and drive in to get some stuff, and I suppose I could come in some evenings and work."

"I'm not a slave driver, Miss Wycherly."

"I know, but it's not fair that you have to make all the sacrifices. You won't have to pay me while I'm gone."

"We'll see. I'll talk to you this evening."

"I'm not fired, am I?"

"Of course not. Goodbye," he grumbled sullenly.

"Goodbye."

I hung up and breathed a sigh of relief. Then I gasped when I realized I'd be taking Mae's place.

It wasn't all that bad. The kids were extra good, and Neil helped out where he could. The house was pretty clean, so I didn't have much to do on that front beyond picking up after the twins. Cooking dinner was the big thing I was afraid of. However, Mae had already done the week's shopping, and had left a menu with notes on which cookbook had whatever recipe. Of course, I still had to cook it. But I'm okay at following recipes, so it wasn't all that hard.

Wednesday turned out to be the big problem, mostly because of how things happened. The day did not start out at all well. Neil's alarm didn't go off and I slept through mine. We were wakened only five minutes late because the twins had woken up early and decided they wanted to make cookies in the kitchen. Flour was everywhere, and on the floor next to the sink, shards of broken honey jar stood up in the golden goo. While I was cleaning the honey up, Ellen discovered that milk beaded up on the dry flour and poured out almost the whole half gallon trying to figure out why it wasn't absorbed immediately. Then Janey couldn't find one of her shoes, and Darby realized at the last minute he hadn't done about five homework problems, and he had math first thing in the morning. I was so happy when Neil took the older two to school.

That still left me with the younger three. Marty and Mitch ran me ragged that morning playing with them. Ellen tagged along, quietly, but persistently, asking me why the milk acted so funny on the flour. I had no idea, and she didn't want to wait until her father got home. After lunch, the twins started throwing blocks at each other, so I sent all three children to their rooms for naps. I knew they wouldn't sleep, but at least they were quarantined for a while, and I could get my head back on.

Since it was the week before Halloween, I had been spending nap times working on Halloween costumes for the kids using Mae's sewing machine. It was a blessing that day, and I as I worked, I could feel the knots in my neck loosening.

At three, ominous thumping sounds from the

twins' room convinced me it was time to let them out. Darby and Janey arrived home right then, and I figured they could keep Marty and Mitch occupied. But Darby wanted to practice piano, and Janey had just gotten three new books from the school book club. Ellen still wanted to know about the flour. I left them all in the living room and hid in the kitchen staring at a package of frozen chicken breasts that I'd forgotten to get out of the freezer two nights before and wondering if I could get them thawed in time to bake them like I was supposed to.

I could hear the bickering rising above the pounded-out beginner exercises. I let it go until it escalated into full-scale shouting.

"Janey! Quit poking me."

"I'm not poking you. It's Ellen."

"Janey! I saw you!"

"Aunt Lisa!" Janey came running in with Darby on her heels, and Ellen pouting behind them. The twins were screaming in the living room.

"Aunt Lisa, she's poking me and blaming it on Ellen!"

"He's lying, Aunt Lisa. I want to read and he's making noise on that stupid piano."

I ignored them and headed to the living room. "What's the matter with your brothers?" The doorbell rang, and I switched directions immediately. "Darby, hold Janey!"

"Let me go, you big brat!"

"Ellen, cut it out!"

I opened the door to a man about average height with light brown hair neatly trimmed, and an equally well-trimmed mustache.

"Hi," he said. "I'm Ned Harris. I go to church with Mae. You must be Lisa."

"Janey, come back here!" Darby yelled.

"Uh, yeah. That's me." I turned inside. "Excuse me. Darby, go stop your brothers from screaming."

"Ellen, stop that!"

I turned back to Harris. "What can I do for you?"

"My wife wanted to know if there was anything we could do while Mae's in the hospital."

Ellen screamed. "Aunt Lisa! Darby hit me!"

"Darby!" I yelped.

"This doesn't seem to be a good time," Harris said smiling.

"I'll have Mae or Neil call you. Thanks." I shut the door.

"Aunt Lisa, Ellen kept messing up my music, and she keeps poking me!"

"But, Aunt Lisa, he won't..."

"I don't care. I've had it! To your rooms, all of you. I don't want to see you until your father comes home. Where's Janey?"

"Upstairs," grumbled Darby.

"Good. Now go!"

Neil took over when he got home, and I assumed cooked dinner. I called up an old girlfriend and we got our own dinner and went to a movie.

The rest of the week passed without a hitch. I had borrowed Neil's car to drive into L.A. twice besides Sunday to make sure all was in order, and it was. Late Friday afternoon, I got a little worried. Friday was the last day on the menu. Fortunately, Mae called and after talking to each of the kids, she spent time conferring with me. Her recovery was quite rapid, and she figured she'd be home the next day, although she'd asked me not to tell the children just yet. After all, she wouldn't be up and around for a while yet. We were just about to decide on what to have Saturday night when Darby yelled from upstairs, where he was cleaning his room.

"Hold on, Mae," I said as Darby's feet pounded down the stairs. "Something's up with Darby." Then I yelled, "What's going on?"

Darby appeared in the kitchen where I was on the phone.

"There's a 450 SL out front!" he exclaimed and left.

Darby had, and still does have, a strong affection

for Mercedes Benz cars and the 450 SL was the top as far as he was concerned.

I peeked out the front window and saw a metallic slate blue fender and groaned.

"What's going on?" asked Mae.

"The boss just pulled up. I'd better call you back." The doorbell rang. "Oh, shoot! Janey! Bye!"

I slammed the phone down and ran through the dining room toward the front. I was too late. Near the big opening into the front hall, I could hear Janey's voice.

"We don't have a Miss Wycherly here," she was saying.

I couldn't see the door and assumed Mr. Hackbirn couldn't see me. There was no point in trying to interrupt Janey. She hung on to her victims like a pit bull.

"Isn't this the O'Malley residence?" I thanked God that Mr. Hackbirn had the sense not to talk down to her.

"Yes."

"I was told she was staying here. Is this your house?"

Janey giggled. "It's my mommy and daddy's. Only my daddy says it's the bank's."

"I don't doubt it. Is your aunt staying here?"

"My aunt?"

"Yes." The funny thing was, he didn't sound angry or annoyed. Just bemused.

"She's here."

"May I talk to her?"

"But you wanted Miss Wycherly."

He chuckled. "I believe that's your aunt."

"I don't have an Aunt Wycherly."

"But you do have an Aunt Lisa."

"Yeah." Janey sounded a little puzzled.

"Well, Wycherly is her last name. Like your last name is O'Malley."

"Then why do you call her Miss Wycherly?"

He paused. "I suppose for the same reason you call your teacher Miss or Mrs. whatever her last name is."

"I call my teacher Sister Francine."

"Oh."

"But Darby calls his teacher by her last name. She's not a nun, you know."

"Oh, I see."

I was about to rescue Mr. Hackbirn when Janey did the last thing that I ever thought she'd do.

"You're a good person," she said blithely. "You can come in."

"Thank you." I heard the door shut. "Would you please get your Aunt Lisa?"

"Aunt Lisa!" Janey bellowed, as loudly as she could, which was pretty loud.

"I'm right here," I said stepping around the corner. "Good afternoon, Mr. Hackbirn, please come in. I see you've already met my niece, Janey. Janey, this is my boss, Mr. Hackbirn."

"Hi." She smiled and flashed her huge hazel eyes.

Mr. Hackbirn smiled, more warmly than I would have thought. "Nice to meet you, Janey."

I looked at her. "Janey, why don't you go finish cleaning your room?"

"Darby isn't cleaning his."

"Where is he?"

"At the car."

"What's that kid doing with my car?" Mr. Hackbirn turned anxiously towards the door.

I somehow beat him there and opened it.

"He's just looking at it," I said, looking to make sure. "He wouldn't touch it."

Mr. Hackbirn looked at me not quite sure.

"Darby!" I yelled. "Come on in and finish cleaning your room. You can look at the car later."

Darby tore himself away and trotted in.

"Darby," I said, shutting the door. "This is my boss, Mr. Hackbirn. Mr. Hackbirn, my nephew, Darby."

I was so proud of Darby. He stepped right up and

shook Mr. Hackbirn's hand.

"Pleased to meet you, sir," he said, the excitement shining in his eyes. "That's one real neat 450 SL you got. I've never seen one that color. You got the hard top for it?"

"At home," said Mr. Hackbirn, smiling.

"If Mr. Hackbirn agrees, you can chat with him later," I said firmly. "Finish your room, first."

"Yes, ma'am." He ran upstairs.

I waited until he had gone, then headed into the family room.

It was littered with the twins' toys. Almost mechanically, I bent and started picking them up.

"So why are you here? Need a manuscript done?" I asked dropping some plastic blocks into a toy box.

"A pickup."

I glanced at the ceiling and shook my head. "I wouldn't talk about that here. The walls are paper thin, and those kids are sharp. You'd have been better off phoning."

"Not on a code one."

I didn't really hear him. At that moment one of the twins started shrieking.

"Crisis," I explained, as I shoved a beat-up doll and bright purple plastic donut into Mr. Hackbirn's hands, then ran upstairs.

What happened next, I wasn't around to see or hear.

[This is what happened – I was in shock, wondering what the hell I was supposed to do with a bald, naked doll and that purple donut thing. I heard the front door open and in walked what had to be Darby's father.

"Hello," he said as if there wasn't anything odd about a total stranger standing in his family room. "I'm Neil O'Malley."

"Afternoon. I'm Sid Hackbirn." I started to shake hands, but I still had the doll.

Neil smiled and set down his briefcase.

"Here let me take those for you," he said, the ice

broken. "You're Lisa's boss. I'm her brother-in-law."

"Nice to meet you," I said.

"You probably want to talk to her."

"Daddy!" Janey came running into the room and tackled her father.

"How's my girl?" said Neil.

"Real good, Daddy."

"Where's your Aunt Lisa?"

"Cuddling Mitch. He tried to take Ellen's book and she hit him real hard with it." She sighed and shook her adorable little head. "Little kids."

She walked over to me, cocked her head to one side, blinked those huge cow-eyes of hers twice, and said, "Aunt Lisa will talk to you as soon as she's done with Mitch. Maybe you'd better stay for dinner. Can he, Daddy?"

"Well," said Neil. "It's alright with me. But you should see if Mr. Hackbirn would like to."

Janey looked at me again and blinked twice. Just two times.

"He'll stay," she said and wandered out of the room.

I wondered how she knew.

"Janey's our little mystic," said Neil apologetically.

At that point, there was more of that god-awful shrieking, and Neil was assaulted by Ellen, followed quickly by the twins, then Darby – SEH]

I heard Neil come in but opted to avoid being trampled and waited to come after the kids.

After greeting each child, Neil sent them back upstairs.

"I've got good news," he said when they had gone. "Mae's coming home tomorrow."

"I know. I just talked to her on the phone," I said, then thought of something. "I guess I'd better plan on sticking around for a while yet, 'til she's in better shape."

Mr. Hackbirn frowned.

"We'll see," said Neil. "Mae said I should call the

Marriage Encounter group. Some of those folks will be willing to help out. I should have done it sooner. Still, I don't want to tell the kids just yet that Mae's coming home. They'll be too excited. In fact, if you could take them somewhere tomorrow. I could get Mae settled in peace and they could get some energy run off."

"Sure, Neil," I said and looked at my watch. It was a little after 4:30. I turned to Mr. Hackbirn. "I've got to get dinner ready..."

"I believe I've already been invited," Mr. Hackbirn said.

"Great." Then another thought hit me. "Oh, shavings. I forgot to defrost the turkey meat."

"Is there anything else?" asked Neil.

"Not enough," I replied, glumly. "Why don't we not tell Mae, and hit the chicken place?"

"Sounds okay to me," Neil replied.

"Whatever." Mr. Hackbirn sounded a little resigned, but I decided to let it go.

"Look," I said, "I'll fix a salad and some green beans, and you won't have to buy all that other stuff."

"Sure," said Neil, noncommittally.

"Daddy, can we come down now?" asked Darby at the top of the stairs.

"Please, Daddy?" asked Ellen.

"Alright, come down," answered their father.

The children noisily trooped down into the family room.

"Dolly," said Marty. "Where dolly?"

I looked at Neil who shrugged.

"I believe it's on the television," said Mr. Hackbirn, unexpectedly. He walked over and handed to doll to Marty. "Here you are."

"What do you say, Marty?" reminded Neil.

"Tank you."

"You're welcome," Mr. Hackbirn replied, then looked down at his legs in astonishment.

Ellen had grabbed a hold of him and was hugging him.

"You're nice," she said looking up at him and smiling.

"You're nice too," replied Mr. Hackbirn, laughing.

I was trying not to laugh. How or why these children had decided to attach themselves to my boss, I couldn't guess, but there was no denying it. I could tell Janey wanted Mr. Hackbirn to sit down, but Darby had already moved in and had engaged him in a conversation about Mercedes Benz. Barely minutes later they were going outside to look at the car. Janey and Ellen followed.

"Can you believe it?" I said, laughing, as soon as I heard the front door.

"I can't believe Janey even let him in," Neil chuckled. "Yet there she is, batting her eyes at him."

"And he says he doesn't like kids."

At that moment Darby burst in.

"He says he'll take me for a ride!" he all but screamed. "Can I, Dad, can I, please?"

"Alright," Neil said reluctantly. "Don't be too long and say..."

"I know!" Darby was already out the door.

Janey came in with Ellen, who was crying.

"Ellen wanted to go," Janey explained. "But I told her there'll be other treats for us, huh, Aunt Lisa?"

"It's not up to me," I said taking Ellen into my arms.

"I know of a treat for Ellen," said Neil. "Would you like to sit at the table with the rest of us?"

Ellen's face lit up with smiles.

"Can I, Daddy?" she asked, sniffling.

"Yes, you can. Now, why don't you go blow your nose, like Daddy's big girl."

Ellen scrambled out of my lap and went running for the tissues.

I was a little nervous about dinner. No, I was a lot nervous. I kept thinking about Mr. Hackbirn's quiet existence in that well-organized house in Beverly Hills and wondering if he was ever going to get over the shock of family life. Worse still, Neil had promised the kids earlier that week that he'd take them to the movies that night so not only were they excited about that, but there was the additional excitement of having a guest for dinner. The fact that he was the much-celebrated Mr. Hackbirn only added to it.

The twins were fed first and sent up to their room to play. Ellen, sitting on a telephone book, just glowed. Of course, I wasn't worried about her. She's the shy one in the family and not too squirmy.

She sat next to Neil at the head of the table and on her other side was Darby. On Neil's other side was Mr. Hackbirn and next to him was Janey, who had insisted on sitting next to him. I sat across from Neil.

I kept my head reverently bowed while we said grace, although I was dying to see Mr. Hackbirn's reaction. Almost right on top of the "amen" Janey started talking about school and pretty much kept the conversation rolling. She was fascinated by the way Mr. Hackbirn separated the chicken meat from the bones with his knife and fork, instead of eating it with his fingers like the rest of us were doing. Darby noticed something else, though.

"He's a picky eater," he mumbled to me at one point in the meal.

I didn't say anything, but Darby was right. Mr. Hackbirn had pulled all the skin and coating off his chicken and set it aside. His salad had no dressing on it, and he hadn't taken any of the mashed potatoes and gravy that Neil had also bought.

At that point, Neil said he had an announcement to make.

"I talked to Mommy's doctor today," he said. "And he said Mommy's coming home tomorrow."

I saw Mr. Hackbirn jump as the kids let out an ecstatic yell.

"And that's not all," Neil's voice rose above the cheering. "To make it easier on Mommy because her knee still hurts her, Aunt Lisa's going to take you out tomorrow, while I get Mommy from the hospital. So, when you come home, she'll be here."

"Are you gonna come too?" Janey asked Mr. Hackbirn.

"Well, I do have..." I could see the light dawn as he changed his mind. "Sure, I will."

The kids yelled again, but I didn't hear it. There was something fishy about that "Sure, I will," and there was something about a code one pickup.

"Absolutely not!" I was trying to stay calm. But I was furious.

Dinner had been cleaned up and Neil and the kids were gone.

"It's priority one, code one," Mr. Hackbirn said with that incredibly aggravating calm manner of his. "There is nothing else that can be done about it."

Anything that passes through the "business" is given a separate priority and code rating. The scales are on a one to five range. For priority, one is the most urgent, namely drop everything and get it moving now. Five means whenever there's time to deal with it. Code implies how secret it is. Technically, no one in Quickline is supposed to know anyone else in the business. Also, anything we get is already given the highest-level top-secret rating possible, which is why we get to handle it. A code five means you can put the information into an associate's hands and all but ask his name, making it easier to pick up a tail. So, you can tell they're not as worried about a code five as they are about a code one, which means no contact at all allowed short of a quick phone call. Priority one, code one means extremely urgent and extremely secret, and in my mind that night, dangerous.

But it wasn't the danger to myself that was bothering me. Mr. Hackbirn wanted me to make the pickup while we were out with the kids the next day. Needless to say, I didn't want them involved. I don't think Mr. Hackbirn wanted them involved either, but there didn't seem to be any other way.

What had happened was that the information had been hidden on a key chain full of keys. The keys were supposed to have been dropped at a time and place

mutually agreeable to Mr. Hackbirn and whoever was
carrying the keys. But the carrier had picked up a tail
and had temporarily ditched the keys in a toy store at
a mall in Brea. [Eduardo Montoya again. Had to have
been. It was coming through the Blue Line and that
guy was hopeless about tails. – SEH] When the carrier
had ditched the tail, he went back to the toy store only
to find that someone else had already found the keys
and turned them into the manager of the store, who in
turn locked them in her desk. By the time the carrier
had returned, the manager had gone home with the
key to the desk.

Assured of the keys' safety, the carrier decided
the toy store was as good as any place for the pickup
and called Mr. Hackbirn. The only problem was that
the assistant manager had seen the carrier, in fact,
talked with him about the keys, and would probably
say something if a man other than the carrier picked
up the keys. So, after conferring with Mr. Hackbirn,
the carrier had called up the toy store and arranged
for his "wife" (me) to pick up the keys. Apparently, Mr.
Hackbirn had assumed Neil would be home to take
care of the kids. To do him justice, it wasn't all that
bad an assumption.

But Neil would be occupied with bringing Mae
home, and Mr. Hackbirn had decided that having
the kids along wouldn't be so bad as long as he could
distract them while I made the actual pick up. I did not
want the kids involved.

"It's too dangerous," I insisted.

"Actually, it's the safest kind of pick up to make."

"I don't care. It'll just have to wait."

"It can't wait. It's been waiting too long already."

"Well, I'm not going to do it. I'm sorry, but I can't.
Not even to save my job."

"I'm not going to fire you. I can't anyway."

"Then I'll quit."

"You can't quit. Remember? Face it, you're stuck."

"Wonderful. We've reached an impasse." I could

feel my control starting to slip. I bit my lip. "You say I will, and I say I won't."

"Will you listen to reason?" There was an edge to his voice that I later learned meant he was getting mad. "There is very little that could go wrong, provided you don't lose your head."

"That was a cheap shot," I snapped.

I looked him right in the eye. He seemed startled at first. Then the bright piercing blue softened, and he actually looked a little ashamed.

"You're right. It was," he said quietly. "I apologize."

"Apology accepted." The fury suddenly left me, leaving me very drained.

Mr. Hackbirn sank into the couch (we were in the living room). He put his fingers to his eyes as if he was going to rub them but didn't. When he removed his fingers, he blinked a few times and looked at me. I noticed his eyes were rather red.

"Look, I don't want to endanger the children," he said slowly. "And frankly, I don't think it will. Consider, in the first place, the tail was successfully ditched and obviously didn't know about the toy store. In the second place, if you'll pardon the cliche, there's safety in numbers. People in our business generally work alone and only rarely in tandem. We'll be seven people total. And in the third place, their very presence will be a type of protection. I mean, who would be crazy enough to bring children on a thing like this?"

I sighed. Unfortunately, he made sense. I had sunk into a chair. I disconsolately gazed at the battered toe of my deck shoe.

"I don't know," I said, not quite ready to give in. I looked at Mr. Hackbirn. "I love those kids. I don't know if you'd understand, but I'm better than Santa Claus to them. They mean the world to me."

"I do understand. If you'd said that to me yesterday, maybe I wouldn't have. But what else are we going to do?"

"I don't know. I guess we'll have to do it. Janey's

got her heart set on you coming anyway."

"What an amazing girl." Mr. Hackbirn smiled gently.

I chuckled. "You certainly seem to be rather fond of her."

He shrugged. "I'm a sucker for big eyes." He got up. I rose with him. "I'll see you tomorrow at nine."

"Okay. Why don't you try dressing casually?"

"Of course."

While trying to get around the piano, the chair, and a soccer ball someone had left, I stumbled into Mr. Hackbirn.

"Oops," he said, catching me.

I looked into his eyes and blushed.

"I'm sorry," I mumbled. Then I frowned.

"Something wrong?" Mr. Hackbirn asked, concerned.

"You've got something in your eye," I said.

He looked away and blinked a couple of times.

"No, I don't."

"Yes, you do. I can see it. It's an eyelash, kind of near the center."

"You got a mirror?"

I was already heading for the kitchen.

"In the bathroom. Hang on, I'm getting a tissue."

"Never mind."

"You got it?" I came back into the hallway. He was looking at something between his forefinger and thumb.

"I didn't think I had anything in there." He walked past me into the bathroom, leaving the door open.

"I know I saw something," I said, standing in the doorway. He pulled a small, flat plastic bottle out of the inside breast pocket of his suit jacket. "It was a little line."

"This is what you saw." Mr. Hackbirn held out his hand. On his forefinger was a light blue curved plastic lens.

"You wear contact lenses?" I couldn't help giggling

a little.

"I am extremely nearsighted." He rubbed a few drops of the liquid from the bottle onto the lens, then rinsed it under the faucet (he'd already pulled the plug). "I admit I got them for pure vanity. But..."

He stopped as he inserted the lens underneath his eyelid.

"Oh, gross." I looked away.

He just chuckled.

"But," he continued. "They have slowed down my eyes from getting worse."

"I'm glad." My stomach was doing mild flipflops.

I left the doorway, and he left the house.

The next morning, I was in the family room French braiding Janey's hair. Right at nine, I heard Darby yell, "He's here!" and the sound of his feet pounding down the stairs. I was doing two braids on Janey. I had the first one done and was midway through the second. Ellen sat on the floor next to us, still in her pajamas with pink sponge rollers in her hair. Neil was upstairs dressing the twins.

"Janey, please hold still," I said as the doorbell rang. "Darby will answer the door."

I have said before that Mr. Hackbirn is an impeccable dresser. To be more specific, he's the type of person that always looks dressed up even in the most casual clothes. That morning he was wearing very tight dark blue dress jeans with a light blue shirt and the inevitable sweater around his shoulders.

"Good morning," he said, smiling. "Why aren't you ready?"

"You are obviously unaware of the logistics involved in getting six people ready to go somewhere," I replied, also smiling.

"They must be incredible." Mr. Hackbirn's eyebrows rose.

"What's logistics?" asked Janey.

"Look it up in the dictionary," I answered automatically.

"I can't. You're doing my hair."

"Then hold still, and you can look it up later."

"Kind of chilly out here," remarked Mr. Hackbirn. "It was sunny in L.A."

In Orange County the sky was overcast, and the air had a definite bite to it.

"Twenty percent chance of rain, I heard," I said.

"I don't think it will." He walked into the hallway, pulling the sweater from his shoulders.

After putting it on, he opened the bathroom door and checked himself in the mirror. He straightened his collar and ran a reassuring hand over his hair. It didn't need it. Even with all its waves, Mr. Hackbirn's hair is always perfect.

"You didn't have to get so dressed up," I said as he came back into the room. "I did say casual."

"I am."

Darby laughed. He was wearing blue jeans with a bright yellow t-shirt that had the Mercedes-Benz logo on it and scuffed running shoes. Janey also had on jeans. But she was wearing a V-necked sweater over a plaid blouse with an eyelet-trimmed collar. She was barefoot, however.

I had opted for a similar outfit, this one including my deck shoes. My deck shoes are my favorite pair of shoes. They were originally white, but now they're a dirty gray. The toes are scuffed up and the heels are starting to wear down. But they don't have any holes in them. Yet.

I finished Janey's braid.

"Ellen, please give me the ponytail band. No, not the dental floss. Thank you." I looped the band around the end of the braid. "Okay, you're done. Go get your shoes on."

Janey got up and ran upstairs. As I stood up, I noticed Mr. Hackbirn subtly but restlessly prowling about the room.

"Why don't you sit down," I said. "I've still got to dress Ellen and get things together. There's no rush anyway. The stores don't open 'til ten."

"Stores?" groaned Darby with shocked disgust. "We're not going shopping, are we?"

"I've got errands to run," I said firmly.

"But I thought we were going someplace neat."

"I want to go to the zoo," said Ellen.

"Some other time, honey," I said, pulling her to her feet. "We haven't got time today."

"I don't want to go shopping," complained Darby. "Couldn't we go to Craig Park at least?"

"Maybe later," I answered. "We'll see what the weather does."

"Stupid weather."

"Please, Darby, no complaints." I felt for him. He hated shopping. "We're going to a nice mall. They have an arcade there, and if you're good, I just might..."

Darby's eyes lit up.

"A surprise?" he asked, grinning and pushing his glasses up on his nose.

"Entirely contingent upon your good behavior."

"What's contingent?"

"Look it up in the dictionary. Come on, Ellen."

I took Ellen upstairs while Darby pulled the big dictionary off the bookshelf.

I put Ellen in a pink dress with a lot of ruffles and black and white oxfords with white ankle socks. Then I brushed out her fine hair and put matching ribbons in it. She looked like a little cherub. I wondered how long it would last. As much as Ellen loves pretty dresses with all the frills, she also loves making messes. How long she stays clean depends a lot on how much supervision she has. That's why she's always the last to be dressed.

Janey had not only put on her running shoes but had found some ribbons for her pigtails and had tied them on, albeit crookedly. I handed Ellen over to her with firm instructions to keep her clean.

I was heading to the twins' room when I heard two small but powerful voices screaming "no shoes!" repeatedly.

"Then you don't go," Neil said firmly, leaving the room and shutting the door behind him.

He winked at me and handed me the diaper bag I had packed earlier with a few toys, diapers, plastic pants, and extra overalls. The twins were in training pants, but accidents were still fairly common.

"Get this downstairs before they catch on," he whispered.

As I headed downstairs, I heard the door open, and a small voice ask for shoes.

When I got to the family room, I dropped the diaper bag next to the couch by my purse. Mr. Hackbirn got up and followed me into the hall. I opened the hall closet and pulled out the twins' stroller. Even folded up, it was large and unwieldy with two seats each facing the other.

"What's that?" he asked, helping me set it against the wall.

"The twins' stroller."

"Why are you bringing it? They can walk."

"That's exactly why I'm bringing it," I explained. Mr. Hackbirn gave me a puzzled frown. "I can strap them down in the stroller. Believe me, Mr. Hackbirn, you don't want to go chasing those two all over the place. Not to mention their talent for getting into trouble." I walked back into the family room.

"Darby," I asked. "Will you help load the stroller in the station wagon, please? The keys are on the couch."

Darby grabbed the keys and ran out. I grabbed my purse and the diaper bag and was about to follow when I saw Mr. Hackbirn carrying the stroller.

"Okay, everybody, time to go!" Neil called, coming down the stairs behind the twins.

Janey and Ellen appeared from the living room where they had been playing and we all went out front to the car. Mr. Hackbirn had just put the stroller in the back. Darby climbed in over it, swiftly followed by Janey. I put Ellen in the middle of the back seat between the twins' car seats and put her seat belt on.

Neil was putting Mitch in the right-hand car seat. I had to chase Marty who had run off halfway down the block.

"Naughty Marty," I scolded when I caught him.

"I run fast." he said happily.

"No kidding," I said and put him in his car seat.

As I straightened up and shut the car door, Neil came up and gave me a big hug.

"Thanks, Lisa," he said warmly. Then he turned to Mr. Hackbirn. "And thank you for going with them."

"It's my pleasure," Mr. Hackbirn said.

"We'll see," replied Neil with a mischievous grin.

"Neil," I groaned, laughing.

Mr. Hackbirn just laughed and got into the car on the passenger side.

We got to the mall without mishap. We spent the morning mostly window shopping. At lunch time we went to the fast-food terrace.

Mae is what I call a health nut. Well, she's not as bad as, say, Mr. Hackbirn, but she won't use salt or refined sugar, refuses to fry anything, and only allows red meat once a week. Her kids are the only kids I know that will eat their vegetables. They have to. They'd go hungry otherwise. Not that Mae underfeeds them. She just doesn't allow snacks and it's a long time between meals if you don't make a point of filling up.

I am the opposite of Mae. If I have one weakness, it's junk food. Actually, I love food in general, but several of my favorite foods are supposedly going to kill me. By rights, I should be very fat and chronically ill. But I'm one of those hated types that never gains weight and almost never gets sick.

Mae knows I feed the kids junk food when I'm out with them. But it's gotten to be a kind of joke that whenever I buy lunch, I swear the kids to secrecy.

After their solemn vow never to tell Mother what Aunt Lisa poisoned them with, I asked them what they wanted. Janey and Ellen are easy to please.

"Hamburgers!" they yelled.

"Hamburgers!" the twins echoed.

"Darby?" I asked.

"I don't know."

"Here," I slipped him a five, "You're old enough to get it yourself."

"Gee, thanks, Aunt Lisa." He ran off happily.

"I'll hold the table," said Mr. Hackbirn.

"You want me to get you something?" I asked.

"No thank you."

"Alright." I swept off with the kids before Janey could ask any questions. I knew Mr. Hackbirn was in sympathy with Mae, and I didn't want his good health to throw a damper on the party.

I returned with the hamburgers, a huge pile of fries, lots of ketchup, four lemon-lime sodas (I would have gotten cola, but I didn't want the kids wired up on the caffeine), and a double chili burger for myself.

Ellen, of course, promptly dribbled ketchup down her front. I sent Janey for a cup of cold water and extra napkins. Darby returned with a large sandwich and a carton of milk. He gave me my change and attacked his sandwich. The twins, as usual, tore up their hamburgers before eating them. To the uninitiated, watching toddlers eat is pretty revolting, but Mr. Hackbirn took it calmly.

"Aunt Lisa," said Janey, handing me the napkins. "They want ten cents for the cup."

"Oh, for heaven's sake," I growled.

Janey was working on getting her fair share of the fries before they were all gone.

"Go ahead and eat, Janey," I said. "I'll get it later."

"Can we go ice skating after lunch, Aunt Lisa?" Darby asked, looking longingly at the rink adjacent to the terrace.

"That'd be fun," I conceded, very tempted. "But what are we going to do with the twins?"

"I don't particularly care to go anyway," said Mr. Hackbirn.

"You could stay with the twins," suggested Darby.

"Darby," said Janey seriously. "That isn't very nice."

"Well, if he doesn't care..." Darby glared at his sister.

"Darby, we're not going skating," I said firmly. "Janey's right. It wouldn't be fair."

"Stupid girl," he grumbled.

"I'm not stupid," Janey yelled.

"Alright, you two," I scolded. "If you're going to bicker, do it someplace else."

Darby finished his sandwich and gulped down his milk.

"Can I go watch the skaters?" he asked, wiping his mouth.

"Would you please get a cup of cold water for me first?" I asked.

"Sure, Aunt Lisa."

"Here." I bent over and grabbed one of the soft drink cups that the twins had spilled. "Rinse this out and get the water from the bathroom."

"Alright."

Darby returned promptly. I washed off Ellen's face and hands, then got as much of the ketchup off her dress as I could. Then I cleaned up the twins and, after removing them, the stroller. Darby was getting impatient, so I gave him charge of Mitch and Marty and Janey charge of Ellen and sent them all to watch the skaters.

"Now would be the time to slip off and go get a salad or something," I said to Mr. Hackbirn.

"I'm not hungry," he said, shaking his head.

"I'll bet."

"When are you going to make that pickup?"

"I was kind of saving the toy store for last if you get my drift. But I suppose we could go when the kids get back."

"I'd just as soon." He sighed a little.

"Well, maybe it'll keep them quiet through my other stops."

"Other stops?" He quirked his eyebrow up.

"I figured if I was 'running errands' I might as well have some errands to run."

"Whatever. Do you have any strategy in mind for the toy store?"

"No. Do you?"

"Not really." He looked over at the skating rink and the kids. "But I would advise having the children as far away as possible."

"No kidding." I thought for a moment. "Maybe we could find someplace to leave the kids. I know. The arcade. You can keep an eye on them while I do my errands."

"I hope it works," he replied with a shrug.

"So do I."

Darby came back with the twins, saying they had to go to the bathroom. Somehow, Mr. Hackbirn got cornered into helping him and off they went.

"It's not hard," I heard Darby say. "They just can't wait all the time, and sometimes..."

His voice was lost in the crowd.

In due time all members of the party were reassembled and on we went. In the camera shop, Darby and I looked over the 35mm S.L.R.'s, trying to decide which one I should buy to replace the one I'd pawned when I was out of work. We concluded that I should go elsewhere because of the price. While we argued I could hear Janey and Mr. Hackbirn discuss good and bad people.

"They're good or bad," she said solemnly. "They fool you. The ones you gotta watch out for are the bad people who do good things. Like I know this one man. He's really bad, but he does real good things, so he fools a lot of people. Not me. I know him."

"Oh," replied Mr. Hackbirn.

"I know you, too."

"I'm a bad person?"

"No! I don't let bad people into my house. You're a good person. But you do bad things."

"Oh, do I?"

"Uh-huh. I can tell. 'Course Mommy said you did, but I could tell anyway."

"Well, nobody's perfect, Janey."

"I know. They're either good or bad."

After that, I made a stop at a dress shop to find a blouse. Almost as if they were cued, the twins began grabbing everything within reach. Mr. Hackbirn was waiting outside with Darby and Ellen. Janey had come in with me.

"This is ridiculous," I grumbled, removing the sleeve of a sweater from Marty's hand. "Come on, Janey."

As we crossed the store's threshold, a loud beeper went off. I groaned and pulled the stroller back into the store. One of the salesclerks and a mall security man ran up. I bent and pulled a dark blouse from Marty's hands. Mr. Hackbirn appeared next to me with a worried frown on his face, and Darby and Ellen at his side.

"Would you remove the children from the stroller," said the security man. It was not a question.

"Certainly." I unstrapped Mitch first.

"What's going on?" asked Mr. Hackbirn.

"A two-year-old kleptomaniac," I replied, shoving Mitch into his arms.

"What's a kleptomaniac?" asked Darby.

Ellen started to cry.

"Are you in trouble, Aunt Lisa?" asked Janey. "Maybe I'd better talk to that man."

"Janey, no!" I grabbed her arm, all too afraid of what her opinion might be. "Listen, you too, Darby. I want the two of you and Ellen to go over to that planter and stay there, do you understand?"

"Yes, ma'am," they mumbled.

I lifted Ellen's chin. "It'll be alright, honey. Really, it will."

The three children left the store and stood by the planter as they were told. I picked up Marty out of the stroller.

"I'm sorry," I said to Mr. Hackbirn.

"This may work to our advantage," he said very quietly.

"May I see your purse," demanded the security man.

"Here," I shifted Marty to my other arm and handed over the purse.

He had already emptied the diaper bag but had not put anything back. A small crowd had gathered. I blushed when he pulled out a certain personal item I'm in the habit of carrying. He looked at the little pouch made of stiff leather attached to my key ring with interest. He opened it and pulled out the can of mace.

"You got a permit for this?" the officer asked.

"In my wallet," I said.

He looked through the wallet, then found the permit and looked at it. He put it back and looked at the rest of the wallet.

"Why do I feel like I'm standing here, stark, staring naked?" I grumbled quietly.

Mr. Hackbirn just smiled his sensual smile, and I felt my heart race and blushed even more.

"Want down," whined Marty, squirming.

"No," I said, sharply.

I looked over at Mitch. He was getting restless also, but at least was sucking his thumb.

"Down," whined Marty again.

"May I put the children back in the stroller, please?" I asked.

"Alright," replied the officer reluctantly. He had finished with my purse and looked at me like he wanted to search me also. He turned to the clerk. "She's clean, and she didn't technically leave the store..." He sounded as if he was sorry I hadn't.

Mr. Hackbirn finished strapping the boys in while I addressed the officer.

"What probably happened was that the blouse was on a lower rack. One of the boys got a hold of it and I didn't see it."

"It is on a lower rack." The clerk eyed me suspiciously as if she didn't believe me.

I started refilling the diaper bag.

"Well, there's no charges to press," said the officer.

The clerk just rolled her eyes skyward and went back further into the store.

I finished with the bag and started putting my things back into the purse.

"The blouse in question is a size sixteen," I said, irritated. The officer just looked at me. "I wear a size eight."

I swung the diaper bag and the purse onto my shoulder and marched out, pushing the twins in front of me.

"I've never been so humiliated in my life." I was seething.

"What's hu—" began Janey.

"Embarrassed," said Darby.

"Well one thing's for sure," I continued. "I can't keep the twins with me, and I've got errands to run."

"Can we go to the arcade?" asked Janey.

I could have kissed her. We went directly there. I gave Darby charge of the twins and told Janey to hold onto Ellen. Mr. Hackbirn lounged in the doorway, keeping one eye on the kids and the other on the young women entering the theater across the way.

I went straight to the toy store. I almost bumped into Ned Harris on the way in.

"Oh! Hello, Mr. Harris."

"Well, hello, Lisa." He grinned. "I hear Mae's getting home today."

"Yeah." I didn't stop to think how he'd heard that. "I've got the kids. Well, they're at the arcade. I'm picking up some surprises."

Harris held up a bag. "I just did."

"Well. Nice talking to you again."

"Nice talking to you."

I waited until he had wandered off before going in.

I asked the girl behind the front register if I could see the manager.

"She's in back," the girl said.

I knocked on the stockroom door.

A young sturdy woman answered. "Yes?"

"Are you the manager?" I asked.

"Yes."

"My name is Mrs. Smith. I believe my husband dropped his keys here the other day."

"Oh, yes, just a minute." She disappeared and came back a minute later with a large bunch of keys on a key ring that had an almost teardrop shaped piece of suede hanging on it. The suede was about two inches long by one inch wide. On the suede was a plastic-coated medallion that had an image of a cannabis leaf on it.

"That's them," I said, smiling and taking them. I slid them into my jeans pocket. "Thank you so much."

I ended up buying each of the children a stuffed animal. Before I headed back to the arcade, I went upstairs to a clothes shop and bought myself a blouse. Leaving that store, I started for the escalators. I stopped for a moment to look in the window of a men's store. I saw a jacket there I liked.

I became aware of the breath on my neck first, then what I guessed to be the barrel of a gun against my spine. I strangled back a scream.

"I wouldn't make any noise, sister," said the voice. "Now, nice and slowly, come with me."

I was pushed slowly along around a corner to a door between two shops. It was labeled for authorized personnel only, but the man had me open the door and pushed me through. The corridor was softly lit. The light brown walls were unfinished with panels of Masonite attached. Several gray doors were interspersed along the walls. Each bore the name of a different shop.

The man twisted my left arm behind me. I dropped the bag containing my blouse. I'd lost the stuffed toys somewhere on the way.

"Alright, where is it?" he demanded.

"Where's what?" I whimpered, then yelped as he twisted harder.

"What you got at the toy store!"

"I don't know. I dropped the bag when you brought me here."

He twisted again. "I'm not talking about toys. I saw you get something from the manager."

"Oh no."

He tossed me onto the ground, then grabbed my purse. Keeping one eye on me, he dumped the contents on the floor, then pawed through them with his foot.

"Alright. Where is it?"

I couldn't answer, I was so scared. He bent and pulled me up by my shoulders. I summoned up what nerve I could and screamed. He backhanded me across the face.

I'm not exactly sure how it happened, but suddenly Mr. Hackbirn was there. He spun the man around and landed a fist on the man's jaw. The man was dazed only for a second. He charged Mr. Hackbirn. Mr. Hackbirn ducked and swung for the man's belly. The man danced back, then let Mr. Hackbirn have it in the eye. Mr. Hackbirn retreated a couple paces and waited. The man flew at him. Mr. Hackbirn ducked, and the man went flying over him.

Somewhere, a door opened. The man scrambled to his feet and went running. The door closed as the man disappeared into the mall.

Mr. Hackbirn, breathing heavily, looked over at me. I was crying.

"Well?" he asked.

"What?" I sniffed.

"Did he get the keys?"

I slid my hand into my pants pocket and drew them out. The keys rattled with the shaking of my hand. His hand gently covered mine. The next thing I knew, he was holding me.

"It's alright, Lisa," he whispered.

I suddenly pulled away, feeling yet another kind of fear.

"Th— the kids," I asked, still shaking. "Where are they?"

"At the arcade, I presume."

"Why'd you leave them?"

"I saw someone I didn't like the looks of, and decided I'd better tail him. It's a good thing I did. I saw that other scum run off with you, and you can figure out the rest. By the way, I found your toys at the door. At least, I assume they're yours. You did buy five stuffed animals, didn't you?"

"Yes." I bent and gathered the contents of my purse together. I began to get angry. "You said there wouldn't be any trouble."

"I said it was unlikely." He rolled his eyes. "There's no way I can guarantee things like that. Are you alright?"

"Yes."

"Lisa, you do know how to defend yourself. Why didn't you?"

"I'm sorry, Mr. Hackbirn. I was scared."

He sighed. "I understand, Miss Wycherly. But you will have to learn to overcome that."

"I will," I said defensively. "Just give me time."

"I hope you've got it." He softened. "I'm sure you'll get there. Are you ready?"

I stood and slung my purse onto my shoulder. Mr. Hackbirn picked up my blouse bag, then at the door to the mall, he retrieved my stuffed toys. He started to put his arm on my shoulders and stopped. He sighed softly.

The kids were waiting for us at the arcade. They had run out of money. They didn't seem to notice my distress as they begged for more quarters. Another half an hour and two dollars to Darby and Janey later, we were headed for home.

As excited as they were, Darby and Janey helped get the others out of the car before running inside. I caught Mr. Hackbirn heading for his Mercedes.

"Come inside," I said. "Mae's already mad that she's the last to meet you. She'll kill me if I let you get away now."

He sighed, nodded, and followed me inside.

The house was full of people. Besides the kids, three couples, friends of Mae and Neil's from church were there. Mae had been settled on the family room couch with her leg propped up on the hassock.

"Thanks so much, Lisa," she said to me as I hugged her and kissed her cheek.

"It's alright," I replied, smiling.

"Well, don't get mad at me, but I'm throwing you back to the wolf."

"What?"

"Your boss, honey. I'm sending you back to work."

"But can you manage?"

Mae jerked her head at the couples sitting around talking.

"They insisted," she said. "I've got the twins and Ellen farmed out. Darby and Janey are old enough to fetch and carry for me, and I've got a meal train coming for the next two weeks. If my knee didn't hurt so bad, I'd have it made."

"Oh, Mae."

"It's not that bad. I can handle it. I take it that's the infamous one hanging back in the doorway, isn't it?"

It was. I turned and waved him over.

"Mae, this is my boss, Mr. Sid Hackbirn."

"Hi, Sid," said Mae, genially. "I've heard a lot about you."

"So, I've been told." He looked at me briefly.

Mae laughed. "Those kids of mine. Couldn't keep a secret for love nor money. It was so sweet of you to go out with them today. I hope they weren't too bad."

Mr. Hackbirn shook his head and smiled. "They're good kids."

"I'd better go pack," I said, heading upstairs.

I packed in less than fifteen minutes. I brought my suitcase downstairs and set it by the door with my purse. I went to the family room where Mr. Hackbirn was chatting with Neil.

"I'm ready," I said to him.

"Well," said Mr. Hackbirn, "I'd like to get going then."

"Alright."

"Kids," Neil called. "Aunt Lisa's leaving now!"

They all gathered around and followed Mr. Hackbirn and me to the front door. I gave them each a hug and a kiss, then turned to pick up my suitcase.

"Goodbye, Uncle Sid," said Janey.

"Uncle what?" Mr. Hackbirn was utterly shocked.

He looked at me for help. I just shrugged and shook my head. He turned to the children.

"Goodbye," he said, still shaken.

Ellen came up and hugged his legs, while Darby shook his hand. Janey motioned for him to bend down to her. He bent politely. She kissed his cheek and hugged him.

"I love you, Uncle Sid," I heard her say.

Deeply touched, he just hugged her back. I think that was the first time somebody had said that to him, at least somebody not in the throes of passion. Quietly, he released her and went to the door. Suitcase in hand, I followed, stopping first to give the okay sign. They cheered.

I let Mr. Hackbirn drive in silence until it got to me.

"You survived that pretty well," I said cautiously.

"Yeah, I did." His voice sounded rather far away.

"So, what now?"

"Hm? Oh." He glanced over at me as he steered the car around another slower one. "What about the keys? I'd like to find out what the fuss was about."

I pulled out the keys that had somehow landed back in my jeans pocket and looked at the suede teardrop. It was two pieces sewn together. Underneath the medallion, a white piece of paper showed through a hole cut in the top layer. I pulled it out and deciphered the code written on it.

"Professor Lipplinger needs extracting," I said after a few minutes. "You've got to go to Washington D.C. to get him and hide him immediately.

"Wonderful," Mr. Hackbirn replied.

"I'll call the airlines when we get home."

"Good, and book me a room, too, will you? You've got my charge card number, right?"

"Yeah."

"By the way, I travel first class."

"It figures."

There was a silence for ten minutes more.

"So, what do you think?" I asked.

"About what?"

"The past two days."

"Interesting." His voice sounded far away again. "Very interesting."

Mr. Hackbirn left before five o'clock the following
morning and had the decency to call a taxi to
take him to the airport. I slept in until eight, ran and
showered and found a note on the breakfast room table
giving me permission to drive his car as needed, but
no instructions about any other work he wanted done.

There was the usual fruit salad in the refrigerator,
but only a small, single serving. I shook my head. There
was bread in the pantry, and I decided to see if there
was anything, like maybe some cereal in the pantry, as
well. In fact, that's where Conchetta found me when
she came in that morning.

"What are you doing in there?" she asked, sounding
pretty annoyed.

"I'm sorry!" I gulped. "I was just looking to see if
there was any cereal or oatmeal or something. The boss
left really early this morning. I guess he made the fruit
salad last night, but he didn't really make enough."

Conchetta looked at me strangely. "That's how
much I make for him when he's alone."

"Oh." I sighed and went back to my search. "What's
this?"

Way in the back of the shelves in the tiny room
were three cans of Dr. Pepper. I pulled one out.
Conchetta laughed loudly, and I almost gaped.

"I didn't know those were still there." She laughed
again, then looked at me, somewhat abashed. "Perhaps
we'd better keep this a secret."

I put the can back. "What do you mean?"

"Sid really likes to eat." Conchetta smiled softly.
"He loved junk food, too." She waved at the cans. "His

favorite breakfast was Dr. Pepper and Cheetos. The crispy ones, not the puffy air ones."

I couldn't help laughing. "That's one of my favorite breakfasts, too."

"Yeah, but he drank two pots of coffee a day, ate steaks day in, day out. I made most of his food out of that French cooking book, by Julia Child, and the really fattening stuff, too. Only about two and a half, three years ago, he started having some real problems with his gut. So, I started making more healthy food for him. He starts eating better and he's a new man."

"Oh." I sighed. "That explains the small portions."

Conchetta shook her head. "That happened a year later. He started gaining weight. Either way, he can't eat that old crap." She paused and winced. "But please don't tell him I told you. He doesn't like admitting he can't eat the way he used to."

"I don't see why I would," I said and frowned. "I can see eating healthy, but I'm still pretty hungry." I winced, too. "I eat a lot. I'm told it's a high metabolism."

"We'll see." Her chuckle was more than a little skeptical. "I'll fix something nice for lunch. What do you like?"

"Pretty much anything. I love to eat."

"Hm." She looked at me warily. "You like Mexican food?"

My eyes lit up. "Love it, and the spicier, the better."

She actually smiled, then glared at me. "We're still not friends."

"Okay."

[I remain amazed that you knew all that so early on and never played my old eating habits against me. – SEH]

Lunch was just chicken salad, but for a change, there was plenty of it. That evening, Conchetta made lots of chicken tacos with a green chile sauce that made my eyes water. I was in Heaven and let her know.

Tuesday, I cleaned up the files, and got spaghetti with meat sauce for lunch, and the most amazing chiles rellenos I'd ever eaten for dinner. I got a little concerned when I hadn't heard from Mr. Hackbirn by Wednesday. But there really wasn't anything I could do about it. On the other hand, I was eating really well. Conchetta made up a huge pot of carnitas, some of which I had for lunch that day with some vinegary cole slaw. Then that night, she grilled a steak and served it with mac and cheese, green beans, and a huge salad on the side.

"Thank you so much!" I crowed as she put the plate on the breakfast room table

"It's nice to change things every now and then." She almost smiled.

"It's nice to be eating good food," I said, grinning. "And to be getting enough food for once." [There is no such thing. – SEH]

She shrugged, then reminded me where the dish should go in the dishwasher. Conchetta was incredibly finicky about where things went in the kitchen, probably because she spent so much time there. When she wasn't slipping invisibly around the house cleaning, she was in the kitchen, usually watching her novelas, or soap operas, on the small TV on the counter. She was gone by five-thirty every afternoon, too. I wondered a little about that and asked her why that Wednesday afternoon.

"Because I need to be home," she said, and left.

That was when I decided that I would find out her story. Most of the time, she was so prickly. She wasn't mean, just really, really wary.

I still hadn't heard anything from Mr. Hackbirn by Thursday. I decided that if I hadn't heard anything by Friday noon, I would call Henry James. Thus resolved, I spent the day making a blouse for myself and wondering what I was going to do about Christmas presents.

I usually make at least one Christmas present for everyone in my family. It's just the way I do things. That and it's cheaper. But that year I had plenty of money. I was already committed to making Christmas sweaters for the twins and Ellen and had Ellen's half-done. I still decided to make things for everyone else but was kind of stuck when I thought about Mr. Hackbirn. He wasn't the type to go for arts and crafts stuff. He had everything he could want. What to do?

I puzzled over the problem until noon when it dawned on me that he was very fond of pullover sweaters. I've been knitting since I was a kid and I make very nice sweaters. I tried to think if there was a type of sweater he didn't have and he didn't have one of those Aran Isles fisherman's sweaters. I'd made one for Neil years ago, so I knew what I was up against. I bit my lip. That certainly seemed like the solution. I just hoped he would like it.

With that problem solved, I went to lunch (a wonderful plate of roast beef sandwiches with mayonnaise, cheese, and mashed avocado) and then back to my sewing.

It was a little after three when I thought I heard the front door open and close. I looked up at the small white box above my door. It had a little red light flashing that told me someone had come in. Nervously, I pulled my Model Thirteen from my bedside table, checked the cylinder, and went to investigate.

Quietly, I slipped through the house to the front hall. Sitting next to the bench there was Mr. Hackbirn's suitcase. So, he was home. I wondered why he hadn't called to have me pick him up. Then I wondered if there was something wrong.

There was, but not anything immediately endangering my health and wellbeing. Well, maybe my health. As I approached the office, I heard a coarse hacking cough from within. Still leery, I stayed clear of the doorway.

"Mr. Hackbirn?" I called.

"Yeah," came the reply. It sounded a little hoarse.

I slid in. The door to his office was open and I saw him looking at a sheet of paper. He raised his fist to his lips, and I heard that awful cough again. I set my gun on my desk and went into his office.

"Are you alright?" I asked.

"I'm fine," he grumbled. "Just picked up a cold."

"I'll say."

He sniffed, then coughed again. He dropped the paper onto his desk and sank into his chair. He looked very tired, his eyes and nose were red, and his cheeks were a little flushed.

"Rough trip?" I asked.

"A complete waste of time," he growled. "Lipplinger won't budge until the end of the term. Says he's got a couple of students that are failing, and he wants to help them."

"That's sweet of him. But couldn't you make him see the danger?"

"I didn't even get to talk to him. I had to go through the guard team." He put his face in his hands for a moment.

I noticed he was wearing a thin gold wedding band on his left hand.

"Did you stop over in Las Vegas?" I asked, completely puzzled.

"What?" He looked at me.

"Your ring."

"Oh." He pulled it off and dropped it onto the desk and coughed. "I was traveling under an assumed name and when Lipplinger wouldn't move I decided to make it feasible for you to come with me next time. I hope you don't mind traveling as my wife."

"As long as I don't have to act like one."

"Fat chance." He sounded miserable.

My heart softened.

"You look terrible," I said gently.

"Thanks."

"Why don't you go to bed?"

"I'm fine," he grumbled. "Where's my mail?"

I walked over and put my hand on his forehead.

"You've got a fever." My fingers probed behind his jaw. "I wonder if your glands are swollen."

"Leave me alone," he snapped angrily, catching my wrist, and pulling it away.

We stared at each other for a tense moment. Then he gently let go of my wrist and looked away.

"I'm sorry," he said. "I'm not feeling very well."

"Why don't you go get into your pajamas and into bed and I'll bring your suitcase and your mail."

Another cough rocked his body.

"Alright," he said meekly.

I watched him go, then gathered up the mail and my gun from my desk. I got the suitcase next. But instead of going to Mr. Hackbirn's room, I stopped first at my own, dropped off the gun and gathered a couple of things from the medicine chest. Then I went to the kitchen to tell Conchetta that the boss was home, but we could still have fried chicken and mashed potatoes because he was sick.

"It's just the flu, I think," I told her. "I've got some cough syrup here, but maybe some hot tea would be good, too."

"It would." She nodded. "He needs chicken soup. I'll make it."

A minute later, I was on the other side of the house where Mr. Hackbirn's bedroom was and knocked on the door.

"Are you in bed?" I called.

There was another cough, and then a weak "yes."

His room is done in dark colors, with dark polished furniture. On one wall is a sliding glass door to the side yard covered with dark drapes pulled back and sheer off-white drapes underneath. On the other side of the glass doors is a small patio with a large hot tub. The wall facing the doors has a long closet with sliding mirrored doors and another door to the bathroom. The long low dresser is next to the door I had come in. On the wall opposite is a king-size waterbed. It has a valance over it with dark drapes tied back to the wall.

I didn't know what I'd been expecting, but I was glad to find there wasn't anything to embarrass me. I put the suitcase down and the mail and other things on top of the dresser. I looked around again. The clothes that Mr. Hackbirn had been wearing had already been put away. Mr. Hackbirn was lying in bed, propped up by pillows. His blankets were pulled to halfway up his bare chest.

"What's that thing around your neck?" he asked.

I looked down.

"It's my tape measure," I said, picking up the thermometer I had brought and shaking it down. "I was working on a blouse when you came in."

"Miss Wycherly, I thought I as paying you well enough for you to avoid such economies."

"You are," I said, checking the mercury and shaking some more. "I can't help it if I'm basically cheap. Besides, I like to sew. It's great therapy." I walked over and put the thermometer in his mouth. "And heaven knows, I need it around here."

"But..."

I put my hand under his chin. "Shut up. If you want me to unpack, just nod."

He nodded sullenly.

A little looking around found two hampers in the bathroom. A quick peek inside told me one was for the dry cleaners, the other, for the laundry.

Mr. Hackbirn watched me as I picked the suitcase up and balanced it on one corner of the bed. I think he was waiting for me to turn purple when I saw his underwear. I got him, though. As easily as I get embarrassed, men's underwear doesn't bother me. While growing up on my parent's resort I did a little bit of everything, including the guests' laundry. I had handled all kinds of underwear, and plenty of it.

"Is everything dirty?" I asked, looking at the neatly packed clothes.

Mr. Hackbirn grunted.

"Oh, shoot." I remembered the thermometer and ran over and pulled it out.

"Yes, it's all dirty," Mr. Hackbirn said.

"Ninety-nine point eight," I replied. "That confirms it. You've got the flu."

"I didn't know you were a doctor."

"I'm not. But after all those years of babysitting Mae's kids, I'm an expert on the flu."

I quickly emptied the suitcase, taking the clothes to the bathroom and dumping them in their respective hampers. I came back into the room puzzled. Something was missing. Mr. Hackbirn coughed again as I checked the suitcase.

"Something wrong?" he asked.

"I think you may have left your pajamas. I can't seem to find any."

"I don't have any pajamas."

I could feel my face turn scarlet as I turned my back to him.

"You don't mean to tell me..."

"That I don't have anything on underneath these covers? No, I don't."

He was enjoying it. I could tell. He loved embarrassing me.

"Mr. Hackbirn..."

"Come on. You'd have never known if you hadn't asked me."

"Then why do I get the feeling that you've just been laying there waiting for me to ask?"

He just laughed, then coughed really hard. Embarrassed or not, I was reminded he wasn't feeling very well. I decided I was not going to let him get the better of me. Taking a deep breath, I turned around.

"We'd better take care of that cough," I said, briskly.

"What do you have in mind?"

I unscrewed the top off a bottle I'd gotten from my medicine cabinet and picked up a spoon.

"This," I said, smiling and going over to him. "It's the best thing for coughs."

"What is in it?" He eyed the unlabeled bottle suspiciously.

"My grandmother makes it," I poured a spoonful.

"Oh, no you don't."

"Oh, yes I do. Relax, Mae gives this to her kids and she's just as finicky as you are."

"What's in it?" He didn't quite trust it, but he opened his mouth.

"Honey, lemon juice and corn liquor." I spooned it in fast and poured another.

"Corn liquor?"

"A.K.A. white lightning, moonshine. My grandpa made his living on his own blend. When he died, I'm told you could hear G-men cheer in three counties. Of course, they neglected to make sure that his still was out of operation. But Grandma just makes the stuff for medicinal purposes."

"Oh, really."

"Mm-hm. Open up." I put the second spoonful in. "You can take two more in four hours. To continue, rest assured. Grandma's a temperance lady except when she runs short of cash. Then she's got a couple of good customers willing to oblige."

"Sounds like an interesting lady."

"She is. But you two wouldn't get along. She takes a very dim view of you-know-what. Some folks say that's why Grandpa died young."

"Was it?"

"I doubt it. Grandpa got around quite a bit. There's a whole bunch of families that, as Grandma would say, have babies with Caulfield features what have no right to have 'em."

Mr. Hackbirn laughed. "So, what did kill your grandfather?"

It was my turn to laugh. "A bad batch of corn liquor."

He looked at the bottle. "That's so reassuring."

"Don't worry. Mama told me it was because he was drunk when he mixed the mash. Grandma doesn't drink, so you're okay."

He coughed, but already it was noticeably gentler.

He sighed and laid his head back against the headboard.

"What about my mail?" he asked.

I put the bottle back on the dresser and picked up the letters.

"Answers to two queries," I said, picking out the envelopes.

"Good. Which ones?"

"The bank one and how to buy a personal computer."

"And...?"

"Both affirmative."

"Terrific. Put the outlines on my desk."

"They're already there. But I'll bring them in here first thing tomorrow. You are staying in bed."

"I suppose. What else?"

"The check for the personal finance piece that you need to endorse. The gas and phone bills, which are already paid. You just need to sign the checks. Several ads, one wishing to sell you the secret to a healthy, happy sex life..."

Mr. Hackbirn chuckled.

"Which I pitched," I continued. "Three fan letters, which I'm putting on your nightstand for you to read at your leisure." Fan letters were what I called the notes from Mr. Hackbirn's various girlfriends. "And this."

I dropped the legal-size envelope on Mr. Hackbirn's chest. It had come that morning, addressed to Mr. Hackbirn in care of me. I had immediately recognized both Darby and Mae's handwriting, Darby having written the return address and Mr. Hackbirn's name and Mae having written the rest. On the back, Darby had written, "Please don't open this, Aunt Lisa." Mr. Hackbirn coughed and looked at it, bewildered.

"What is it?" he asked.

I shrugged. "I have no idea. I was asked not to open it."

He shook his head and opened the letter. Dying of curiosity, but equally determined not to pry, I took the rest of the mail back to the dresser.

"What on earth?" he muttered. "Would you mind explaining this to me?"

"What's the matter?" I walked over to him. "Can't read Darby's handwriting?"

"Oh, I can read it. It's just... Here."

I took the letter. The writing was Darby's.

"Dear Uncle Sid," it said. "We O'Malley's got together Sunday night and had a family meeting. We talked about you and decided that you should be made an official family friend. This means that you are automatically invited to all family celebrations and holidays and can come at any time to visit and we hope you will. This means too that if you need us, we are here. We love you."

It was signed by the whole family, even Mitch and Marty.

"Wow," I exclaimed softly.

"They sent this, too."

He handed me another piece of paper. This one was parchment, of sorts. It had a purple scrollwork border and it proclaimed that Mr. Sid Hackbirn (carefully printed in) was an official Friend of the O'Malley family, entitled to all privileges, etc., and signed again by the whole family.

"So that was what they were squabbling about," I said.

"Who?"

"Darby and Janey. Don't you remember? Last Saturday. They were fighting over something in the stationery store. This must have been it."

"Hm. But what does it mean?"

"Just what it says, I expect. It looks like you've been adopted, boss."

"Hm." He sounded bemused.

I left him still looking over the letter and the certificate.

Friday morning, I went running when Mr. Hackbirn reminded me that I needed to. I think he figured I'd conveniently forgot while he was gone. I hadn't entirely, but I had missed a couple days. His cough was still pretty bad, so he spent the day in bed. That afternoon I decided to ask him about my sitting room.

"I'd like to move the couch and the coffee table out," I told him.

He shrugged and sniffled. "I don't care. You can do whatever you want in there." He coughed. "In fact, I'll call the decorator."

"No. Don't. I'll fix it up, myself. It will feel more like it's mine that way."

"Whatever." His eyebrow lifted. "So. You're staying here."

"Yeah. It is convenient."

"Yeah." He smiled, then coughed.

The poor thing was still feeling pretty lousy. I went shopping on Saturday and found an enormous red velvet Victorian couch with intricate carvings on the oak frame that I really liked, plus another desk, and more bookshelves. I also ordered a full-sized cutting table with shelving underneath that I'd seen in one of my sewing magazines. Sunday, I put up the bookshelves and arranged the two desks and couch to fit around the coming cutting table, and the new ironing board and iron that I'd also bought. I looked around with great satisfaction. I felt so at home there.

Mr. Hackbirn wasn't back to normal until Monday. Even then he was still a little drained and sniffling. I hadn't said anything about Lipplinger the whole time he was sick, although I had a strong feeling there was more to be said on the subject. I waited until an hour after lunch when I brought the printed drafts of the two articles he had written over the weekend into his office.

"Looks good," he said, flipping through them.

"Thanks," I replied. There was a pause. "Um. May I ask you a question?"

"Yes."

"What's going to happen with Lipplinger? I

remember you said something about next time."

"Yeah. We're going to have to take him physically."

"Kidnap?"

"Not exactly. We just have to get to him and if necessary, use force."

I sighed.

"Don't worry," Mr. Hackbirn said. "I'm sure it won't come to that."

"I hope not. I don't know if I could hit a nice old man over the head and drag him off."

Mr. Hackbirn smiled. "We don't do that anyway. The worst we'd do is stick a gun in his ribs. But I think I can talk him into seeing reason."

"How are you going to talk to him when you couldn't get through last time?"

"That's what took so long. We'll have to go through his sister, who is Ms. Hattie Mitchell."

"Is that someone I'm supposed to know?" I asked with a nervous smile.

Mr. Hackbirn shrugged. "She's made a name for herself among the Fortune 500 gang. Her husband was Damon Mitchell, founder and owner of Mitchell Electronics, Inc."

"Oh."

"Less than twenty years ago it was just a one-man office. Thanks to government contracts, Mitchell built it into a defense electronics empire in seven years, then died, left it all to his wife, and she turned around and built a major conglomerate."

"And the wife is Hattie Mitchell."

"Uh-huh."

"How's she going to help?"

"Well, under my assumed name, on the pretext of interviewing her for an article, I spent a lovely afternoon chatting with Ms. Mitchell and managed to get an invitation for Mr. Ed Donaldson and his lovely wife to join Hattie and her brother for Thanksgiving dinner."

"You being Ed Donaldson, with me as his lovely

wife."

"You got it."

"You don't." I was very irritated by the way he had casually overlooked my feelings in the matter. "Did it ever occur to you that your lovely wife has a family, and she wants to spend Thanksgiving with them?"

"For a brief moment. However, remember the objective is getting to Lipplinger. Thanksgiving is the next time he'll be seeing Hattie and therefore is the only chance we'll have to talk to him."

"But I can't miss Thanksgiving with my family!" I blinked back tears.

"I'm afraid you'll have to."

I was shocked. "That's asking too much."

"Miss Wycherly," Mr. Hackbirn sounded very tired. "We've already established that I cannot fire you and you cannot quit. So will you please accept the fact that you will not be spending Thanksgiving with your family and bear in mind that it is in the interest of helping to ensure that there will be other Thanksgivings to spend with them that you are doing so."

I swallowed. He was right. But I still felt like crying. I didn't somehow.

"I suppose." I got up to go, very downcast.

"It can't be all that bad," said Mr. Hackbirn.

I looked at him. "Yes, it is."

"You have dinner with them almost every Sunday. What's so special about one Thursday?"

I stared at him, unbelieving. "Is that all it is to you? Just a Thursday?"

"In effect, yes."

"But it's Thanksgiving."

"A part of Capitalistic propaganda to convince the people they are not oppressed and dedicated to a god that doesn't exist."

"Do you really believe that?"

"No. I gave up Communism, remember? But that was my aunt's philosophy, and therefore how I was raised."

"You never celebrated Thanksgiving?"

"Or Christmas, Easter, Mother's Day, Fourth of July, Labor Day, Halloween. In fact, the only day I've ever celebrated was New Year's Eve."

"That's awful."

"Not really. Never having done it, I never missed it."

"But when your friends did..."

Mr. Hackbirn was silent for a long moment.

"I don't want you to feel sorry for me because there is nothing to feel sorry for." He stopped and looked at me. "But I've only had a couple friends who were that close to me. I am what is commonly called a loner by my own choice. I have always been that way. I'm used to seeing people do things I've never done. I grew up that way and it never bothered me."

I sank back into my chair. The tears I could no longer hold back ran down my cheeks.

"I was afraid you'd do that." Mr. Hackbirn sighed and pushed the box of tissues on his desk towards me.

"I'm sorry." I sniffed and took one. "I can't help it."

"Miss Wycherly, my lonely lot in life really doesn't bother me."

"I know. Why do you think I'm crying?"

As the week passed, I found out a couple other things about Mr. Hackbirn that made me thank God for the miracle that had caused Mae and the family to attach themselves to him. One was that he was an atheist. Well, I had more or less figured that he was. But he actually admitted it over dinner one night.

The other thing was about his aunt. We were shopping for, believe it or not, wedding rings for Mrs. Donaldson. Mr. Hackbirn says it's the details that can trip you up faster than anything when you're undercover. I made some comment about getting my Christmas cards out. In the discussion that ensued it came out that Mr. Hackbirn had not spoken to his aunt in over thirteen years. I stopped dead in my tracks.

"How could you?" I exclaimed.

"It was not my idea," replied Mr. Hackbirn calmly. "It was her idea to kick me out."

"But what happened?"

"I allowed myself to be drafted by the U.S. Army instead of going off to Canada. Aside from the fact that I did not share my aunt's beliefs, Canada was too cold for me, and I didn't particularly want to be a fugitive." [Yeah, the excuse I always made. – SEH]

"How sad. You must have been devastated."

Mr. Hackbirn shook his head. "I don't talk about it."

"Oh, Mr. Hackbirn."

"Now don't start crying again." He shifted uncomfortably. "You and I both know I don't like it, but it's a fact of my life and there's no point in blubbering about it."

"I'll try, sir."

"Alright. Let's get that stupid ring bought and get going."

"Yes, sir."

"And don't 'sir' me. This isn't the army."

I couldn't squelch a giggle at his irritation. He glared at me, then laughed.

"At least that's a little closer to the role you're playing," he said.

"I'm sorry I can't hang all over you," I replied. "It just isn't right for me."

"Fine. But do me a favor and don't blush when the salesperson asks to help us."

Mr. Hackbirn held open the door to a jewelry store for me. I entered and cast a quick glance over the glass cases. That's when I saw it. It wasn't a ring. It was a necklace, a fine gold chain with a pendant. The pendant wasn't more than three-quarters of an inch tall or wide. It was two open rectangles, one was brushed gold, the other polished. In the middle of the polished rectangle was oval opal surrounded by tiny diamonds. I was entranced. It was so delicate and beautiful.

"That necklace," I whispered.

"We're looking for rings," said Mr. Hackbirn. I hadn't noticed that he had his arm around my waist, I was so fascinated.

"I know. But that necklace is so beautiful. I really like it."

"So, buy it."

I shook my head. "I don't like keeping fine jewelry. It makes me nervous. I'm always afraid I'll lose it. I wonder how much it is."

"May I help you?" asked the salesclerk, a woman around Mr. Hackbirn's age.

"How much is that necklace, the one with the opal?" I asked before Mr. Hackbirn could say anything.

"We're not here for that," he said, amused.

"I know. Just let me find out how much it is and then we'll go look at rings."

"It's two hundred dollars," replied the clerk.

"That's a lot," I said, shaking my head.

"No, it isn't," said Mr. Hackbirn, and considering the store we were in, it wasn't. "If you like it, buy it."

"No," I sighed. "I— I don't think so. We're not here for that."

I forced my attention to the rings. Mr. Hackbirn made the actual selection. The engagement ring had a one-carat round-cut diamond. The rest of the ring looked like the diamond had been set at the top of a wing of filigreed gold that curled around the main diamond, with tiny diamonds scattered throughout. The band part had a row of diamonds, although it was mostly hidden under the wing part of the engagement ring. Fortunately, the set fit as it was, so we could take it with us. As we left the store, I took one long parting look at the opal necklace. I sighed and went out.

Mr. Hackbirn rolled his eyes skyward.

"I've never met anybody before so tight with the bucks," he sighed, as we walked to his car.

"You try scrounging sometime."

"But that's the point." He shook his head and held out his hands. "You do not have to scrounge. That necklace would have barely dented your bank balance."

"I know."

"Then why are you so tight?"

"It's just my nature, I guess."

Tight with the bucks or not, that necklace haunted my thoughts. After about a week, I decided that maybe Mr. Hackbirn was right. I went back to the store to look at it. It was gone. I asked the salesclerk, and she assured me it had been sold. Downcast, I left the store.

November 18-26, 1982

When two people work together as closely as Mr. Hackbirn and I do, there's bound to be some friction. In truth, we get along very well. Aside from our individual value systems, which are radically opposed, we have a lot in common and we complement each other. We have managed to develop a very good relationship. But we both had some growing to do first and it wasn't easy.

Part of the problem revolved around those various idiosyncrasies that each person has that drive another person nuts. Well, I shouldn't say that they were part of the problem because they were more the catalyst for the unrest that got Mr. Hackbirn and me into the biggest fight I have ever had in my life, and I have had some doozies.

On my part, my singing bothered Mr. Hackbirn, although it was not my voice because even he admits I sing fairly well. What he objected to was that I did it constantly. I could see his point. He'd be in his office trying to work when he'd hear this soft snatch of music. Some days it'd be just the same refrain over and over again, other days whole songs. A couple of times, I sang whole shows. He tried turning on the radio to drown me out, but I just sang along with that and louder, too.

Then he never could understand why I was so cheap. To be truthful, I couldn't either. I'd always been that way. I think that's what helped me survive the year I was out of work. Anyway, it would drive him nuts every time I'd shake my head and say, "But that's too much!"

The thing that really got to him, though, was my appetite. When he first picked me up, he sort of understood. I'd been out of work for a year. I was starving. But when it never slowed down, it got on his nerves. Worse still, I never gained an ounce. That must have been what really bugged him, because although he won't admit it, he does have to keep an eye on his weight.

On the other side of the coin, I was hungry, and when I said so, I got a lecture. Those lectures were incredible. Mr. Hackbirn would go into every possible consequence of poor eating habits he could think of with anatomical precision. He even threatened to take me to the county morgue a couple of times so I could see for myself what I was doing to my insides.

When he wasn't lecturing me about food, he was teasing me. He could turn anything I said into something smutty and often did, just to make me blush. Woe to me if I tried to one up him, too. I was incredibly naive, so I didn't stand a chance and I ended up twice as embarrassed.

The only thing that was worse was his habit of chewing ice. It made me laugh. I tried not to, but I couldn't help it. He finally got fed up and asked me what was so funny.

"It's really stupid," I said, still giggling.

It was a chilly day and for some reason, he was drinking ice water and chomping away.

"I can imagine," he said dryly. "So, tell me."

"Well, when I was in high school, there were certain things one didn't do. They were stupid little things that were supposed to mean other things and it didn't matter if they did or not because of that being the way things were. You may even have heard of some. Like green M&M's."

"Green M&M's?"

"You know, the little candies."

"I know. But what did they mean?"

"They were supposed to make you horny. We all knew it was ridiculous. But go to any party and by the middle of the evening, the M&M's bowl would have nothing but green ones in it and everyone avoiding it like it had V.D. Until some stupid freshman got to it, or some guy trying to tell somebody something. It was like wintergreen Lifesavers. Guys carried them around all the time, but no girl would be caught dead with them."

"They were supposed to spark against your teeth in the dark, right?"

"Right."

"I outgrew that ploy when I was seven."

"I'm sure you did."

"So, what was chewing ice?"

I giggled and blushed. "Sexually frustrated."

He looked at me, then at his glass, then back at me. I could hear the ice crunching between his teeth.

"That is obviously not true," he said and bit down on another ice cube.

After that, it began to get on my nerves, because I began to wonder if he was trying to tell me something. I was pretty sure it was unconscious, but with Mr. Hackbirn, one never knew.

The fight that all this aggravation led to started shortly before we left for Washington and lasted to its final cataclysm the day after Thanksgiving, just about a week. It sounds kind of funny, but it was Mr. Hackbirn who started it, and it was his fault it lasted so long. [Sigh. I know. – SEH]

About two weeks before we left, just before we'd gotten the ring, Mr. Hackbirn got a phone call from one of his girlfriends.

"Sid? I've got some bad news..." was all I heard (and wanted to hear) before I hung up. I figured she was pregnant and trying to hang it on Mr. Hackbirn. It was a short conversation because I heard him angrily bang down the phone in a rare display of emotion. So much for her baby.

Then a week and a half later, the pharmacy called and said Mr. Hackbirn's prescription was ready. I was on my way out on an errand already, so I didn't bother him. I just put it on my list and went out.

The prescription was for penicillin. I was puzzled.

Mr. Hackbirn had been rather grumpy that morning, but he didn't seem to be having any trouble swallowing, or anything else wrong with him for that matter. Then I remembered the bad news phone call. I put the pieces together and what I came up with wasn't strep throat.

I snickered and then realized he needed my sympathy. However he got it, he probably wasn't feeling very well.

I came sailing cheerfully into the house. Mr. Hackbirn stopped me in my office.

"What took you so long?" he growled.

"There was a sale at the sporting goods store, so I picked up some cold weather gear. The climate's a little different in Washington, you know." I opened up one of my bags and pulled out the leather fleece lined gloves. "You like?"

"Hm." He barely even glanced at them and went into his office.

I picked up the bag from the pharmacy and followed him.

"I picked up your prescription," I said, laying it on his desk.

"What did you do that for?" he snapped.

"Well, they called, and I was going out, so I thought I'd save you a trip."

"You didn't save me anything."

"I'm sorry." There was a pause. "I can't take the gloves back, but if you don't want them, you don't have to reimburse me."

"Miss Wycherly, the gloves are fine. Now, will you leave?"

I glared at him. "You could say thank you."

"For what?" He glared right back. "Thinking on your own? That's what I pay you for."

"I was just trying to surprise you. I thought you might appreciate it."

"Just as much as you appreciate the chance to stuff your face behind my back."

"Don't you give me another lecture," I snapped.

"I've had it with anatomy. At least you don't see me gaining any weight."

Mr. Hackbirn's voice got very tight and quiet. "That will be all, Miss Wycherly."

Still steaming, I left, slamming the door behind me. Back in my office, I hoped we could clear the air before we left in three days.

Mr. Hackbirn refused to play ball. The next day we got word that Gannett had escaped. He'd been seen hanging around Georgetown University, and the best anyone could figure was that he was trying to find another buyer for his information.

The news just made Mr. Hackbirn grouchier. He sulked about the house, not saying one more word to me than he had to. Every time I tried to bring the subject up, he'd just say, "I don't wish to discuss it, Miss Wycherly."

"Well, I'm afraid we're going to have to," I finally said on Sunday evening after getting home from my sister's. We were due to leave the next morning. "We've got a job to do, and we need to be able to communicate."

"We are communicating good enough to do it."

We were in my office, working out a couple last second details.

"Oh, we are?" I shook my head. "Well, I don't call your sulking all day and night good communication. Let's face it, I'm mad and you're mad, so let's get this thing settled."

"There's nothing to settle."

"Then why are we so mad?"

"I have no idea. There must be no reason, so we shouldn't be mad. There, all settled. Are you happy?"

"You've got to be kidding. That is the worst line of reasoning I have ever heard in my life."

"That's too bad." He started out of the office.

"I don't believe you," I said following him. "Why can't you admit that we've got a problem here and deal with it?"

He stopped and turned on me. "Because I see no

problem. I refuse to get emotional just because you think you can't talk to me."

"Wait a minute, who's the one who's been saying 'I don't wish to discuss it'?"

"Who's the one who's letting her emotions interfere with her job?"

I gaped. "That's not fair!"

"See, Miss Wycherly? Now you know why I didn't wish to discuss it." He walked off to his bedroom.

"You're impossible!" I screamed, then immediately regretted it.

I decided if he could play his little detached game so could I. I sure as heck wasn't getting anywhere confronting him.

The next five days were miserable, except for the time on the plane. Mr. Hackbirn got into his seat, popped his contacts out, and promptly went to sleep.

At the hotel, if the bellhop noticed the tension, he didn't say anything. Mr. Hackbirn had booked the room himself, a three-room suite. It had a sitting room and two bedrooms, one on either side of the sitting room. It was very nice with quiet tasteful furniture, a raised area, two steps up, in the back in front of the windows and near the bedroom doors, and a wet bar on one side.

As soon as the bellhop left, we each picked up our individual suitcases and went to our bedrooms without saying a word. I don't know what Mr. Hackbirn did that night. I assume he was making phone calls to contacts. I stayed in my room and pored over some maps and a visitors guide. Mr. Hackbirn hadn't said a word about anything to do before Thanksgiving Day, so I decided I'd go sightseeing. It'd get me away from him. I'd never been to the nation's capital before, anyway, and I wanted to see it.

Mr. Hackbirn was in the sitting room the next morning reading a newspaper when I came out.

"Any plans for today?" I asked.

"Absolutely nothing," he replied without looking up.

"Good." I put on my dress coat, arranged a wool cap over my hair and ears, and slipped on some wool gloves.

"Where are you going?" Mr. Hackbirn finally looked up.

"Sightseeing." I picked up my purse and the camera I'd finally bought. "I'm going to make the most of this fiasco."

We'd been taking pot shots at each other the whole week before. The standard response was none, or at least to remain as unruffled as possible. So far, Mr. Hackbirn was winning in that respect.

"Remember to stay away from Georgetown," he said.

"I wasn't planning on going anywhere near there."

"And don't bring anyone back here." He returned to his paper.

"You reprobate, you're telling me that?"

"I meant a tail, Little Miss Ice Cube."

I stormed out, slamming the door.

If I hadn't been so angry, it would have been wonderful fun. The weather was cold with a nice crisp bite to the air, just the way I like it. Washington D.C. is a wonderful place and, corny as it sounds, very inspiring. If only I hadn't been trying to escape Mr. Hackbirn. I got back to the hotel before dark and ate in the restaurant and went straight to my room.

Wednesday, I went out again. Late that afternoon, I realized that I'd gotten myself turned around and found myself walking right onto the Georgetown campus, the very last place I was supposed to be. After all, Gannett was supposedly in the neighborhood, and he had seen me and knew I was an operative.

Trying desperately to stay cool, I hurried back into the city, checking for tails all the way. Now, if you really want to keep someone tailed, you use a team, so the person being tailed doesn't notice the same person behind all the time. Being as inexperienced as I was, I forgot about that possibility, so I wasn't looking when I crossed the alley, which was stupid.

I didn't see anything. I just felt the hand clamped over my mouth and the cold metal uncomfortably close to my jugular vein. I was dragged back into the alley, where my captor spun me around and shoved me, back first, against the wall.

"Well, well, well," he said, his knife dancing perilously close to my face. "My chauffeur."

I gasped.

"So, you recognize me," Gannett snickered maliciously and waved off the person who had just entered the alley, presumably his partner.

"Uh..."

"I escaped. I had no choice. But you're a long way from home."

"I get around."

"And you just happen to be in the same town where dear old Professor Lipplinger lives."

"Who?"

He backhanded me hard across the face. I cried out in pain and tasted the blood where my teeth had cut open the inside of my cheek.

"Don't tell me you don't know about him. It's just too convenient, having you pop up on campus this afternoon."

I thought I saw a policeman at the entrance to the alley. I bolted for it, shoving hard against Gannett, and running. I could feel my upper left arm sting as his knife bit through my coat to the skin.

"Rape!" I bellowed as loud as I could, then tripped and fell forward.

Gannett gripped my shoulder and started pulling me up. I felt the point of his knife press against my spine.

"That was real stupid, sister."

"Police! Freeze!" The officer at the head of the alley had his gun pointed at us.

As the grip on my shoulder relaxed, I sank to my knees in relief. Gannett bolted, assuming, perhaps correctly, that with me between him and the cop his chances were reasonably good. In any case, he got away. The cop shot at him twice and then chased him, but not for long. I stayed where I had collapsed, trying to get myself together. It was just as well, I figured, to let myself be afraid. If it really had been attempted rape, I would have been pretty distraught.

"It's alright, honey," I heard the officer's gentle voice say to me. He was a medium-sized Black man with dark skin.

I gasped in pain as he took my left arm, helping me up.

"My arm," I said softly.

"Here, let's see." He pulled out his handkerchief and opened the slash in my coat to inspect the wound. "It doesn't look too bad. Here, hold this tight against it."

I held the handkerchief to my arm. Gently, he escorted me out of the alley and down the street a block to a call box.

"I'm going to call a squad car," he explained. "By the way, I'm Officer Marshall, Rob Marshall."

"Hi."

"And what's your name?"

"Janet. Janet Donaldson." I fidgeted with the wedding set I was wearing.

Officer Marshall made the call quickly. I knew I was going to have to make some decisions fast. They were going to be asking a lot of questions, which was understandable. I knew I didn't have to make a statement, but it occurred to me that I might be better off doing so. Not making a statement might arouse suspicion, and with a statement, they'd be looking for Gannett.

"Alright, Mrs. Donaldson, they're on their way." Officer Marshall smiled at me. "Why don't you tell me about yourself."

"Like what?"

"Where you live. How we can get a hold of your

husband."

"W— we don't live here. We're from California."

"I see. Where are you staying?"

I gave him the name of the hotel.

Fortunately, the squad car pulled up.

I was taken first to the infirmary where the doctor looked at my cut and said it wasn't bad enough to need stitches. The nurse was very kind and talked to me merrily about her children as she bandaged my arm. After that, I was taken to the squad room.

Mr. Hackbirn was there waiting. He seemed concerned and relieved to see I was alright. In fact, he was very much the loving husband. Giving gentle reassurances, he came up to me. But when he hugged me, he hissed "Relax, damn it, I'm supposed to be your husband," into my ear.

I had calmed down considerably. I gave my statement accurately, except for the conversation. Mr. Hackbirn had driven to the station in a rented car and now drove me back to the hotel. We took a circuitous route, because of the tail he'd picked up. He didn't say anything, but I could tell he was mad.

Back in our room, though, he said a lot.

"Beautiful. Just beautiful," he growled, prowling around the room. "I don't suppose it was a coincidence that we picked up a tail at the police station?"

I sank stiffly onto the couch. "Uh, no. Gannett found me."

"Gannett? How the hell did he do that?"

"Well..." I bit my lip and tried not to cry. "I was looking for a phone. I was lost. And I asked this man where one was, and he gave me directions, only they led me right onto the Georgetown campus, and I got out of there as fast as I could without calling attention to myself, but he saw me, I guess, and caught me in the alley."

"And you called the cops in on top of it." He rolled his eyes as he paced. "Of all the stupid things to do."

"Well, it was either that or get carved up. You've

got to admit the alternatives weren't exactly the greatest."

He turned on me. "And what do you think is going to happen if they catch him and he spills his guts?"

"Do you honestly think they're going to believe a crazy story like that?" I held my hands out. "If anybody, I'm the one they're going to believe, just so long as neither one of us gives the cops any reason to believe we're not on the level. Heck, I've even got a knife wound to help. Not to mention the fact that my good winter coat is ruined. The sleeve's slashed open and the front's all shredded."

"From what?"

"I tripped and fell spread-eagled."

"On your knees?" Mr. Hackbirn looked concerned.

"Yes."

"I'd better take a look at them." He sounded resigned.

"At what?"

"Your knees."

"Anything to grab a feel, huh?"

He pressed his lips together then said in a tight angry voice, "Miss Wycherly, I have enough trouble with your weak knee-ed attitude. I don't need any trouble with the real article."

Unfortunately, he made sense.

"Alright, turn around."

"Why?"

"I've got to take off my tights."

"Oh, for the love of Pete." He was completely exasperated, but he did turn around. I hurriedly slipped off the tights as he complained. "What do you think I'm going to see anyway? Your underwear? Big deal."

"Well, pardon me. I happen to believe in common decency. I'm ready."

He turned around and bent to look. His hands were warm and soft and very gentle, and, angry as I was, I caught my breath at his touch.

"Can you move okay?" he asked gruffly.

I flexed each leg a couple of times and nodded.

"They're just a little bruised," he said. "Put a heating pad on them tonight."

"I don't have one."

"A hot-water bottle, then, and I hope it keeps you company." Mr. Hackbirn started for his room.

"Look," I snapped. "If you want me that badly, then why don't you just rape me and get it over with."

He stopped and turned to me. I was afraid he would.

"I wouldn't give you the satisfaction," he said in a low, controlled voice.

He turned back and left, shutting his door quietly behind him.

The next day was Thanksgiving. I spent the morning in my room, crying quietly because I felt so lonely and homesick. We drove to Hattie Mitchell's place in Mount Vernon around one. Neither one of us broke the silence during the ride. But as we pulled into the estate, Mr. Hackbirn finally spoke.

"Try and be nice," he said. "We are supposed to be a happily married couple visiting friends on a happy occasion."

"Would you do me the same favor?"

He just snorted and parked the car.

"Stay put," he growled.

I did as I was told, while he walked around the car. When he opened the door for me, he was smiling. The mask was on, the curtain had risen, and he was in character.

I smiled in return and got out.

"Thank you, darling," I said, as he shut the door.

I stiffened when he put his arm around me as we walked up to the front door.

"Loosen up, lady," he growled behind his teeth.

I took a deep breath and tried to relax. I nervously put my arm around him. I really did try to look natural. But being that close to him did things to me that had nothing to do with how angry I was, and I was scared.

The afternoon was spent congenially chatting with Hattie, who was a lovely woman in her middle fifties, and her son James and his wife, Mary. They didn't have any children, so it was a quiet afternoon. It would have been quite nice, but the lack of children only made me miss being at Mae's more. Also, Professor Lipplinger wasn't there. I could tell Mr. Hackbirn was worried by his absence, as I was. But there was nothing to be done.

As is always the case when you hear a lot about a person before actually meeting him or her, you form a mental image of what that person is like. My image of Professor Lipplinger was a kindly old gentleman with white hair and glasses, a gentle darling so devoted to his students he would rather risk his life than allow them to fail.

When he finally showed up (just in time for cocktails), he did conform to that image physically. He was a little shorter than Mr. Hackbirn with white hair and wire-rimmed glasses. He even stooped a little.

When introduced to us, he nodded curtly and asked Mr. Hackbirn what he did for a living. Mr. Hackbirn said he was a freelance writer. The professor looked at me a long moment then addressed Mr. Hackbirn again.

"That's a fine piece of meat you got there. What's she good for?"

"I also write," My hackles were rising.

"Published?"

"Not yet."

"You don't write." He turned and walked off, bellowing, "Hattie! Where are those drinks?"

"Coming, Miles." Hattie walked over to us. "I'm afraid I must apologize for my brother. Unfortunately, there is no excuse for his behavior." She sighed. "Oh well, what'll you have, Ed?"

I was a little surprised when Mr. Hackbirn opted for bourbon and water. I made a point of asking for wine.

At dinner, things only got worse. To begin with, nobody said grace. Then everyone was stiffly polite, except Lipplinger. He complained about everything and made lewd comments. Hattie and her son and daughter-in-law had obviously long since given up being embarrassed for him. To be honest, it didn't take me long either. I was too upset as it was and he just made things worse.

About an hour after dinner, Mr. Hackbirn got a chance to talk to Lipplinger alone long enough to let him know we had to talk to him away from everyone else.

"Hattie," he yelled. "I've got to talk to these two privately. I'll be in the library. Don't bother us."

"Whatever you like, Miles." Hattie was long past being surprised at anything her brother did.

Once in the library, Mr. Hackbirn sharply told me to watch the door.

"So, you want my formula," said Lipplinger.

"Wrong," replied Mr. Hackbirn. "I want you to see your next birthday. Somebody knows you've got something, and they want it, and they won't make any bones about taking you to get it."

"What are you going to do about it?" Lipplinger grinned as if there wasn't anything we could do.

"We're here to take you into hiding."

"Where?"

"To a safe house."

Lipplinger looked at both of us for a long time, but mostly at Mr. Hackbirn.

"I don't know if I should trust you or not," the professor finally said. "I was told that a Sid Hackbirn was coming to get me. You fit the description, but why are you using an alias?"

I gulped, my stomach doing loop the loops. Mr. Hackbirn somehow kept his face straight.

"Because that's usually how we function," Mr. Hackbirn said slowly. "But, yes, my real name is Sid Hackbirn and this is my secretary, Lisa Wycherly."

"Convenient way to keep meat on the hoof," the old man chuckled.

"I don't do that," I snapped.

"Unfortunately," replied Mr. Hackbirn.

I just glared at him.

"What if I don't want to go?" Lipplinger folded his arms across his chest and grinned.

"Professor, we are here to move you quickly and efficiently to safety." Mr. Hackbirn remained calm. "We will be most efficient with your cooperation. But we do not need it. I want to make it perfectly clear that we are prepared to use force. Is that understood?"

"Well, I guess those two are failing badly enough not to need my help anymore. Give me tomorrow to get my affairs in order. I'll be here Saturday."

"Alright, and Professor, not a word to anyone."

"Of course not. Good evening."

He left. Mr. Hackbirn took a deep breath and let it out again.

"Let's go," he said finally.

We went and said goodbye to Hattie.

"It was an excellent dinner, and we appreciate your having us," Mr. Hackbirn said.

"Well, thank you for coming. It was wonderful having you, Ed. And, Janet, I must tell you it was so nice to see someone sit and really eat. I see so many women just pick, it's a real treat to see you enjoy your food and not be afraid to ask for seconds."

"Thank you, Hattie," I replied with real warmth. "I can't tell you how nice it was of you to say that."

Mr. Hackbirn just smiled, but I knew I had one on him.

"To be completely honest," Hattie continued, blushing a little, "I was beginning to wonder if you were pregnant."

"She's not pregnant," Lipplinger said, coming up. "She's frustrated."

"Well, goodbye," said Hattie, ignoring him. "It was wonderful having you."

The ride back was silent, also, and again Mr. Hackbirn broke it when we were back in our suite.

"We've got contacts to make tomorrow," he said on his way to his room. "Be ready to go early."

I stopped my tears long enough to call Mae and family. Hearing their voices only made me feel worse. They say it's the next best thing, but that night it was a lousy second best. I cried myself to sleep.

The next morning, as I got dressed, my depression deepened into a black fog so thick it seemed suffocating. I wasn't about to let Mr. Hackbirn see it, though. I feigned cheerfulness until we traded angry words that morning over my coat. The slash in the sleeve and the holes in the front I'd more or less repaired and, as the coat was dark colored, didn't show much. Mr. Hackbirn wanted to know why I didn't just buy a new one and I wanted to know when I was supposed to have been able to do that. Neither question had been answered.

An hour later found us in a low rent district, in another alley, this one spilling out onto a dead-end street lined with parked cars. Mr. Hackbirn's tan overcoat was hanging open so that he could get to the gun in his shoulder holster easily. I, also, had a shoulder holster on. Even so, I had buttoned my coat and tied it.

The tension in the air was incredible. The silent routine continued. Mr. Hackbirn remained cool even though he paced restlessly. Something had gone wrong. Our contact was fifteen minutes late.

I looked out at the street, then at my shoes. Out of the corner of my eye, I noticed something light colored laying among some trash barrels a few yards away. I went over to look. It was a hand. The arm it was connected to disappeared behind the barrels. I pulled one away and two bulging sightless eyes stared up at me. I screamed.

"What's the matter?" Mr. Hackbirn walked over.

I just pointed.

"Terrific," he grumbled and started to move the other barrels away.

"I can't look." I turned away and leaned on a wall,

facing it.

"It's just a corpse," Mr. Hackbirn said callously. "Hasn't been one too long. It's probably our contact. We'd better get out of here."

The only way out of the alley was onto the street. Just as we got onto the sidewalk the shots rang out. I screamed.

"Get down, you idiot!" Mr. Hackbirn grabbed my belt and pulled me down next to where he was hiding behind a parked car.

I just sat there trembling.

"I thought you were used to guns," Mr. Hackbirn growled.

"None of them were shooting at me."

There was another shot and the glass in the car we were hiding behind shattered, and with it what little calm I had.

"We're gonna die," I moaned.

"If you keep that up, we will." He had his gun drawn. "You stay put. I'm gonna see if I can find out where it's coming from."

He moved away. I could hear more gunshots and glass shattering.

"Well, well, here we are again."

I looked up and saw Gannett. This time, instead of a knife, he had a gun trained on me.

"Oh my god," I whimpered, then watched in horror as he jerked and crumpled backward with a hole in his chest.

Seconds later, Mr. Hackbirn was by my side.

"It's a sniper, alright," he muttered.

"You killed him."

He looked at the corpse next to us and sighed.

"Yeah," he said, shortly.

"But..."

"Look, did you want him to kill you?" His eyes flashed. He wasn't happy about it either. "The sniper's on the roof across from us. He's got a lot of mobility. We've got to stay low and behind the cars. We can't go that way, that's the dead end. We can't go in the alley, 'cause that's a dead end. We've got to make it to the corner and across the street if we're going to have a chance. He's got a high-powered rifle up there."

I just nodded.

"Alright, you ready?"

I nodded again but didn't follow him. Blocking my way was the corpse.

"Come on!" Mr. Hackbirn yelled from two cars down. I couldn't move. I pointed at the body. "He's dead. He can't hurt you."

I still couldn't move. Mr. Hackbirn cursed angrily and shoved the body out of the way.

"Come on, now." Just to make sure, he grabbed my hand and pulled me.

As we got to the corner, I could hear the police sirens. Several police cars pulled up at roughly the same time. They were followed closely by a SWAT truck.

There was a police car not far from us, maybe a hundred feet.

"See that car?" Mr. Hackbirn asked. "Get behind it and you're safe. I'll cover you. You stay low and run like hell. You got that?"

I nodded.

"Okay, go!"

He practically kicked me. I ran. I didn't stop until I ran smack into Officer Marshall, of all people.

"Mrs. Donaldson!" he exclaimed.

"It's not been my week," I replied, sobbing.

Then Mr. Hackbirn slid up next to us.

"It's alright now, honey," he said, his hand on my back and then addressed Marshall. "Where's your captain?"

"Over there."

"Get him. I need to talk to him."

Marshall left. Mr. Hackbirn reluctantly put his arms around me and let me cry on his shoulder.

Officer Marshall and the captain reappeared in

record time.

"Captain Pete Laing," he said tersely. "What do you want?"

"Ed Donaldson, F.B.I." Mr. Hackbirn replied, pulling something from his suit coat. "I'm here on vacation, but it looks like the job followed me."

I stopped crying and looked up. The captain was inspecting a small billfold which I assumed had the F.B.I. I.D.

"What happened?" the captain asked, handing back the billfold.

"A friend of ours asked us to meet him here. We found him dead in the alley, and that other guy on the sidewalk waiting for us."

Captain Laing shifted to look at the body, then back to Mr. Hackbirn, who shook his head.

"He's gone, and yes, I did. Self-defense."

The captain nodded. "You said it's connected to something you're working on?"

"Back in L.A. It's top secret, so I can't talk about it. What I need from you is a lift out of here in an unmarked car."

"That's damned irregular."

"Code twenty-three, twelve-A. You can call Henry James, L.A. office. In the meantime, can you get me and my wife out of here?"

Laing nodded. Mr. Hackbirn surrendered his gun and a short time later, we were bundled off in a dark green car. Mr. Hackbirn remained silent through the whole trip but kept checking behind us for a tail.

"Here we go again," I grumbled as he shoved me into the suite.

"You really did it this time, Wycherly," he growled. "You don't know how lucky you are you're alive!"

He headed for his room.

"Where are you going?" I demanded, thoroughly fed up.

"To change clothes." The door shut behind him.

I took off my coat and laid it on a chair near the

window. I kicked off my shoes. I'd had it. I was going to wait for him, and we were going to thrash this out once and for all.

He came out dressed in brown tweed pleated pants, light shirt, and sweater and headed for the door.

"Where do you think you're going?" I asked firmly.

"To the bar."

"No, you're not."

He stopped, turned slowly, and looked at me.

"And why not?" he asked quietly.

"Because I've had it." My voice was shaking but still in control. "Because these past few days have been the pits."

"Oh, they have?"

"Yes, they have. My patience, my calm, my entire emotional stability was already strained to the limit this morning. What with your potshots and your insinuations and your bad mood and Lipplinger with his 'meat on the hoof' and 'she's frustrated.' And then on top of all that, we've got today."

"I'll admit, today was no picnic." Mr. Hackbirn walked over to the wet bar and pulled out a bottle of bourbon and a glass. His hands shook a little as he reached into the ice bucket. "But who's fault was that, may I ask?"

"Oh, I suppose it was mine. But have a little sympathy. I've never even been to a funeral. Now I've got my first corpse presented to me in a trash barrel, then I get shot at and to top it all off, you blithely make another corpse for me, fresh!"

"I don't like killing people!"

"I can tell. You just agonize over it for an hour, then go plug a couple more."

I winced as Mr. Hackbirn threw his glass at the bar. He turned on me.

"That was low, Wycherly, damned low!"

"Good. Because I don't like the way things have been lately. I don't like your evasionary tactics. I don't like your snide comments. I don't like being called an ice cube, and I'm beginning not to like you. I'm very angry right now, Sid Hackbirn, and what is making me angrier than anything else is that all the tension, all the potshots, all the bad mood is because you can't admit you've got a lousy case of the clap!"

"If you know so much about it, then why can't you just leave me alone?"

"Why can't you just admit you're not feeling well?"

"I feel fine."

"There you go, denying it again."

"I'm not denying anything. I feel perfectly alright. I do not feel sick because you don't feel sick with gonorrhea."

"Then what has all this bad mood been about?"

"Oh, for Pete's sake, think about it, Lisa. It's been three weeks. I'm extremely horny. I tried to tell you there was nothing to settle. I'm going to be this way until I can get myself between a nice pair..."

"You can spare me all the graphic details. I know how it works."

"You do? That's a surprise."

"See, you're doing it again."

"Then leave me alone."

"It's too late. It was too late the day you picked me up. You're stuck with me now."

"You'd better remember that." He headed for the door.

"That's right, Hackbirn, run away. Just like you always do. Any time you've got a problem with a relationship, you just ditch it. Well, you can't ditch this one. Go ahead and run. But I'll still be here, and I'll be here every time you try to run away."

"Okay, we're stuck." He put his hand on the doorknob. "But I can make life pretty miserable for you if I want to."

"That's a two-way street," I shot back. He stopped. I took a deep breath and continued. "I don't think we have to go that way. But that depends on whether you're willing to take some risks, if and only if you're

willing to admit we've got a real problem here, and
if and only if you're willing to face it and fight it out.
It's a big risk, I'll grant you. You're going to have to
do some digging. You might have to face yourself, and
worse still, let me see it. It's a pretty big gamble. But
we're already miserable, and personally, I'm willing to
chance that it won't get worse because I happen to like
the odds on it getting a lot better."

"What are you talking about?" he asked quietly.
But at least he came away from the door.

"Human relationships. One thing your education
was real short on. I may not know much about the spy
business, but I've got relationships down real well."

"Then what do you propose is wrong with our
relationship?"

I sank down into the couch. "I don't know."

"Aw, geez." Okay, that wasn't what he really said.
"After all that you can't tell me what's wrong?"

"Even if I could, it wouldn't do you a bit of good
until you found it yourself."

He paced the room, frustrated.

"You know what I think is wrong with you?" he
said, finally. "It's your snotty attitude towards my
lifestyle." That hurt, but I had to admit there was some
truth in it. "I've run into it before. All you damned
church types running around saying no and all the
time you're jealous of those of us who say yes."

My stomach twisted. "I think you just hit the nail
on the head."

"What?" His face contorted into a puzzled frown.

"Look, we've both got a list of petty grievances.
But I don't think that's the real issue here."

"Then what is?" He stopped pacing long enough to
look at me.

"Neither one of us has a tremendous amount of
respect for the other's values."

He snorted. "I respect your values. Why do you
think you're still a virgin?"

"Because if you laid one hand on me, it'd be bye-

bye Lisa, Quickline or not and you know it."

He thought about that a minute. "I've always thought I did."

"So did I. I thought I was being wonderfully accepting of you." I got up from the couch. "But think about it. Haven't most of the potshots we've been taking at each other the past week been direct attacks on the other's values?"

"Yeah, I s'pose." There was a pause. "I guess I just don't understand. I'm not hurting anybody. I can't even get a girl pregnant. So, why not?"

"Are you sure you're not hurting anybody? What about your little social disease?"

"Well, I guess. But still..." He shrugged his shoulders.

"I can only speak for myself. But..." I paused. I couldn't believe how hard it was to say it. "I say no because God said no. That probably sounds silly to you. I admit I took it on blind faith. But the more I look at the world around me, the more I think God is right. I look at Mae and Neil and what a good thing they've got, and then I look at you and it seems so empty."

"I am content." And he clearly was.

"Maybe you're lucky. But I know so many people who aren't."

There was a pause as he watched me start pacing. "Lisa, I want you to know that I find you extremely attractive. But, at the same time, I do not want to violate you."

"Why are you saying that?"

He winced. "Because of something that's been bothering me about you for a long time."

"What? Is it my cheapness, the singing, or the appetite?"

"No." He shook his head. "Those are petty things. Yeah, they bother me, but that's part of being alive and in close quarters. It's that I get the feeling you're scared of me. I come close to you, you draw away. I touch you, you stiffen up like a board. I'm not trying anything."

"Really?"

"Really."

I looked at him. He was being honest.

"I guess maybe you're not." I looked down at my hands because all along I had known that he wasn't. "You say you're attracted to me. Well, it may surprise you, but the feeling is very, very mutual. You come close to me, and I'm aroused like I have never been aroused in my life. You touch me and I have to stiffen up, or I'll give in, and we both know the guilt would kill me." I looked at him, flushing. "And the worst of it is, it's purely physical. I've never met anyone who could do that to me. You think I'm scared of you? You bet I am, but I'm just as scared of myself."

He smiled softly. "There may come a time, Lisa, when we do find ourselves in each other's arms. I wouldn't be averse to it."

"Neither would I." I swallowed and shook my head. "But don't count on it. For that time to come, one of us is going to have to do a complete one-hundred-and-eighty-degree turn. I don't think I can and I'm not sure you could either."

He sighed. "No. Not now, at any rate. In the meantime, can we both be a little more tolerant?"

"And open?"

"Sure. Friends?" He offered me his hand.

"Friends," I said, taking it.

"Whew," he said, pacing the room. "I don't think I've ever been that angry in my life."

"I don't think I have, either," I said, then stopped.

He was looking at the glass he had broken. I guess he was remembering why he'd thrown it.

"I'm sorry about saying that," I said, softly. "I didn't realize how deep I was hitting."

"You couldn't have. I'd better clean this up."

I could see his hands shaking, so I got up and put my hand over his.

"Let me do it," I said.

"No." He shook his head as he picked up the larger

bits of glass. "Like you say, I've got to face it."

"Face what?" I brought over a wastebasket.

"What I did today." He stared at the sink. "Every time it happens, it brings to mind things I want to forget."

"Vietnam?"

He nodded. "In war, you do what you have to do. But you wouldn't believe the rationalization. We told ourselves that they weren't like us, they were less than human. One day, I stuck a knife into a man and watched his blood and his life slip away. It was him or me. Just like today. Only it was you also."

I made a face. "I think I would rather it was me."

"So do I, sometimes." He shook his head and went back to picking up bits of glass and dropping them in the wastebasket. "But you have to remember, Lisa, the next time it'll be Lipplinger. And someone else, the time after that, and on it goes, until the next time it's Neil and Mae and the kids."

"It still won't be easy for me to pull the trigger." I shuddered.

"Let's hope it's never easy for either of us."

Silently we finished picking up the broken glass, then he went and got a washcloth and wiped up the spilled bourbon.

"Anybody'd think we had one hell of a fight in here," he joked.

"We did."

"Yeah, I guess so. I hope we never fight again."

I chuckled. "There's nothing wrong with fighting. It's the not resolving it and clearing the air that's the problem. Heck, we could have had this all over before we left."

He smiled sheepishly at me. "You tried to tell me, didn't you?"

"Mm-hm." I put the wastebasket where it belonged and flopped down on the couch. He followed me and sat on the arm.

"You know, Lisa, I've told you things that I've

never told anybody."

"Even yourself, maybe?"

"Maybe. But you've gotten closer to me in three months than Henry James has in all the years he's known me, and he's closer than anybody. Heaven knows, he's tried hard enough."

"It's funny what comes out of a resolved fight."

"You know, Lisa..." Then he stopped as a thought struck him.

The same thought occurred to me. He'd been using my first name. It also dawned on me that I had never used his first name. He said so.

"Why don't you?" he asked.

"Same reason I got bugged about you touching me. I had to keep the distance, I guess."

"Do you still have to?" His eyes danced softly.

I smiled and took a deep breath. "I guess I don't."

"Good."

He bent to kiss me, and I almost did. There was nothing I wanted more than to feel his lips against mine. But I was only too aware of what would follow if he did. So, at the last moment, I placed my fingers on his lips and shook my head.

"Please don't misunderstand me," I said. "I— I know you're only trying to say thank you, I like you, all those nice things. But, please, not that way. You're too strong for me."

He pulled back and patted my shoulder.

"I'm sorry," I said.

"Don't worry," he chuckled. "You're doing wonderful things for my ego."

I gasped, then groaned, then clobbered him with a pillow. He laughed.

"I'll ego you," I yelped, laughing also, and hitting him repeatedly with my pillow. "If there's anything that doesn't need help, it's your ego."

"Hey! Hey!" He grabbed another pillow and launched a counterattack.

Poor Sid. He was new to pillow fights, and I showed

no mercy.

I still sing and he still chews ice. We both still bicker over the way the other eats or doesn't eat. But he's trying to stop the innuendoes and I'm trying to be a little easier about spending money. Like I said, we have a very good relationship. [A very, very good relationship. – SEH]

Unfortunately, the story doesn't end there. Relationship-wise, Sid and I were doing very well. Lipplinger-wise, we weren't out of the woods by a long shot.

Friday night, we took advantage of room service for dinner, then Sid called Henry James and made arrangements for the next day. It turned out that the contact who had been killed that day was going to help us set up the safe house for Lipplinger. The really bad news was that meant Lipplinger was going to have to stay with us at Sid's house.

The next morning, I woke up with cramps, bad ones.

We drove to Hattie Mitchell's estate in our third rented car. The first one, Sid had traded in after the alley incident and the second we'd left behind at the shootout. I'd asked Sid what we were going to do about that second car, and he told me it was being taken care of. [The F.B.I. had it towed, and Ed Donaldson paid for it all, out of my paycheck. Talk about government fleecing. It's a good thing we didn't have to live on the pittance they paid us. – SEH]

I was nervous and holding my belly.

"We've had knives, guns," I said as we drove along. "The only thing they've got left for us is bombs."

"Will you cut that out?" Sid was still smiling. "You're making me nervous."

"You? Hah!"

"I have my moments." Then he turned serious. "Is, uh, something wrong? You don't seem to be in peak form this morning. You're not still mad at me, are you?"

"No. Not in the least." I winced as we hit a pothole.

"Well, something's wrong."

"Oh. It's nothing."

Sid glared at me. "I seem to remember getting yelled at pretty soundly yesterday for not owning up to my little infirmity."

The flush spread over my face. "Sid, it's real embarrassing."

"And me getting caught with my pants down isn't."

"Alright," I groaned. "I'm just cramped up, okay?"

"Ah hah! Something you ate."

"Nice try."

"Then what?"

I glared out the window. "That time of the month cramps."

"Oh." Sid chuckled. "My condolences." He looked at me, mildly concerned. "Are you going to be up to it if things get rough?"

I shrugged. "I should be. Cramps have never slowed me down. It's just uncomfortable."

"Well, I hope you'll be alright, and not just physically."

"So do I. But I shouldn't flip too badly. I've been through it before and the emotional strain I was under yesterday has been resolved."

"Except for Lipplinger."

I shook my head. "He won't bother me."

"Be careful. He knows how to push your button."

"Uh-oh," I said. But not about Lipplinger.

Hattie's estate was just about a block away. Two cars were parked next to the gates.

"Looks like we might have some company," replied Sid.

Yet we got through the gates without hindrance. Hattie met us at the door.

"He's packed and ready to go," she said. "But I want to talk to you two first."

She led us into the room we'd been in two nights before.

"Miles told me you were his contacts after all," she said.

"How do you mean?" Sid asked, again keeping his face neutral.

"His magic formula." Hattie rolled her eyes. "I was the one who called The Company about it. They put me on to your organization head, code name The Dragon."

I shrugged, but Sid obviously knew the name.

"And your security code?" Sid asked.

"Twenty-one Beta Delta."

Sid's eyebrows rose. "So why didn't you get our code names?"

"The Dragon wants us to have a visible relationship with each other."

"Okay." Sid did a really good job keeping his face straight.

Hattie chuckled. "I've been working with our intelligence community since before my husband died. I oversee a lot of the covert activity in our defense plants, which means I need to be in relatively frequent contact with the two of you, since you're stationed in Southern California. So, we'll need some plausible way to continue contact. Fortunately, I have my fingers in a lot of different pies, and once I knew who you were, I decided to enter the world of magazine publishing." She smiled at our surprised looks. "Don't be so shocked. I've been accused of playing the dilettante before, and I've yet to fall on my face. Last week, I bought On Our Own, that singles magazine that was about to go under?"

Sid's eyebrow lifted. "I'm surprised it lasted as long as it did."

"Well, it has a new life now, but without the sophomoric content and bad layout. You see, I don't enter these enterprises without some knowledge of what I'm doing. In any case, Mr. Hackbirn, or may I call you Sid?"

"Call me what you like," he said with a mildly lecherous smile.

Hattie returned it. "I would like to confirm that your relationship with Miss Wycherly is not of the sort in which exploring the west coast singles scene would cause trouble between you."

I shrugged. "I wouldn't mind. It might be fun."

Sid laughed. "Not the kind of fun you like, my dear. But don't worry, Hattie, we each have our own lives."

"Good. Then you'll be my west coast correspondent. I've seen your F.B.I. column and I like how you've approached it. However, I've been warned your spelling and grammar can be a little rough."

"Not anymore," I said smugly.

"She's been cleaning up after me," said Sid.

"Excellent. I'll expect your first column on the thirteenth. It's for the April issue, fifteen hundred words, seventy-five cents a word."

"A dollar a word and you've got a deal."

"A dollar a word, it is."

They grinned at each other.

"We do have to get out of here alive, first," I pointed out.

"True," said Sid.

I added, "I might also say, that while I'm a little shaky at setting those kinds of odds, they don't look too good, considering the two cars out front."

"Oh dear," said Hattie. "Maybe I'd better call the police."

"Please don't," replied Sid, getting a little antsy. "We'll have to make do without. They've been involved far too much already."

"I don't want to know." Hattie thought a moment. "You know, there is a path that runs through the woods out back. It goes to the road. I'm sure we could get a car down it."

"A back way out of here?" Sid's face lit up. "Hattie, I could just kiss you."

"Oh, Sid, please do."

That reprobate. Sid, I mean. He kissed her, alright. Boy, did he kiss her. When they finally got around to pulling away from each other, he winked at her, and she let out a prim little sigh.

"Well," she said, smoothing her dress. "Let's go get

my brother."

We got him, bad temper, lewd comments, and all. The car did go down the path very easily. We got onto the highway without mishap. But to get back to the city and National airport, we had to go past the front of the estate. After we passed it, I heard tires squealing. I looked out the back window.

"Step on it, Sid! They're coming after us!"

Sid stepped on the accelerator.

"Get on the floor, Professor," said Sid. He looked at me quickly. "You'd better get down too."

"I don't see why," growled Lipplinger. "It's undignified and I'll wrinkle my suit."

A bullet glanced off the roof.

"It's a lot safer, that's why," I yelled. I reached over the front seat and pushed him down as a second bullet embedded itself in the trunk.

"Get down, Lisa," Sid yelled.

"I'm getting!"

I slumped down in my seat. I reached into my carry-on and pulled out my gun, then rolled down the window.

"What are you doing?" snapped Sid.

"I'm going to shoot their tires," I said. I turned around in my seat and started out the window.

"Oh, no you're not." Sid grabbed me with one hand and pulled me back. The car swerved dangerously. "Do you want to get yourself killed?"

"You'll get us all killed if you keep on driving like that," Lipplinger yelled from the back.

"Shut up, Lipplinger. Don't worry, Lisa, they'll stop shooting at us when we get into traffic. Not that there's ever any around when you need it."

I shoved my gun back into the special case that would get it past the metal detectors at the airport.

"Got anything you can't replace in your suitcase?" Sid asked me softly.

"No, I put all my valuables in my carry-on like you said."

"Good. How about you, Professor? Got anything in your suitcase you can't replace?"

"Of course not. Too many thieves around to carry valuables."

"Good. We're ditching the luggage."

"Why?" I asked.

"It'll make it easier for us to change planes at the last minute. Maybe we'll lose our tail."

"Aren't you going to ditch them before we get to the airport?"

"Not much point in it. They're probably watching it anyway. With any luck at all, we can put them off our track."

"Holy Jesus in Heaven, please," I prayed, crossing myself.

"Whatever."

At the airport, we dropped the car at the rental place and ran through three terminals before Sid found a flight he liked. Even then we had to run to catch it. Lipplinger complained every step of the way.

The flight was a puddle jumper to La Guardia airport.

"Think we'll lose them in New York City?" I asked Sid as we were taking off.

"If you can't lose someone in New York, you're in big trouble." Sid yawned. "Keep an eye on the Professor for me, will you?" And he dropped off.

In New York, Sid promised the cab driver a handsome tip if he could get us across Queens to Kennedy airport in under thirty minutes without anyone following us. I didn't dare look. Sid was looking out the back window for tails, so I just kept my eyes fastened to the back of the seat.

We still switched planes two more times and got into Los Angeles shortly after midnight. I was never so glad to see that house in my life. I was also exhausted. Sid wasn't. He'd slept most of the way. Cheerfully, he drove Lipplinger downtown to an all-night market to get some of the necessities of life left behind in

Washington.

The next day, they went shopping and I went to Mae's. It was so nice being there. I blithely forgot about Lipplinger and risking my neck in the spy business and happily spent the afternoon risking my neck running around on the roof helping Neil and Darby put up the Christmas lights.

I also told Mae a little about the fight Sid and I'd had, and she agreed it was the best thing for him.

"He's not going to make you go away for Christmas, is he?" she asked.

"He'd better not," I said. "Of course, it is a little hard for him to understand how I feel. He's never celebrated holidays."

"You're kidding."

"'Fraid not, Mae."

"Well, he knows he's invited here."

"You'd better confirm that. I told you how he reacted to that letter."

"It's not late, I'll do it now."

Mae had been back on her feet for some time, and it didn't take her long to get Sid on the other end of the line.

"Sid?" I heard her say. "This is Mae O'Malley. You got any plans for Christmas Day...? Then I won't take no for an answer. You're spending it here and that's final. You plan to be here at ten thirty a.m. sharp. Any later, and the kids'll have to wait to open their presents and they'll be mad... Alright, talk to you later."

She hung up and smiled. "See? It's all settled."

On Monday, two things happened which made me very happy. At breakfast, Sid gave me permission to decorate the house for Christmas.

"You'll have to buy all the decorations, though," he said.

"Oh, that's no problem." I grinned.

Sid's eyebrow lifted, as if he wasn't quite sure what to make of my response. Well, I am pretty cheap.

"Waste of time and money," said the professor.

"Shut up, Lipplinger," said Sid.

Sid drew the line on outside lights, however, and with good reason. We would be the only house with them, and we did not need to be conspicuous.

Then shortly after noon, I got the results of a project I had started in the middle of November.

"Is Sid around?" Henry James asked on the phone.

I wasn't sure where Sid was, but he wasn't in the office.

"Looks like the coast is clear," I said.

"Alright, here's the information you wanted. She's in Coral Gables, Florida."

"Shoot, that's near where all my family's from."

"You want the address and phone?"

"You got that?" I copied them down. "Thanks."

"We aim to please," continued Henry. "How's it goin' between you and Sid?"

"Fine."

"Are you sure?"

"Positive. Thanks for the info, Henry. You're a doll."

"Well, good luck, kid. I've got a feeling you'll need

it."

But his warning couldn't dampen my spirits. I slipped into the library and shut the door. It took me three tries to get through, but finally, the other phone rang, and an elderly female voice answered.

"Is this Stella Hackbirn?" I asked.

"Could be." The voice had a rather light drawl for that part of the country.

"My name is Lisa Wycherly. I'm calling on behalf of someone you haven't talked to in a while."

"I see."

"You see, Ms. Hackbirn. I work for your nephew."

"I do see, but I'm afraid you don't. He does not want to talk to me, so we no longer speak."

"But haven't you wondered at all about him?"

There was a pause. "It sounds to me like you're trying to effect a reconciliation."

"I'm not asking much. Just send him a card or something. Here's the address."

I gave it to her so quickly I don't know if she got it down.

"You got that?"

"I don't need it."

"But..."

The line went dead, and then the dial tone. I just sat there, utterly amazed.

Sid opened the library door and stood in the doorway. "I could have told you she wouldn't."

"What? How...?"

"I had a feeling you'd try. So, when I saw you sneaking in here, I listened in."

"You weren't supposed to know."

"Just in case she said no, so it wouldn't hurt my feelings?"

I nodded, my happy mood dashed.

"I appreciate your trying." Sid sighed and shook his head.

"I'm just sorry you found out."

"Okay. It hurts." He shrugged and an odd look

came over his face. "But... I have to confess, it's as much my fault as it is hers. She, uh, called me soon after I got back from Vietnam." He sat down at the piano. "I, eh, was not in very good shape at that time. I didn't know what to say and hung up on her."

"I'm so sorry, Sid."

"It's one of the many, many reasons why I do not talk about that time in my life." He looked at me again. "I'm a little shocked that I've told you as much as I did."

"I'm glad you have," I said softly.

"There you are, Hackbirn." Lipplinger's voice shattered the moment. "We've got some talking to do." He stopped when he saw me. "What? You still have your clothes on?" He leered at me. "Hackbirn, you should make her go naked."

Sid glared at him. "That is not why she's in this house."

"So what. Listen, Hackbirn, we've got to discuss this setup. I need space, room to work. This room would suit me fine."

When I thought of that old grouch taking over one of my favorite retreats, I got angry.

"Something else will have to do," I said firmly. "This is a common recreational area."

"She's right," said Sid. "You have your room. If there's a problem, I'll have the decorator in tomorrow."

"Well, if that's the best I'm going to get." He shuffled off, muttering.

"That's darned good, Lipplinger," I shouted after him. I looked at Sid, who was chuckling. "There's something about that man that brings out the worst in me."

Sid chuckled. "I suspect you're not the only one."

That night, I put out the first of my holiday decorations, an Advent wreath, on the breakfast room table. Sid was bemused as I explained the three purple candles and one pink candle, after lighting the first purple one. Lipplinger rolled his eyes and Sid shot him one ugly glare.

Tuesday, I went, for the first time, to the Single Adults Bible Study. I'd met Frank Lonnergan at Mass a few weeks before and he'd invited me. That Tuesday was the first chance I'd had to go, and I was glad I did. The next morning, however, Sid was not in a happy mood. Well, he'd had to spend the evening with Lipplinger because we didn't both want to leave the house while he was there, especially after what Lipplinger had said about the library. I mean, we did in the early mornings to go run, but Lipplinger slept quite late, so I doubt he noticed.

I did get out a red, green, and white afghan that I'd made some years before and put it on the living room couch. It was one of the few things that I'd had left from when I'd sold everything the year before. Given the soft blues in the room with goldenrod accent pillows, the afghan didn't exactly go, but I thought it looked festive enough. The next morning, as I went from the breakfast room to my office, I looked into the living room and sighed.

"What's the matter?" Sid asked as I slid into my desk chair.

"I guess the living room is off-limits for Christmas decorations," I said with a sigh.

Sid looked at me strangely. "No. I saw the afghan. It's fine."

"It's gone."

Sid growled and went in search of Lipplinger. Sure enough, he'd taken the afghan. I told Sid to leave it. When I went out that night to shop for decorations, I got enough yarn to make another afghan, and found a really cute pattern for a sweater for myself and bought that yarn, too. Friday afternoon, we were caught up on writing work, so I went ahead and decorated the rumpus room, put out a beautiful floral display in the dining room, and twined holly garlands with red ribbons over the fireplace mantle in the living room, and stuck elves all over the shelves in the library. Sid chuckled and Lipplinger made several obscene comments.

Sid went out that evening, but apparently, he'd had enough of Lipplinger. I spent the weekend over at Mae's and was quite happy when I came home on Monday morning to find him gone.

"You didn't throttle him without telling me, did you?" I asked Sid when we were both in the office.

"Nope."

I grinned. "Shoot him and not let me get any shots in?"

"Nope. I found another house for him."

"People you're not very fond of, I hope."

"Don't know them at all."

"That's good." I sank into my desk chair. "Well, Praise the Lord, he's gone!"

The days passed quickly. Christmas was well on its way, which put me in a very good mood, although I was busier than a one-armed paper hanger, what with all the various projects I had going for different people. I'd found twelve-inch high plastic Christmas trees and got one each for Sid's and my desks. Sid was startled Wednesday night when he found me watching Christmas movies in the rumpus room and knitting furiously.

"You knit, too?" he asked.

"Yep."

He frowned at the bright red and green bits of fabric hanging off of my circular needle.

"What on earth are you making?" he asked sinking into a bright orange bean bag chair next to me.

"Sweaters for the twins." I said, and pointed out which pieces were for the sleeves, backs and fronts. I often knit all four pieces of a sweater at the same time, especially if I'm doing stripes, because it's easier to keep everything all lined up and matching.

Sid just nodded, then looked at the TV screen. "What are you watching?"

"Rudolph, the Red-Nosed Reindeer," I replied, putting the tape on pause with the remote. "I taped it earlier this week." I looked over at him. "Haven't you seen it?"

Sid looked at the screen and frowned. "I don't think so. I seem to remember seeing a couple somethings or other with my buddies when I was in high school." He paused. "I did tell you that I have never celebrated Christmas before, right?"

"Well, yeah, but didn't you go for Christmas dinner or anything? Send cards? You've been getting them."

He chuckled. "Yeah. But, no. I don't send cards, haven't gone for Christmas dinner. Didn't even know those elves in the library existed, let alone put any out."

"So, this is your first Christmas?" I grinned.

"Yeah. I guess so."

"This will be fun."

"We'll see." He got up and wandered elsewhere in the house.

I put my tape back on, then watched another Christmas special I'd taped and got the twins sweaters knitted. I just had to block them, then sew them together.

Friday afternoon, after lunch, I checked to be sure Conchetta wasn't anywhere within earshot, then slid into Sid's office and shut the door.

"What's up?" he asked.

"What do I get Conchetta for Christmas?" I sat down in the chair in front of the desk.

He looked up from an article he was reading. "What do you mean?"

"I'd like to get something nice for her. She works so hard and she's so good to us." I did avoid telling him about the extra lunches she'd been leaving for me in the fridge.

"I give her a generous end of the year bonus," he said, then turned back to the article.

"Oh. Do you know what she likes?"

"Yeah. Being left alone." He sighed and looked at me. "Look, Lisa, I don't know the whole of it, but there are some good reasons why Conchetta is so prickly. According to Lydia James, she's had a hard time."

"Lydia?"

"Henry's wife." Sid shrugged. "You'll meet her soon enough, I'm sure. Anyway, after I moved here in seventy-six, I asked Henry about getting a housekeeper. He talked to Lydia, who found Conchetta. Or maybe knew her already. I don't know. But Lydia told me that Conchetta came to the U.S. from Mexico when she was fourteen and had to go to work cleaning houses right away. She eventually married a guy who worked for a concert promoter as a roadie, which explains her t-shirt collection. Anyway, after twenty-plus years of cleaning houses, and producing five children, her husband had worked his way up in the organization and was doing well enough that she was able to quit. Until he dumped her, and while she got a good alimony settlement, her oldest daughter, who's a nurse, had a baby that needed constant care. I forget how old the kid is now, but that kind of specialized care is really expensive, so Conchetta needed to go back to housekeeping right around the time I asked Henry for a housekeeper, and Lydia set us up, after getting Conchetta screened and cleared. That's why she only works the hours she does and why I'm happy to make things as easy for her as I can."

"Oh." I bit my lip. "Then I really should get something nice for her. I just wonder what."

"Whatever." Sid went back to his article.

Saturday morning, at breakfast, Sid finally broke down. He'd been getting a little grumpy in the days before and he finally admitted that he was getting nervous about Christmas with my family.

"I've never done this," he said, setting out the non-fat milk and his prune juice.

"You've bought presents for people before, haven't you?" I put the bowl of fruit salad on the table.

That was another gift from Conchetta. Ever since Sid's bout with the flu in early November, there had been a lot more fruit salad in the bowl than before. Sid dished out his preferred portion.

"Well, for birthdays and just for the fun of it, but not for Christmas." He winced. "I should probably get your family some presents, shouldn't I?"

I grinned. "That's up to you. But you'll be getting them. Mama's probably already got your name on your Christmas stocking."

Sid swore. "All right. What do I get them?"

I shrugged, but I soon found myself at the Beverly Center, where we settled on perfume for Mae, a classical record for Neil, a very nice souvenir book on Mercedes-Benz for Darby (I said it was too expensive, but Sid insisted), a copy of "The Wizard of Oz" for Janey, a picture dictionary for Ellen, and toy cars for the twins.

Sid also took me out to an early dinner that night where I told him that he shouldn't feel obligated to get me anything.

"I don't want to put you on the spot," I said.

"Then don't get me anything."

I paused. "Sid, it's too late."

"I thought so. Well, I'm not going to make any promises, then." [Of course, it was too late for me, too, although I hadn't intended it as a Christmas present. Still, I needed an opportunity, so, what else could I do? – SEH]

That closed the issue, of course. I would have made the deal, but I'd already finished the sweater and after all that work, I couldn't bear not to give it to him.

If I had been happy to see Professor Lipplinger leave, you can imagine how I felt when, a week and a half before Christmas, I answered the door and found him on the doorstep, suitcases in hand.

"What are you doing here?" I asked.

He walked in and set down his suitcases. "I'm moving in."

"Oh, no you're not," I said picking up his cases and putting them on the porch.

"I'm afraid he is," said Sid, coming into the hallway. "I just got the call. His other house kicked him out."

"I believe it."

Lipplinger, with an air of triumph, picked his cases up and walked past me with a smug grin on his face.

"Always did like your place, Hackbirn. No noise, decent scenery, even if you can't touch her."

"You're staying here on one condition," warned Sid. "You stay in your room. I will not have you harassing my secretary or my housekeeper, nor do I want to listen to your tripe. Is that clear?"

"Perfectly. All I require is privacy and three hot meals a day."

"You will get what you want, provided you stay out of our way. This is my house, remember."

"Of course. Don't bother showing me. I know the way, Hackbirn." He shuffled off.

I shut the door and looked at Sid.

"Couldn't we just ship him to the Soviets with a note that says, 'Here he is, you can have him if you can stand him'?" I smiled weakly.

"Nice idea," Sid replied. "There's just one problem."

"What?"

"They'd ship him right back and we'd be stuck with him again."

We both laughed.

It was one week before Christmas.

"Sid!" I ran into the house bellowing that Friday. "Hurry up! Come here! Sid!"

He came out of the library with a worried frown on his face.

"What's going on?" he asked.

"I got it! Hurry up and see!"

I grabbed his hand and started towards the front of the house.

"What are you talking about?"

"What you loaned me the car for. The Christmas tree. I got it. It's out front. Come on. It's a real beauty, too. I can't believe I did it again."

"Did you make that drop?" He followed me out through the tiny Japanese garden in front of the house.

"Of course, I did. It went smooth as silk. I told you it would work. I was a little late. The guy was already at the lost and found counter asking for it. I just handed it over. No sweat."

"Good."

I stopped at the edge of the driveway. "There it is. What do you think?"

Sid winced. "I think there's a tree tied to my car. I just had it waxed, too."

"Quit fussing. I put a blanket down first. Help me get it inside. It's absolutely perfect. Another year and I did it again."

I had to run inside first and get some scissors to cut the twine. After we got the tree off the car, I ran ahead to open the double front door all the way.

"Bring it in bottom first," I called.

"I'll bring it in whichever way I can get it!"

With much grunting and groaning, he got it into the hallway.

"Where do you want it?" he asked, sighing.

"I told you. In the living room, right in front of the bay window. It's going to be so gorgeous! I can't believe I did it again."

"If I remember correctly, there is a very nice Queen Anne bench in front of that window."

"Not anymore. Don't panic. I just did a little rearranging this morning."

"Miss Wycherly." Sid heaved the tree along to the living room. "You have already dug deep inside me and turned me around, must you also rearrange my house?"

"Sure. But relax, it's only temporary, just through the holidays."

We stood the tree up on its pine cross bars. The top branches scraped "snow" off the acoustical ceiling. Sid looked up at it and sighed.

"Lisa, that tree is at least five inches too tall for this room."

"And it's not even in the stand." I looked it up and down. "Yep. I did it again."

We finally got it up and decorated, after first going out again to buy a stand, a saw (I couldn't believe he didn't have one) lights and the decorations. I guess Sid got caught up in the excitement in spite of himself, because I knew he'd planned on going out that night, but he stayed home to help me with the tree. Conchetta left some lovely eggnog for us, and Sid spiked it with something or other. [One of my lesser bourbons. – SEH]

The tree was so beautiful. Even Lipplinger admired it when we let him out of his room for the occasion.

"It's decent," he said. "Just the sort of thing you need a woman for, Hackbirn."

"Hey, I helped too," Sid replied, laughing.

Lipplinger snorted. "It only confirms my opinion of you. Nice piece like that and you're not laying her. What a waste. Of course, I've always thought that about your kind."

"Are you suggesting I'm gay?" Sid's voice was calm, but it had that edge to it.

I tried to suppress a laugh. I could see where one could accuse him of it. He wasn't swishy or had that kind of high-pitched voice (although I know a lot of gays don't). But he was terribly clothes-conscious and there was a gentleness about him that could be labeled effeminate.

Lipplinger just shuffled off, muttering.

"What are you laughing at?" Sid grumbled, picking up his cup of eggnog.

"You? Gay?"

"It's not funny." There was something strange about his discomfort.

"You haven't...tried it, have you?" I was actually kind of curious.

"No. That would make me bi-sexual, and I'm not that, either." He looked at me, trying to figure something out. "I don't know how you feel about the whole gay thing, but I have friends who are gays and lesbians and it's no big deal."

"It's not for me, either," I said.

"I don't usually fool gay men, but it does sometimes happen that one thinks I might be, and that doesn't bother me." Sid sighed. "I hate it when a straight guy calls me gay because then he's being as insulting as he can be."

"Yeah. That would be." I shook my head, then smiled at the ornament boxes all over the living room.

I started stacking the boxes up so I could put them in the hall closet. Sid watched me for a moment, then chuckled softly.

"What are you laughing at?" I asked.

"You. You won't spend twenty dollars on a blouse you need, and yet you spent a bundle today, and for what? A tree."

I walked over to the tree, smiling at the softly twinkling lights.

"O Tannenbaum, O Tannenbaum," I sang softly. "Wie treu sind deine Blaetter."

"I don't speak German."

"The message of the evergreen, Sid. Its leaves are always green. They don't change with the weather. The evergreen is unchanging, just like God's love." I looked at him and blushed. "Sorry, I didn't mean to preach."

He just shrugged. "I seem to remember reading somewhere that the Christmas tree was originally a pagan symbol of fertility."

I laughed and picked up my eggnog.

"Well, then, a toast." I raised my cup and so did Sid. "To fertility."

"Fertility?" he laughed.

"A fertile mind, for new ideas and a fertile heart, for love."

"To fertility, then, because I'm not and you probably are."

December 20-25, 1982

Monday morning, I was surprised I was lighting the fourth candle on my advent wreath and told Sid so. He just shrugged. He was mostly amused by my advent wreath.

He did finally break down and came home from an errand that afternoon with his own contribution to the Christmas spirit. Of course, it was mistletoe.

"It figures," I said, shaking my head.

"Admittedly, it's pagan," said Sid, "but that's okay because I'm a pagan."

I thought about it. "I don't think you are, technically. Pagans believed in multiple deities, and you've said you don't believe in any."

"This is true." Sid looked around my office. "Now, where to put it. Ah, the front window."

He reached up and attached the twigs to the top of the mini blinds. Suddenly, he stopped and pulled the blinds apart.

"Oh no," he grumbled.

"What's the matter?" Worried, I got up from my desk and joined him.

His arm landed across my shoulder.

"Gotcha!" His eyes twinkled as he glanced at the mistletoe above us.

"You stinker," I groaned. Sid moved in, his mouth open. I put on my best Madeleine Kahn voice. "No tongues."

"No fun." He sighed heavily, then gently, so gently, his lips pressed against mine. I was drawn in and found myself returning it in good measure. As he pulled away, I scrambled free.

"One of these days, I'm going to end up slugging you," I said, going back to my desk. But my lips were still warm and tingling, and come to think of it, I was tingling all over. [You were tingling. I'll give three guesses what you'd done to me. – SEH]

Mae called that afternoon to let me know that my parents had arrived safe and sound. They live in Southern Florida during the winter. They'd flown into LAX, but Mae had gone to get them. I would have met them there, but that would have meant borrowing Sid's car and possibly bringing Sid. Mae and I had already decided that the airport was not a good place for my parents to meet Sid.

Both the writing and the spy businesses had completely slowed down, so there wasn't much work to do in the office. I managed to get all my projects done early that afternoon, so, that evening after dinner, I landed in the library with a knitting project for me. Sid appeared in the doorway, dressed in jeans and a sport shirt.

"Mind if I join you?" he asked.

I shrugged. "I don't see why not."

"What are you knitting now?"

"A sweater for me" I grinned and held it up. It was mostly navy blue, but the front had a big, red-nosed reindeer in brown and black on it. It's called intarsia, where you drop in different colors into your knitting. I'd also added a cable down the sleeves. "Isn't it cool?"

Sid winced and sighed. "I don't get you. Last fall, those couple times we went shopping, you gagged over anything the least bit cutesy, but now you're knitting a reindeer."

I shrugged. "I didn't say I was consistent. Besides, it's Christmas. I love Christmas." I took a deep breath. "I love the smell of a douglas fir in the house. I love the decorations, shopping and making presents, singing Christmas carols. In fact, I have a book of them. I put it on the piano."

"So, is that a request?" Sid slid onto the piano bench.

"Not really. Do you even know any of those tunes?"

"I'm sure I've heard some of them." He picked up the music book and thumbed through it. "Besides, I can sight read. Ah. I think this is a classic."

He played Silent Night. I tried singing along.

"A little high for you?" Sid chuckled, then played a couple scales.

"Mae is the soprano." I said, but the next thing I knew, he was playing the old hymn in a key I could sing.

It was Wednesday and three days before Christmas. We got the good news that a new holding place for Lipplinger had been found. It was much more secret and better protected. The only hitch was he couldn't go there until after the holidays. No matter. He'd mostly been keeping to his room, but he'd come out and be obnoxious every so often. Sid couldn't wait to be rid of the old man.

Then Hattie called. Sid was out making a pickup, so I got it.

"Miles is begging to come home," she said. "He says he wants to spend the holidays with his family, though why he does, I haven't the faintest idea. He does nothing but complain when he's here."

"Well, I don't know that there's anything I can do about it," I said. "We sure wouldn't mind sending him, but there's no way of knowing if it would be safe."

"That's the most important part," said Hattie. "If he can come home for Christmas, it would be nice, but unless it's one hundred percent safe for him, keep him there, I don't care how much he howls."

Sid was anything but thrilled when he heard that. Worse yet, the latest intelligence we had said that Hattie's was the worst place Lipplinger could go. She'd been under heavy observation since Lipplinger left. Lipplinger agreed to stay put without too much fuss. We should have known.

On Thursday, since Conchetta would be off on Friday, Christmas Eve, I found a moment to hand her a wrapped box. I had managed to worm out of her that she still liked going to concerts and had found tickets from a band I'd seen on one of her t-shirts.

"What's this?" she growled at me.

"A Christmas present to say thank you for all your hard work."

Conchetta sighed and shook her head. "We are not friends."

"I know," I said simply.

"You don't understand, do you?" She glared at me. "Every time someone I work for tells me we are friends, or worse, one of the family, I get fired. I don't want to lose this job."

I shrugged. "But I can't fire you. I'm not the boss."

"True." Conchetta thought it over, then muttered under her breath in Spanish. I was fairly sure it was something obscene. "Thank you."

I went back to my office and debated what to do next, since there really wasn't that much to do. I was also getting a little worried.

It was about my parents. When Mae called Sid to have him come over for Christmas, I should have remembered that my parents would be there. But it was too late, and the thought of Sid and my daddy getting together had me more than a little tense.

I love my father. He is the sweetest, most wonderful father a girl could ever have. He's very much the he-man type, strong and silent. He taught me how to backpack, shoot, fly fish, ride horses, rock climb, all sorts of things. He's usually very open-minded and always taught me that all human beings are God's creatures and deserving of respect, regardless of sex, age, race, or creed, unless the man happened to be dating Mae or me. I think the only reason he got along with Neil was because Neil had worked for him for so long (Neil had put himself through college and dental school working summers and breaks at the resort in Tahoe.)

Personally, I enjoyed my boss's smooth cosmopolitan sophistication. But I knew Daddy wouldn't. I wasn't sure if Daddy would be suspicious of Sid or what. Either way, it was not going to be easy on Sid. As much as I looked forward to Christmas, I began to dread the inevitable confrontation.

I didn't want Sid to drive me into Orange County on Christmas Eve. But Sid insisted, saying that Mae had invited him to lunch. We pulled up in front of Mae's house a little after ten in the morning. As we got out of the car, the front door opened and the kids came streaming out, yelling. Despite the noise, I still heard a sweet female voice with a wonderfully familiar southern drawl to it.

"Lisa Jane! Lisa Jane!"

"Mama!" I ran to her.

Mama is an exceptional woman. She's small and pert, the perfect southern lady. She reminds me of a tiny brown sparrow with a southern drawl. I hugged her.

"It's so good to see you, Mama," I said, kissing her.

"Well, now, Lisle, just let me get a look at you." Lisle is my parents' pet name for me. She stepped back to admire me. "Aren't you looking pretty as a picture."

I was wearing a nice pair of jeans, an oxford shirt, and a rust tweed sports coat with leather patches on the elbows, and of course, my beloved deck shoes. Sid still sighs every time he sees them.

"Thank you, Mama."

"Well, now, you go unload your stuff, then come on in and we'll talk."

"Oh, Mama, come meet my boss."

Sid was loading Janey and Darby up with the presents we had brought. Because he was planning on returning to Los Angeles, he was decked out in his standard three-piece suit, complete with pin under the tie. When he looked up and smiled, Mama just looked at him with a puzzled frown.

"Mama, this is my boss, Sid Hackbirn," I said, not quite aware of what was happening to her.

"How do you do, Mrs. Wycherly." Sid extended his

hand.

"I'm Althea," she replied, mechanically shaking his hand. "Pardon me, but have we met before?"

Sid looked at her, then away, trying to think if he had.

"I don't believe so."

Mama smiled. "Well, I guess it's just silly me. Still... Oh, never mind. Lisle, you get yourself settled and then we can talk. I'll be in the kitchen."

She walked back in the house, shaking her head.

"What's with Grandma?" Darby asked, struggling underneath several wrapped boxes, and trying to pick up my overnight case.

"Beats me," I replied. "Darby, can you carry all that? Let me take my case."

"No way, Aunt Lisa, that's my job!"

"I'll take these," said Sid, removing a couple of boxes from Darby's load. "Now, scoot." Darby hurried in. Sid turned to me. "Why don't you go talk to your mother? I'll supervise the unloading."

"And you've got to see the tree," said Janey. "It's beautiful."

"And presents," replied Ellen quietly, still attached to Sid's leg. "Lots of presents. But we can't open them 'til tomorrow."

"Nope," said Janey, running after the twins, who were screaming "Jingle Bells" repeatedly.

"Alright," I said, then grabbed each of the twins and headed in. I figured that unloading the car, seeing the tree, and inspecting the largess underneath would keep Sid occupied for a while.

"Well, maybe he's been up to Tahoe," Mae said as I walked into the kitchen.

"Where's Daddy?" I asked as Marty and Mitch stumbled their way upstairs.

"Him and Neil went up to the market," replied Mama, more concerned with another problem.

"Mama's been having fits over your boss," explained Mae.

"I have not been havin' fits, Mae Alice. I just know I seen that face before, and I can't think where."

"I have no idea, Mama. It could be Tahoe," I said, although I doubted it. Sid had said he'd never been to my parents' place or store.

"No, it wasn't Tahoe. It was Dade County for sure. I keep thinking Homestead, but that don't seem likely."

I shrugged. It didn't seem likely. Homestead, Florida, was where my folks were raised. Right next to the Everglades, it wasn't exactly Sid's kind of place.

"The thing that keeps throwing me is that's he's so young," Mama continued. "I keep thinking it was years and years ago." She slammed her hand down on the kitchen table. "John! John Caponetti. Went steady with him for three months in high school, would you believe? Had money too. Mama said I should've married him for it when he asked me. But I was bound and determined not to marry a man from Dade County." She laughed.

Mae and I smiled. It was an old story, how Mama and Daddy met. They'd both come from the same town but didn't know each other until they met in college in New York. Grandma Caulfield had never liked the idea of her girl going to college, let alone a Yankee one. But Mama had gotten a scholarship and there was no stopping her determination to get out of Homestead and Dade County. Of course, Daddy brought her back for a little while. Then just after I was born, the opportunity to buy the resort in Tahoe came up and they took it.

Mama laughed a little. "My, my. John Caponetti. Haven't thought about him in years. But I tell you, Lisle, your Sid Hackbirn is the spit and image of John Caponetti."

Mae and I looked at each other with guilty grins. We were both wondering if we'd stumbled on Sid's missing father. Mama had to catch us.

"Now, I know what you two are thinking, but if there's any relation, you can bet it's on the wrong side of the blankets, hear? So, I don't want you two saying anything. 'Tisn't nice. There were all sorts of cleft-chinned babies in families what had no right to have 'em, just as there was Caulfield babies. Remember that, now."

"Sure, Mama," I said.

"Mommy!" called Janey running in, followed by Darby and Ellen and, further behind and slower, by Sid. "Mommy, can Uncle Sid sleep over tonight? Can he, please?"

"Pretty please, Mom?" begged Darby. "He can sleep in my bed. I won't mind a sleeping bag. Can he, please?"

Mae and I were both laughing at the uproar.

"Settle down," said Mae. "He can—" The kids yelled. "Hush up! He can if he wants to." She turned to Sid. "Really, Sid, you're more than welcome, but I don't want you to feel obligated. If there's anything you need, I'm sure Lisa won't mind running you down to the store."

"She won't have to." Sid paused. "I, uh, am in the habit of carrying an overnight case in the car."

I bit my lip. I didn't want to laugh. I could see Mae biting hers, too.

"Now, why on earth would you carry an overnight case?" Mama asked innocently. She hadn't heard that much about Sid.

I put my hand to my mouth and held it. I didn't dare look at Mae. Sid, mercifully, ignored us.

"I like to maintain a flexible lifestyle," he replied.

"Well, now as a writer, I s'pose you would," Mama said.

"I guess I'm staying, then." Sid was drowned out by cheers. "Come on, Darby, let's get my case."

He left with Darby and Ellen.

"Now, what is your problem, you two?" Mama's eyes flashed as she turned to us. "I admit it seems a little silly, carrying a bag, but it's certainly convenient."

"Oh, no! I can't hold it!" I was laughing. So was Mae.

"Mama, you did it again," gasped Mae. "Walked

right into it."

Mama glared at us. "What are you on about?"

"The overnight case," I said. "It is really convenient for him."

"Well, honey, if he doesn't know where's he going to be at night."

"Or in whose bed," giggled Mae. I giggled with her.

"Girls!" Mama glared at us. "'Tisn't nice!"

"What's so funny about an overnight case?" asked Janey, bewildered. She was too young to know about Sid.

I picked her up and set her on my lap.

"Janey," I said, squeezing her. "Sometime, when you are older and a lot wiser in the ways of the world, I'll explain."

"Just nobody say anything to Grandpa," warned Mae.

At that moment, Sid and Darby came in. Darby was carrying a garment bag. As I thought about it, I realized I'd seen it behind Sid's seat and wondered what it was for.

"Darby, please go hang that up in your room," said Mae, then to Sid, "I just put fresh sheets on his bed this morning."

"Is there anything in there that the kids can't see?" I whispered in his ear.

"Not if they don't look," he whispered back.

"Darby, put the latch on the door when you leave," I yelled, then explained, "He's not going to want the twins going through his stuff, and you know if it's not locked up, it's fair game."

"They're not old enough to know better," added Mae, who was wishing they were. "Well, I'd better get lunch started."

Darby came running downstairs.

"All locked up!" he reported and then went out back, taking his sisters with him.

"Sid," asked Mae. "Are you going to be comfortable all dressed up like that?"

"Sure," he shrugged, then thought a moment. "Maybe I will change."

"Lisa, why don't you show him Darby's room."

As we came into the front hall, Neil and Daddy came in from the store.

"Hi, Daddy!" I came up and hugged him.

"Hi, Lisle. How's my baby?"

"Real good, Daddy. How are you?"

"Good."

"Oh, Daddy, this is my boss, Sid Hackbirn."

They stood there for a minute, like two dogs on the street, sizing the other up, only it was like a terrier and a German shepherd. Daddy is a big man. His face is a little on the stern side, but both Janey and I have his huge round eyes. He used to play football in college, and he looks like he could have gone pro. Sid isn't that small, but he's not more than three inches taller than me and I'm average.

Sid broke the silence first.

"How do you do, sir," he said putting out his hand.

Daddy took it, shook it firmly and nodded his head.

"How de do," he mumbled, then walked into the family room.

Sid raised an eyebrow and smiled at me.

"You seem relieved," he said.

I started up the stairs.

"He doesn't dislike you." I paused. "Yet."

"I see."

When we got to Darby's room, I undid the latch, then paused.

"Sid, are you planning on wearing a sweater?" I asked in a low voice.

"I usually do."

"Then I'd strongly suggest wearing it all the way or not at all."

His eyebrow quirked up. "What do you mean?"

"You know how you usually do, around the shoulders?"

"Yes."

I winced. "Daddy doesn't think that much of that kind of style."

"Ah. I see. Well, this is going to be interesting."

"You said it."

There wasn't much he could have done about the blue tweed pleated-front pants. But he was wearing the sweater all the way when he came downstairs. He sat quietly at the kitchen table listening to the rest of us gossip about the family.

I wouldn't have believed it was possible. Daddy was not only suspicious of Sid, but Mae and I agreed by lunchtime, he was certainly jealous of Sid. It did make lunch a little strained.

"You poor thing," Mae whispered to me.

We were cleaning up in the kitchen while the other adults lingered in the dining room and the kids were outside playing.

"Poor Sid, you mean," I whispered back.

"Isn't Daddy awful?" Mae giggled. "Remember that one boy you brought home from college? The one who had his hands all over you?"

"Rory? Oh my, do I." I laughed, though at the time Daddy had hit the roof. "I was amazed Daddy let me finish my degree."

"Thank God, I talked you out of moving into Rory's house with him and his friends."

"And thank God, you didn't talk me out of moving to Sid's place." I was amazed I'd said it but not half as amazed as Mae. I mean, I had been meaning to tell her, but I just never got around to it.

"Are you joking?" she gasped.

I glanced at the closed dining room door, then quickly shook my head.

"Lisa!"

"Sh. It's completely kosher, I promise. His room is on one side of the house and mine is on the other. There's a whole big house between us. He hasn't touched me."

"But why?"

"I'm on twenty-four-hour call. I told you the guy was eccentric." I was shaking, although I was tremendously relieved at finally having told her.

"So why didn't you tell me in the first place?"

"Because I was desperate, and I was afraid you'd try to talk me out of it."

"I probably would have, so I suppose it's just as well now."

"Mae, I don't even know why I signed on with him. I could have worked at the resort."

Mae patted my arm. "Well, it's a good thing you did, Lisa. He needs us."

"There really isn't anything going on, Mae. I promise."

"I believe you."

I swallowed. "It's just that he wishes there was and a lot of times, so do I."

"Of course, you do. He's had my heart racing a couple of times, too."

"It scares me, Mae. I've been horny before, but this is different."

"Well, you just stand firm. He'll come around."

"It'll be a long time before that happens, if at all."

"Don't worry. I'm here. It'll be like AA. You just call when temptation hits. I'll be praying for you, too."

"Thanks, Mae."

Sid wandered in at that point.

"It may be my imagination," he said to us slowly. "But I get the impression that your father does not like me."

"Oh, don't worry, Sid," replied Mae. "It's not you. He doesn't like anybody that comes near his little girl."

Sid noticed I'd been blushing since he came in. He smiled mischievously.

"Is there a reason why your face is so red, Lisa?" he asked.

"Oh, we were just talking about you, Sid," Mae giggled. "I hear you got my little sister shacked up at your place."

Sid looked surprised for a moment then burst out laughing.

"You, shut up!" I backhanded him in the arm.

He only laughed harder. "You mean you never did tell your own sister where you were living?"

"No," I groaned. "I just didn't. I haven't even told my parents, really."

"You can't," gasped Mae. She had stopped laughing and was deadly serious.

"Mae, I'm going to have to sooner or later."

She glanced back at the dining room. "Are you kidding? What do you think Daddy's gonna do? He'll be furious, and if he loses his temper..."

"Well, Sid can handle himself." I looked over at him.

"I really don't care to be involved in physical violence," he said.

"Lisa, you can't tell them where you're living, unless you want Daddy getting into one nasty fight, then physically dragging you back to Tahoe."

"What on earth is going on in here?" asked Mama as she came in.

"Just joking around, Mama," said Mae, with a quick laugh.

"I wish," I muttered as I turned on the faucet.

"Sid, you'd better go back and join the men," said Mama. "We'll take care of the mess. This is woman's work."

"That's okay," replied Sid. "I'm liberated."

"No, Sid," I said. "Daddy thinks it's woman's work."

"I think I'll go join Neil and your father."

"He's certainly trying," said Mae when he had gone.

"I just hope Daddy doesn't make any insinuations," I sighed.

"Like nocturnal activity?" Mae giggled.

"Mae, what are you getting on about?" Mama asked in that voice that said she knew darned well what Mae was getting on about and didn't like it one bit.

"Mama," I replied. "Remember the overnight case? Sid fools around a lot."

"Oh, dear," Mama sighed. "He seems like such a nice man, too."

"He is," I said. "What he does with his time is his business and I've no right to judge. Just don't worry. He's not fooling around with me. I only work for him."

"I never doubted that for a minute, Lisle, honey. And don't you worry about your daddy either. I told him to behave himself."

I must give Daddy credit. He did behave himself. But it was obvious Sid and he were not going to be great friends. There was one tense moment that afternoon. Sid was relaxing and chatting with Neil in the living room. Janey came in, holding her grandfather's hand. Seeing Sid, she dropped Grandpa and ran over to Sid. She climbed into his lap and gave him a big hug and a kiss on the cheek. Sid naturally hugged her back and cuddled her while he went on talking to Neil. He didn't even see Daddy.

But I did and I groaned silently. Janey is the apple of Daddy's eye and the joy of his middle age. Now, Daddy would be jealous of Sid over two females.

The awkward moment happened when Mama decided that Sid should get one of his presents early. She'd pulled him into the dining room after checking to be sure that the kids weren't anywhere around.

"I know you've got your night things with you, but I thought this might be a little more in the spirit of the day," she said softly, handing him the gaily wrapped floppy package.

"Thanks, Althea." He glanced at me, then pulled the paper off.

I put my hand over my mouth. In a way, I was really glad Mama had decided to give it to him before the next morning. And Mama had chosen a more, um, subtle pattern for Sid's Christmas pajamas, namely a red and green plaid. [Which was comparatively subtle. I can't unsee some of the others she's gotten me, and she only got worse when the Internet happened. – SEH]

"That's quite an unusual gift," he said looking at the freshly-washed flannel top and bottoms.

"Everybody in the family has Christmas pajamas." Mama laughed and patted his arm. "I got them all out of the dryer just now, but thought I'd wrap yours to make them special. Mae said they'd adopted you and I didn't want to assume you had them."

"That's very kind of you, Althea." Sid swallowed and balled up the paper as Mama went back to the living room.

"Are you okay?" I asked.

"I'm not expected to put these on, am I?"

"It might be more appropriate in front of Darby," I said. "Given that you don't wear usually wear anything."

"I was going to sack out in undershirt and shorts." He sighed. "We'll see."

Despite five wired kids, Christmas Eve with my family is the most peaceful, contented time of the whole year for me. I could see Sid was enjoying it, too. We spent the evening in the living room. The tree lights were turned on, giving everything a nice soft glow. Darby was being as adult as he could. The four younger children were taking turns in everybody's laps.

Then Darby decided we should be singing Christmas carols. I tried to talk Darby into playing the piano for us. He said he wasn't good enough. Then I suggested he find someone else. Sid glared at me but succumbed to Janey's pleading to hear "Fur Elise," her favorite.

The kids kept him busy after that. He finally put his foot down and told them to ask me to sing "Silent Night." He had to have his revenge. He played it in my key and without the music. I must admit I was impressed. By the time I finished, the twins and Ellen had fallen asleep, and Janey was nodding. Darby soon followed them upstairs. He knew about Santa Claus and had been promoted to look out the year before.

While we waited for his clearance, Mama unwittingly asked an awkward question that nearly started a scene.

"How'd you and Sid meet? Did he run an ad in the paper or something?"

Mae, Neil, Sid, and I looked at each other nervously. We knew we were on thin ice.

I looked at Sid.

"Shall I...?" I asked, hoping he'd see I was trying to give him a chance to save face. Of the two of us, he had the most to lose.

"I picked her up in a bar," Sid said, grinning mischievously.

"You, Lisa?" Mama couldn't believe her ears.

I saw his strategy.

"Oh, he's just trying to shock you," I said with feigned disgust. "I was out on a blind date. The guy turned out to be a jerk, so I ditched him. Mae and Neil weren't home when I called. Sid popped up, eventually sent the jerk on his way, bought me dinner and that's all. Two days later he called up and offered me a job."

"You never went out with men you didn't know before, Lisa," Daddy spoke deliberately.

"Well, Daddy, I was hungry. Heck, it had been a year since I'd worked, and things were tight."

"You could have had a job." Daddy glared at Sid for some reason.

"Now, Bill," Mama interrupted sternly. "I thought you weren't going to bring that up."

"It's alright, Mama," I said gloomily. I hadn't wanted to hurt Daddy's feelings when I'd decided not to go to Tahoe, but I got the feeling he'd still been hurt. "I'm sorry, Daddy. I like Tahoe and I loved working for you. But I guess I figured I'd be stuck in Tahoe for good if I went then, and I wouldn't be able to get my PhD. Besides, you would have had to fire someone to put me in and all those people have kids to support, and I don't."

"Well," grumbled Daddy. "I always said it was

your life."

"I really like what I'm doing now, Daddy. It's different."

Sid smiled at me. He alone knew just how different it was.

"Hey," hissed Darby from the top of the stairs. "It's all clear."

"Alright, Darby. Goodnight," said Mae.

"Goodnight, Mom."

We waited five seconds in silence. After that, quiet chaos reigned. Poor Sid sat and watched, bewildered, as we all sprang to our appointed tasks. Daddy and I worked on putting toys together while Neil and Mama concentrated on stuffing stockings. Mama finally took Sid under her wing and had him helping her. Mae tried assembling a dollhouse. Daddy and I are the only ones who are any good at putting things together. Well, we were the only ones. At one point Mae groaned in utter frustration. Sid automatically reached over and set her straight. I put him on assembly detail.

Thanks to Sid's help, we were done in record time. Even so, it was well after midnight when we finished. Thoroughly exhausted, but happy, I went to bed.

On Christmas morning, the kids are allowed to take down their stockings and play with the presents Santa has brought them, which are the ones left unwrapped. The wrapped presents must wait until after church.

I got to sleep until shortly before seven, when I was awakened by the girls, whose room I was sharing. I wake up slowly, and I was still half asleep when I followed Janey and Ellen downstairs, after putting their robes on over their Christmas nightgowns. I was also bundled neck to toe in a flannel nightgown with long sleeves and elves dancing throughout the fabric.

"My ice skates!" crowed Janey with delight.

"Nice," I mumbled and headed for the kitchen.

I was a little surprised to see Sid coming in the front door, wearing a running suit and even more surprised to see Darby, also.

"We went running," Darby said and ran to his sisters in the living room.

"You would," I grumbled with tired disgust, then yawned. "You gonna shower?"

"I was planning on it," replied Sid.

"Then do it now and be quick. Towels are under the sink."

"You wouldn't happen to have a blow dryer, would you?"

"In my case, in the girls' room."

"Thanks, and uh, Merry Christmas."

"Mm."

Twenty minutes later, I was sipping hot herb tea and somewhat more alert. Daddy came down in his robe and red-striped pajamas and sat down next to me.

"Any coffee?" he asked without much hope.

"Just instant. You know Mae."

"I went past Darby's room. Know what he was doing in there?"

I assumed "he" meant Sid.

"Dressing?"

"Blow drying his hair."

"Oh, come on, Daddy. It's the thing now. Even Neil does sometimes."

He just snorted. "He coming to church?"

I paused, realizing Sid's religious beliefs, or rather lack of them, would just cause more conflict. But then there wasn't much I could do about it.

"I don't know," I said finally. "I haven't asked him."

"He ain't Catholic, is he?"

"No, Daddy."

"I don't know, Lisle. I know you're just working for him, but, honey, that boy's dangerous."

"I know."

"Then why're you still with him?"

"I like him. Don't worry, I'll be alright. He knows how I feel, and he respects that."

"Well, Lisle, I just don't want to see you get hurt."

"I know, Daddy." I reached out and patted his hand. "You gonna come early to church with me and save seats?"

"Wouldn't miss it for nothing."

Janey came running in with a box. "Merry Christmas, Grandpa. I got ice skates."

He took her in his lap. "Well, now, let's see 'em."

Sid chose that moment to walk in, fully dressed in the suit he'd been wearing the day before.

"Uncle Sid, you're ready for church," proclaimed Janey.

"Well, I..," he started to protest. But then he saw all three pairs of our big eyes staring at him expectantly. "I thought I might take it in."

A few minutes later as I went upstairs, Sid followed me.

"Lisa, I have never been to a church service before in my life," he whispered rather frantically. "What do I do?"

"It's no sweat," I replied, a little moodily. "Just stand when we stand, sit when we're not standing and try to look like you're paying attention. They've got little books in the pews that'll help you follow along."

I yawned and went to change.

Sid went early with Janey, Daddy, and me to help save seats for the slower moving ones at home. He did look a little uncomfortable when we all genuflected before entering the pew but wisely decided against trying it. Otherwise, he made it through mass okay. Janey had managed to sit between him and me and stayed in the pew with him when we all went for communion.

After mass, chaos broke loose. Mae and Neil's friends are mostly people they know from church and there were quite a few there. Janey and Darby both go to the parish school, so they had friends, also. Even I was delighted, though not terribly surprised, to see a couple of old friends from college there.

There was a great deal of helloing and hugging

and talking. Sid would have gotten lost in the shuffle, but every few seconds he was being introduced to somebody. Mama and Daddy had left right away with the younger three, so Mae and Neil took their time.

Almost twenty minutes after Mass had ended, people for the next mass were coming in, and we were still in the vestibule talking and saying hi.

I turned to see Sid standing next to me.

"Well?" I asked.

"They're talking," he replied, noncommittally.

"Uncle Sid, I want you to meet my teacher," piped up Janey.

We turned to face Sister Francine.

From the look on Sid's face, I think he'd "heard about" nuns before. But things have changed a lot since most of those stories got started. Sister Francine was not a face in a long heavy black habit.

She was a fresh, pretty, young woman dressed in a conservatively cut navy blue suit that had a wooden pin of the Sacred Heart order on the lapel. She wasn't even wearing a veil.

Sid recovered himself to say "How do you do" to her and shake her hand.

"Janey's very fond of you," Sister Francine said, smiling.

"Well, I'm very fond of her," Sid replied, as Janey grabbed his hand and leaned against him.

"Oh, Lisa, Sid!" called Mae. "I've got somebody here I want you to meet."

I don't know if Sid really wanted to meet whomever it was Mae was talking about. But I know he wanted away from Sister Francine.

"Nice to meet you," he said, politely. "Excuse me."

He walked towards Mae, still holding on to Janey. I followed behind.

"Lisa, Sid, I want you to meet one of Fullerton's premier citizens," Mae said. "He just joined our parish last September. Ned, this is my sister Lisa and her boss..."

Ned Harris was carrying one of his children, a one-year-old girl. When he first saw Sid, he looked startled for a second, then broke into a huge grin.

"Well, if it isn't Sid Hackbirn," he said, with happy surprise.

"How are you, Ned?" Sid replied quietly.

He was smiling, but there was something about his reserve that told me he wasn't nearly as happy to see Ned as Ned was to see him. At the same time, Janey was a sight to see. Her lips were drawn into a tight thin line and her eyes had a fierce look in them. Obviously, she did not like Ned Harris.

"You two know each other?" Mae was amazed.

"Sure," said Ned. "We were in the army together. So how are you, Sid?"

"Very well, and yourself?"

"Couldn't be happier. Got a beautiful wife and kids, good business. Doing terrific. I'll bet you're still single."

"Yes."

"You've still changed. Look at where you are. The last place I would have ever expected to find you would be in a church."

"Actually, I just came along for the ride."

"Yeah, still cool as a cucumber. So, what are you doing for a living?"

"I write."

"Books?"

"Freelance, for magazines."

"No kidding. Does it pay well?"

"Enough."

"Great. I'm in the travel business, myself. Inflight Travel Agency. Doing really well."

"Good."

"Listen, I gotta get inside. Say, look me up real soon, will you? I'd love to have a chance to chew over old times."

"Whatever."

Ned left, after shaking hands with Sid.

"He's a bad man, Uncle Sid," said Janey. "He does good things, but he's real bad."

Sid just lifted an eyebrow.

"Hm," was all he would say.

On the way to the car, Mae held me back a little.

"Sid sure reacted strangely to Ned Harris," she said softly to me.

"Sid was in Vietnam. He doesn't like to be reminded of it."

"That's right. Ned was, too. That must be it."

"I don't know. Janey doesn't like him."

Mae sighed. "I know. Still, he is a very sweet man, and his wife is just as nice. Janey likes her well enough."

We both shrugged.

"Hurry up, you two," called Neil.

Mama already had the turkey in the oven when we got home. The next order of business was to unwrap the huge mound of presents underneath the tree. It's a time-consuming process because Daddy hands out each present one at a time and waits until the present has been opened and duly admired before handing out the next one. Of course, the kids got most of it. But I cleaned up pretty nicely myself and Sid was surprised when there were several packages for him even though I'd told him there would be.

I admit I was a bit nervous when Daddy handed Sid a box from me.

"Very nice," he said, smiling and nodding when he saw the sweater.

"Lisle, is that one you knitted?" asked Mama.

I could have kissed her. Sid looked at me, surprised.

"Did you make this?" he asked.

"Every stitch," I replied, blushing as usual.

"That's beautiful. Thank you."

Several packages later, I got a long, thin one from Sid.

"I said you didn't have to," I complained.

He just smirked and went back to thumbing

through a book Neil and Mae had given him. But I noticed he kept one eye on me.

"Go on, you ingrate. Open it." Mama was used to my protests over receiving presents.

I slid the ribbon off, carefully undid the tape, pulled the paper away and opened the box. Laying on the cotton, suspended from a fine gold chain was a pendant of two rectangles, one polished, one brushed. In the middle of the brushed one was an opal encircled by tiny diamonds. The diamonds sparkled in the morning light.

"My necklace," I said quietly and looked at him.

He smiled gently and nodded. I looked at it again.

"I went back a week later, and it was gone." I returned my gaze to him. "I guess you bought it."

"Let's see, Aunt Lisa," begged Janey.

"Why don't you put it on?" said Mae. "That way we can all see."

"Alright." I lifted it out. My fingers fumbled on the catch. "Oh dear, my hands are shaking."

"Here, I'll put it on you." Mae took it and had it on in seconds. "Oh, Lisa, it's beautiful."

"Thanks." Still shaking, I turned to Sid. "Thank you, Sid."

"You're welcome." He went back to the book.

Opening presents seemed to last forever. It didn't, but it was almost one by the time the last one had been opened. I helped Mae and Sid clean up the paper in the living room, while Mama checked the turkey.

Neil and Mae must have conferenced about Daddy and Sid the night before because Neil shooed Mama out of the kitchen and took over, drafting Daddy and Sid to help. Even Darby got to help peel the potatoes.

But when dinner time came, Neil, Sid, and Darby dropped the liberated bit and became perfect gentlemen; Darby seating Mae, Sid my mother, and Neil me.

I confess, I was a little nervous about how everything would taste. But Neil's a fairly good cook and Sid's very good at finding his way around the kitchen, even though he seldom does. Daddy's basically hopeless, but he can follow directions.

He followed them very well because everything tasted wonderful. I pigged out. I caught Sid glaring at me when I asked for seconds. I just smiled happily, cleaned my plate, and asked for thirds.

We were all finishing up and debating whether we should eat dessert just yet when the phone rang. Mae answered.

"Hello...? Oh, hi Ned... Merry Christmas to you too... We're just eating... No, you're not interrupting a thing... Well, my sister works for him. He came down when she was babysitting while I was in the hospital with my knee... Oh, the kids just love him... Well, I expect he was pretty surprised too... It's a small world, Ned. He's still here, do you want to talk to him...? It's no trouble. Sid, it's Ned Harris. Hello? Hello? That's funny." Mae hung up. "Never mind, Sid. We got cut off."

"Hm." Sid had obviously heard the conversation and was now mulling it over in his mind.

All too soon it was time to say goodbye. It was dark when we left.

"What a time," I sighed as we pulled onto the freeway.

"It's been a very enjoyable two days," Sid replied.

"I want to thank you for my necklace." I put my hand on the pendant that still dangled from my neck.

"I thought it would surprise you."

"It certainly did." I frowned as something occurred to me. "If you bought this before I went back, then you got this in November, didn't you?"

"Yes. So?"

"But two weeks ago, you told me that you didn't give Christmas gifts."

"I don't. Or I didn't until this year." He shrugged then checked his blind spot before changing lanes. "I just knew you liked it and bought it figuring I'd find some excuse to give it to you."

"I guess you did, then."

Sid chuckled and was silent.

"What are you thinking about?" I asked after a bit.

"Hm? Oh." He shrugged. "A lot of things. The sweater. It's a very nice piece of work."

"I made that one 'cause it was the only kind you didn't have."

"It's the only kind I don't wear."

"Oh no." My heart sank to the floor.

"However." He started to pat my knee, thought better of it, and put his hand back on the steering wheel. "I am going to make a point of wearing this one."

"You don't have to if you don't want to."

"That's just it. I want to, very much. There's something about the work that makes it a very valuable thing."

"It's one heck of a pattern. It's funny, but it's as close as I've gotten to knitting a perfect sweater."

"I didn't see any mistakes."

"I see them, but I know they're there."

There was another silence.

"What do you think of Ned Harris?" Sid asked suddenly.

"I don't know. I've only met him a couple of times. He seems alright, but..."

"Janey doesn't like him."

"I noticed. Why did you ask about him?"

"Back in 'Nam, I was investigating him for selling secrets. My, eh, commanding officer insisted that Ned was only walking the fence and doing a good job for us."

"That's interesting. It must have been quite a surprise to see him at church this morning."

"It is and it isn't." Sid gazed out at the traffic, dodging cars without really seeing them. "I've been told that I might end up working with him again, and actually, catching him at church makes perfect sense. Ned was always very good at appearances, which is why he was so good at what he did. He'd been a volunteer aide for the Catholic chaplains, and they stuck up for him. That phone call's bothering me. Getting cut off was a little too convenient. I think I'll talk to Henry about it tomorrow."

"Good idea."

I put Ned Harris out of my mind and let my thoughts drift.

[I didn't realize this until years later, but what made that first Christmas so incredible wasn't just that it was the first time I'd celebrated the holiday. It was the first time I was part of an extended family. It had always been just Stella and me, and while the two of us were a family, she didn't have any relatives to speak of. And it was also that I was becoming a part of your family, which is and was amazing. – SEH]

December 26, 1982 – January 1, 1983

The next morning after breakfast, I took the long way to the front door, going past Lipplinger's room.

"Good morning, Professor," I called after pounding on the door.

No answer. That wasn't surprising. Lipplinger never said anything to me unless he absolutely had to. I went on to Sunday mass without thinking about it.

When I got back, I found Sid hadn't lost any time calling Henry James.

"Well, I'd appreciate it, Henry," he told the living room phone as I entered the house. There was a pause as Henry spoke. "No, she's doing really good. We had some tense moments, but she came out okay... What do you mean you can reassign her if she wants?"

"I don't," I said, going into the living room.

Sid looked at me.

"I see... When was this...?" Sid sighed in response. "That's been settled. She'll stay with me... No, she's standing right here." He handed me the phone. "He wants to talk to you."

"Hello, Henry," I said into the receiver.

"Sid says you've patched things up."

"A long time ago. Really. I'm fine."

"Well, the option's there. Getting rid of Quickline you won't be able to do, but if Sid's a problem I can get you reassigned."

"You haven't done anything yet?"

"No."

"Please don't, then. I'm very happy where I'm at."

"That's a different song than the one you were singing last November."

"I know, Henry. But we settled it."

"Alright, goodbye."

I handed the phone back to Sid, who hung it up.

"I didn't know you called Henry during that fight," he said, hurt.

"I was pretty upset. It didn't matter. He couldn't do anything anyway."

Sid sighed.

"It looks like we're not as stuck as we thought." He looked like he wished we were.

"Maybe not by the business."

He looked at me and smiled.

"Even then it won't be that easy." He paused, then looked away. "Which, perhaps, is just as well."

I just smiled and left the living room.

Later that afternoon a call came through on the business line. (The other two lines are Sid's and my private lines.) I didn't listen in, being busy with a new dress I was putting together. When I saw that Sid had hung up, my curiosity got the better of me. After all, people hardly ever called us on the business line on Sundays. I went looking for Sid and found him in his office. He sat behind his desk with his chin in one hand. He glanced at me briefly and went back to staring into space.

"Something's up," he said. "Harris is being a little too chummy."

"Is that who called just now?"

"Mm-hmm."

"Could he be wanting to bury the hatchet?"

"That's what he says. But I seriously doubt it. Last fall when we were at that mall with the kids, I saw him there. I'm pretty sure he didn't see me. I thought he might have been talking into a radio. I tailed him just out of curiosity, then saw you in trouble, so I dropped him. At the time I thought I was just being paranoid. But now I'm really wondering."

"I'm more than wondering. I ran into him just outside of the toy store." I frowned. "And there's something else, too. Mae introduced me to Ned on Christmas morning."

"Me, too."

"I know. But Ned had already met me back in October. He came to the door when Mae was in the hospital, and he knew my name. Now, if he was new in the parish, like he said, and Mae didn't think we'd met, how did he know my name last October?"

"That is an excellent question." Sid frowned. "The funny thing is, he didn't say why, but Henry thinks we should definitely be keeping an eye on Harris."

I bit my lip. "Sid, you said he'd been walking the fence when you knew him. Could he be doing it again?"

"I would say probably." Sid thought. "But does Harris know us as operatives? It would almost seem likely if he knew your name without Mae giving it to him. The problem is Lipplinger. Nobody has come for him, and we haven't had any tails."

"True. But what are we going to do about Ned?"

"That is indeed the crucial question. We'll have to keep an eye on him. That's another thing that bothers me. He practically paved the way."

"How?"

"We were talking about city government, and he suggested it might be a good magazine article. I said it would take some research and he said he'd be happy to help me."

"Oh."

Sid lifted an eyebrow. "It would make a good piece if I can get the right angle on it. I think I will play Harris's game."

"What if it's a trap?"

"It's quite possible. But I get the impression Harris is trying to feel me out more than anything else. He had no reason to suspect I was an operative back in 'Nam. He's definitely wondering about me, but if he was certain, he'd be more likely to set up an attack or just watch us and try to blow up our operation. Which is why I'm taking his bait. If I were only a freelance writer, I'd think Ned's being a little pushy and trying to grandstand, but I'd still do the article."

"Well, be careful. I don't want to end up in the unemployment lines again." Then a thought hit me. "You mind if I do some research, too?"

"Your sister?"

"Uh-huh. I don't know what she could tell me, but it couldn't hurt."

"I think it could. We don't want her to get suspicious."

"If she's going to get suspicious, then she already is by now. She noticed you were a little put off track when you met him. I wrote it off by telling her it was Vietnam. With all the current concern over about Vietnam vets, she won't think twice about Ned Harris bothering you."

Sid frowned, then sighed. "That does make sense."

"Good. I'll call her in a little while. No sense in pushing it."

A little while turned out to be the next day. Mae was very happy I called.

"Any chance I can get to sit down," she sighed.

"Knee bothering you?"

"Just a little. So, what's up? Did Ned Harris get a hold of Sid?"

"Unfortunately. Sid's been really moody since he did."

"The Vietnam thing?"

"I think so. Listen, Mae, what can you tell me about Ned?"

"Well, I don't know. He's a very nice, very active man. What more can I say?"

"He's a travel agent, isn't he?"

"Mm-hm."

"How does he strike you, as a person?"

"Just a good All-American type, I guess. A little pushy sometimes. He seems a little closed, too, like he's not quite willing to let you see him. Hold on a second, Lisa." Then more softly, "Ellen, you stay out of that, or

I'll paddle your seat."

I heard a soft chuckle. Sid was listening in.

"What was that?" asked Mae. So, she had heard it, too.

"Just some interference on the line, I expect." I got up from my desk and walked over to the doorway where I could see Sid with the phone to his ear. I felt a little like my privacy was being invaded, but decided he had a right to listen this time. "Do you know much about Ned's business?"

"Not really, except that it's doing very well. They've got plenty of money and a nice place up in Sunny Hills."

"He's on the city council, right?"

"Yeah."

"When's the next meeting?"

"Sometime the week after New Year's. Why do you want to know?"

"Ned kind of hinted that Sid should do an article on city government and Sid's thinking about it. He also thinks Ned's grandstanding a little."

"That may be. I wonder why Sid's so bugged about him."

"I have no idea." I looked away from Sid. "Bad wartime memories, I guess. Sid absolutely refuses to talk about it. The only reason I found out he was in Vietnam was that I was cleaning out his files and found his army papers."

I said goodbye to Mae shortly after and hung up. Sid came into my office.

"So, now what?" I asked.

"We wait." He seemed bugged.

"Sid, did I say anything wrong?"

He paused. "Not per se. If anything, you were a little too accurate. I, uh, really don't like remembering that time in my life."

"So, you've said. That bad, huh?"

"There are no words to describe it, Lisa."

He looked back at his office, then ambled out into the hall. A few minutes later, I heard piano music from the library. I later found out that the piece was the first of Chopin's Twenty-Four preludes, Opus 28. Sid played all twenty-four.

The next day, Harris took second place for a while to a greater concern: Lipplinger. He'd been very good about staying in his rooms before Christmas, so neither Sid nor I thought anything of it when we didn't see him after. Until Conchetta came into the office. It was her first day back after the holiday.

"You have sent the old man away again?" she asked.

"Not 'til after New Year's," I said. "Why?"

"I haven't seen him."

"He has been staying in his room since he came back."

"No. His room is empty and his breakfast is still on the tray."

"Uh-oh." I turned and called out, "Sid. We've got a problem."

"What?" He came out of his office.

I was on my way out. "Conchetta thinks Lipplinger's missing."

"His room is empty," she said, as she and Sid followed me to Lipplinger's room.

I opened the door. The room looked alright except for the full breakfast tray and the fact that Lipplinger wasn't in it. Sid came in past me and went straight to the bathroom.

"He's not there," he said coming back in.

I noticed a piece of paper lying on the dresser. I picked it up.

"That idiot," I grumbled, and handed it to Sid.

"'I'll be back after the holidays.' What does he think he's doing?" Sid slipped the note into his pocket as he cursed. "He must have gone to Hattie's. I'd better call her."

In the office, I listened in. The butler answered.

"Yes, may I speak to Hattie Mitchell?" said Sid. "It's rather important."

"Just a minute."

There was a delay before Hattie's voice came over the wires.

"Hello?" She sounded particularly cheerful.

"Hi, it's me, is your brother there?"

"Oh, hello, Sid. I thought Miles was with you."

"Not at the moment. Have you heard from him at all?"

"Actually, I haven't. I was a little surprised when he didn't call at Christmas, but I didn't think anything of it. You know Miles." Her voice caught. "Sid, if you don't know where he is..."

"We're on top of it. Don't worry. In the meantime, you are under surveillance by the other side. I'd be careful."

Hattie laughed. "Oh, don't worry. My phones are clean, and so is my house. I'm very certain of that."

"There are other ways to listen in."

"Sid, it's sweet of you to be concerned, but believe me, half my business is electronic surveillance. I know what's out there and how to thwart it."

"Alright. We'll get back to you as soon as we know anything."

He wasn't happy as he hung up. I walked into his office.

"What do you think?" he asked me.

"There goes Mammoth." I'd been planning on spending New Year's skiing at Mammoth Lakes with the Single Adults Bible Study.

"I think you'll make it."

The phone rang. This time, it was Henry. I went back to my office and debated what to do next.

"Lisa," Sid called.

I went back to his office. He scribbled something on a notepad.

"Yeah, thanks a lot, Henry." He hung up and slid the cap on his pen.

"What's up?" I asked.

"Sit down. We've got a hot one." Sid set the pen on

the desk and leaned back in his chair. "Henry finally got something solid. Apparently, Lipplinger is one of our operatives. He made up the formula to draw out Gannett and another operative fairly high up in our organization. That's one of the reasons why we were brought in on this. They were thinking that other operative was based out here. Just this morning, they traced a satellite signal from an enemy bird to a transponder in Fullerton."

"Ned Harris?" I slid into the chair in front of his desk.

"Very probably. The receiving transponder was one of ours. They haven't got the code completely broken yet, but there was something about a special traveler in two weeks."

"You know, Ned Harris is a travel agent."

"Mighty convenient, don't you think?"

I sighed. "It is. It just seems so weird. I mean we're only guessing at this point. How can we know for sure?"

Sid smiled. "That, my dear, is the difference between knowing what has happened and proving it in court. But Henry finally told me why Harris knew your name. Not only is he a regional supervisor..."

"As in fairly high up in the organization."

"He was the one checking you out when I first hired you."

"Oh, crud!" I got up and started pacing. "And Mae said he joined the parish in late September." I gasped. "Sid, he must have been trying to use Mae to get to me!"

"I know." Sid looked a little guilty. "That's why we have to keep our secret from your family. It's safer for them. The good news is that we've got a couple weeks to do some more digging before that prisoner transfer."

"I don't know, Sid. Why two weeks? If they've got Lipplinger now, why don't they ship him right away?"

"Traveling with a prisoner, especially when you don't want anyone to know he's a prisoner, is not an easy thing to do. And then there are arrangements to be made. You don't just charter a Soviet plane or boat on a moment's notice."

I nodded. "I guess this really puts the clamps on Mammoth."

"Why? We've got two weeks."

"They could have gotten it wrong, or they might move it up."

"We're making arrangements. If Ned leaves Fullerton or has any guests, we'll know."

"And what about Lipplinger?"

"They've got him, for the moment. Let them deal with him." He looked at me for a moment, thinking something over. "Actually, I think you'd better go to Mammoth as originally planned. It's possible we're being watched, and I want us to stay as clean as possible. Henry agreed, which means we're shutting down business. Any plans we've made I don't want to change unless something legitimate comes up. It might arouse suspicion if we do."

There was something fishy about that. Shutting down business, I could see. But letting me go running off to Mammoth...?

"Are you trying to get rid of me that weekend for some reason?" I asked.

"Well," Sid's grin was guilty as all get out. "I have been planning a small party here."

"Not the kind I'd like, I take it. Okay. I'll lock all my doors before I go. Don't get too drunk."

"I won't be drinking that much. Alcohol doesn't do much for lovers either."

"And heaven forbid you should not always be in peak form." Then another thought hit me. "There won't be any illegal substances floating around, will there?"

Sid shrugged. "It's not unlikely. That's one thing you can't always control. I don't think there'll be much pot. I try to discourage it. It doesn't do much for the sex drive, besides being hard on the lungs. But coke is a whole other kettle of fish. This town is loaded with it, and you can't get around it, even though the stories are exaggerated."

"You don't..."

Sid snorted. "Lisa, you know better than that. It's far too dangerous in our business, and I probably wouldn't anyway. Sex is my only vice."

I looked at him, my curiosity getting the better of me again.

"Did you ever do drugs?"

"I once did coke and will never do it again." He shrugged. "But I did do marijuana every so often. It was as common as tobacco among the people I grew up with. When I was in high school nobody could understand why I was so bored about it. A few kids thought I was doing the hard stuff. But I wasn't. I'd seen too much of what that does to people. I just smoked the occasional joint to be part of the gang."

Sid's reminiscent mood infected me also.

"I was just the opposite. I knew there were drugs around, but I never really believed it. In a resort city, you get all kinds of people. I was still very sheltered. I remember once this girl I knew told me drugs were to be had as easily as asking for them. I never believed her. I was in college before I saw my first joint."

"Such innocence." He chuckled, then got serious. "You know, there are times when I could kick myself for getting you involved in this business. You're too good. You don't deserve guys shooting at you."

"So, what do I deserve?" I asked smiling.

"Something like what Mae's got. A husband and family, a nice peaceful life."

"Did it ever occur to you that I don't want that?"

Sid was surprised. "You don't?"

"No." I laughed. "Sure, I like being at Mae's, and, sure, I love the kids. But I've got a good thing going. When those kids get cranky, Mae and Neil get them. When diapers had to be changed, Mae and Neil did it. When the kids have to be disciplined, that's Mae and Neil's job. I get to share all the good times and only rarely do I have to deal with the bad. That week I spent babysitting only reinforced that. In some ways, I'd like to get married and settle down, and maybe there'll come a time when I will. I'm not ready to close the door on that option yet. But the more I think about it, the more I want to stay single. That's mostly the reason why I didn't want to work for my dad. If I had gone back to Tahoe, or even to Florida, I would have worked for a while. But it wouldn't have been a career. It would have been just marking time until I found a husband, and I don't want one. I like my freedom. Of course, I couldn't tell that to my parents. Even as independent as Mama is, she's in the resort business because Daddy is. With them, it's either the convent or the home, and I won't be settled to them until I've chosen one or the other. Even if I'm eighty."

"I hope you don't choose the convent."

"Don't think I haven't thought about it. It would be nice and there's certainly a great deal of job security in it. But I really don't think I am, if you'll pardon the expression, called to it."

The jangling of the phone totally shattered the mood. It was Mae, calling to give me the date of the next Fullerton city council meeting. It was approximately two weeks away.

New Year's Day, I entered the house very cautiously. Well, it was closer to the day after New Year's at that point. The lights were still on, so I knew Sid wasn't in bed yet, or rather asleep for the night.

"Sid?" I called loudly. "I'm home."

There was no answer, but that wasn't surprising. As I dropped my luggage in my room, I thought I heard glassware jangling from the rumpus room. So, I went to investigate.

He was straightening up the bar. There was a pile of dirty glasses on one end and next to it a dustpan with a broom on the floor.

I yawned and flopped down into a bean bag.

"Have a good time?" Sid asked without looking up.

"Uh-huh, and yourself?"

"Quite nice, thank you. Any casualties?"

"Just a couple of sunburns. Myself included. Dummy me forgot my sunscreen."

Sid looked at me and smiled. "You look like a raccoon."

"I know. They changed my nickname from Teacher to Bandit."

"Teacher?"

"My past has been haunting me. I used to be, among other things, a ski instructor in Tahoe. There were a couple people with us who had never skied before, so guess who got elected to teach them."

"Elected? If I know you, you told them not to spend the money on lessons as you could teach them just as well." His blue eyes glittered with mischief.

"Better than the twit they had. I have my pride."

"Oh, well, my condolences on not getting to the good slopes."

"Oh, I did. How do you think I got sunburned so badly? Even got a little night skiing in."

Sid yawned and came around the front of the bar for the broom. I noticed that not only was he just wearing a shirt and dark pants, he was in his stocking feet. His hair was still perfect, though. I shook my head and smiled.

"I take it your party was a success."

Sid nodded and began sweeping behind the bar. I yawned again and stretched. I noticed something with lace on it sticking out from underneath the beanbag next to me. I reached over and pulled it out. It was a pair of women's bikini underpants.

"One of your friends left something." I tossed them at him. He caught them and looked at them, lifting an eyebrow.

"Whoever these are, I'll bet it's not the first time it's happened to her," he said. He looked at me. "If I had them washed, would you want them?"

I think he was being tacky just to tease me.

"No thanks," I said, for once playing it cool. "Lace itches me."

Sid dumped them in the waist can and went on sweeping. I got up, walked to the door, and turned back to him.

"It might amuse you to know," I said, languidly leaning against the door jamb. "That yours truly has a genuine real live date, scheduled for the end of this month, provided my boss doesn't cart me off on one of his infamous capricious whims."

"Congratulations. With who, may I ask?"

"I don't ask who your dates are. Of course, it's impossible to keep track. His name is George Hernandez and he's a class A-one sweetheart. He's part of my church group."

"Well, if I have to behave, he darned well better."

"I'm sure he will. Good night, Sid."

"Good night, Lisa."

January 11, 1983

I suppose jeans, even nice dress jeans, are not really appropriate for a city council meeting, even if the city is a smallish Southern California suburb. But I was dressing for comfort and mobility that night. We'd learned, through Henry, that Ned Harris had met twice since New Year's with a man who had contacts among known Soviet operatives and that preparations were underway to pick up a passenger the night of the council meeting.

Along with my dress jeans, I was wearing an oxford shirt and a camel-colored blazer. Unseen underneath the blazer, I was also wearing a shoulder holster and a miniature transmitter and microphone. I also had on my armored running shoes, the ones with the false soles. Mae wasn't much more dressed up, though definitely unarmed. She would have died if she'd known what I was really up to.

I was supposed to be attending the meeting as part of Sid's research on the city government article. Sid had gone ahead full steam on it and found himself genuinely interested. He'd already talked to all of the council members. I was at the meeting more or less incognito because Sid wanted as natural a meeting as possible, and he was afraid his presence would cause the council members to start grandstanding. Or that's what he said. Frankly, I think Sid knew it was going to be a dreadful bore and didn't want to go.

Mae had decided to go also because she was mad again at the overnight parking law (you can't park your car overnight on the streets in Fullerton). She picked me up at the train station and drove us to City Hall.

"Well, Ned's here already," she said as we walked through the parking lot to the council chambers.

"How do you know?" I asked.

"That's his car." She pointed to a white Cadillac with a tan top about three cars down from us.

"You sure?"

Mae laughed. "You can't miss it, or that license plate."

I began digging through my purse. "Now where's that pen?"

Sure enough, the Caddy's license plate read "INFLIT 1." I stopped, and continued digging, not looking for my pen, but for a round leather case that looked like a compact, but actually held a micro transmitter.

"Can't you get your pen out inside?" Mae asked impatiently.

"I've almost got it. Nope. Besides, I've got to be ready before I get in that door. You never know when somebody will say something." I slid the transmitter into my hand, then dropped a notebook and three pens. "Shavings."

Two of the pens obligingly rolled under the Caddy's bumper. Mae groaned and scrambled for the other pen and the notepad.

"Lisa, you are so disorganized."

I ignored her and quickly stuck the transmitter's magnet to the inside of the bumper. Mae just rolled her eyes as we got up and got going.

We sat together in the middle, on an aisle. I set my purse on the floor and left it open. Inside was a very good cassette recorder. I was taking notes also, but more on the people than what they were saying since that was being taped. All that was for the article.

The meeting dragged on and on and on. It finally broke up about ten. Sighing with relief, I turned off the tape recorder and put my pad and pen back in my purse. Mae was fussed because she hadn't had a chance to have her say. She went after Ned Harris, but he had gone. We got outside the chambers just in time to see him get in his car and drive off.

My hand slid under my shirt and tapped out a code on the transmitter I wore. I couldn't hear it or see it, but somewhere in the sky, a helicopter waited to follow the micro transmitter's signal. Static filled my right ear.

"This is G-2," said a voice. I looked over at Mae, certain that she had heard. [I told you no one would. - SEH] "We read you, Little Red. Tracer's working just fine. Over."

"I'll just have to call him tomorrow," complained Mae. "Lisa, are you alright?"

"Oh. I... I'm fine. Did you hear anything funny just now?"

"No. What did you hear?"

"Just somebody's radio."

"That's another thing I've got to talk to Ned about. Those stupid stereo boxes the kids are running around with and playing so loudly. There must be some ordinance they can enforce on those things."

Mae drove us back to her house because I was supposedly spending the night.

"What's Sid doing here?" Mae asked as we drove up. His car was parked in front of the house.

"I have no idea," I said, although I did. "Probably has some problem for me. I swear he's just like a little kid sometimes."

"Wanna trade?" Mae asked, then set the brake.

"Not on your life."

I took my overnight bag out of the car and followed Mae into the house. Sid was there waiting for us. He was wearing jeans (as always dark blue and discreetly, but very tight) a white shirt, black running shoes, and light blue tweed blazer, which meant he was armed to the teeth, and to the soles. I also knew he had hidden on his person somewhere a transmitter and mike similar to mine, and probably some other stuff. I couldn't see the receiver parked behind his ear, but I knew it was there.

"Okay, boss," I groaned. "What's the problem?"

"Hattie Mitchell called and moved up a deadline."

"And I thought she was a friend," I sighed. "Well, so much for spending the night."

I kissed Mae and Neil good night, got my overnight case, and followed Sid out of the house.

At the car, we checked before we got in to make sure no one was looking. Sid nodded and we quickly exchanged our blazers for ski jackets. We weren't terribly sure of where we were headed, but it was probably going to be a long night and January nights are chilly in Southern California.

"Here we go," said Sid, starting the engine.

I opened the glove compartment and turned on the radio equipment there. I took a deep breath and glanced at Sid as I picked up the microphone.

"This is Big Red/Little Red to G2. Do you read me? Over." I said into it.

"G2 here, Big Red/Little Red. I read you loud and clear. Over."

"We are in motion, G2. Over."

"Affirmative. Your friend is heading east on California 91. Over."

"We copy G2. Over and out."

I put the microphone back but left the equipment on.

"The Riverside freeway," I said. "He's headed for the desert."

"It figures. Nice, quiet, flat place to land a plane. It was either that or the beach."

Once on the freeway, Sid drove fast, eighty miles an hour, dodging between the other cars. The freeway was clear but there are always plenty of people driving somewhere in Southern California, even late on a Tuesday night. The further out we got, though, the less traffic there was.

"I hope the C.H.P. doesn't pull us over," I said.

"They won't," Sid replied. The way he said it implied that that had been arranged. He looked at me nervously. "It's going to be rough tonight."

"Why do you say that?"

"Because if and when Harris sees us, he's not going to let us live unless we get him first."

"That shouldn't be any problem."

"It's going to be harder than you think, Lisa." Sid took a deep breath. "The reason I couldn't go to that meeting tonight was that I had a break-in to do."

"Oh." I was hurt that he hadn't taken me.

"Lisa, break-ins are tough, and you've never done one. You don't want your first to be a high risk, early evening job."

"I suppose not. So, what went down?"

"Harris's office. Hit the jackpot big time and I had to trigger the alarm. The Feds are all over it by now."

"What did you find?"

"Satellite equipment, code books and files."

"That doesn't mean things are going to be more difficult tonight."

"Except that while I was in the office, Harris got a transmission which said that if he wanted to ship an extra package or two tonight, there was room."

"You mean if he had an extra prisoner."

"Or two."

"Oh."

I really didn't like the sound of that, but there wasn't much I could do about it. I just shrugged and gazed out at the darkness around us.

G2, the helicopter monitoring the tracer's signal, broke in periodically to tell us our "friend" had changed freeways. From 91 he changed to 60, and then I-10. Sid drove as fast as the traffic and road would let him, hitting over 100 a couple of times. But there's a very narrow curvy place on the 60 between Riverside and Beaumont where Sid was forced to slow to 65. Still, each time G2 reported we could tell we were gaining on our friend.

It was getting close to midnight when G2 reported that Harris had turned onto highway 62. We had just passed the turnoff to Palm Springs about five miles back.

"Should be picking him up any time now," said Sid.

I nodded. A few minutes later, just after we turned onto 62, to Joshua Tree, a small red light flashed on one of the consoles in the glove compartment. I flipped the switch, and a small monitor came to life with a line drawing of the road ahead, a compass in the upper left-hand corner and a small green flashing blip near the top of the screen. The tracking equipment was basically a combination radar and signal receiver that was tuned to the micro transmitter on Harris's car.

I picked up the microphone. "This is Big Red/Little Red. We have our friend. See you at the rendezvous. Over and out."

I put the microphone up. Sid had slowed down considerably, remaining about a half a mile behind Harris's car. We drove on for another thirty minutes. Neither one of us were tired, having slept most of that afternoon in preparation. The tension and the naps kept us alert.

The small green blip left its place between the lines.

"He's leaving the road," I said. "Heading south."

"There's where he's going." Sid pointed to a small orange light burning on the horizon to our right.

I could barely make out Harris's headlights in the pitch black. Sid slowed the car some. I aimed the light magnifying binoculars at the distant light.

"I can see a campfire and a plane there, but not much else," I said. "We should probably get in closer."

"There's no way we can get closer from here without our headlamps being spotted, and I'm not driving in the dark."

We drove past the dirt road Harris had taken. A tall hill rose and blocked the campfire. Sighing, Sid turned off the road and followed the edge of the hill around for about half a mile.

"We'll hide the car here," said Sid, stopping and killing the engine.

As silently as possible, we walked around the hill to the side where we'd seen the campfire. We could see its glow but nothing else. Above and behind us, the hill had long ago crumbled, leaving a sheer, rocky face. Sid looked through the binoculars and frowned.

"I can't see a thing from here," he grumbled. "The angle's wrong."

"We must be lower than the road. What are we going to do?"

He headed for the face of the bluff. "Climb up there and look."

"That's awful steep, Sid. Do you know what you're doing?"

"How hard can climbing a rock be?"

"Plenty. I've done a lot of rock climbing in my time. Let me go."

"Alright, if you really want to. Your wiring on?"

"Yeah." I pulled out a pair of knit gloves with leather faces and put them on. Sid handed me the binoculars and I was on my way.

"Am I coming in okay?" I heard Sid's voice in my ear.

"Loud and clear," I said a little breathlessly. "Am I?"

"Clear as a bell. Don't go too high up."

"I won't." I grunted and pulled myself a little higher.

It took me about ten minutes to climb to a small ledge where I was reasonably secure. Looking down I could barely make out Sid leaning casually against a rock. I lifted the binoculars to my eyes.

"I can see three men," I said. "One of them is getting on the plane. There's another one there, and yeah, it's Lipplinger. He's bound and gagged."

"Good for them," Sid replied.

"I don't see Harris, though. His car's there but I can't see him. The plane's moving. It's taking off. Lipplinger's still there."

The plane roared away above me.

"I still can't see Harris," I continued. "I don't think he's in the car. The men are sitting around, waiting, I think."

"Someone's coming," Sid announced quietly.

I could just barely make out the sound of an engine and wheels turning over rocks. I turned the binoculars on where Sid was. The sound died out. Sid stiffened and I could see his right hand reaching into his open ski jacket.

"Where are they coming from?" I asked.

"About two o'clock."

The night was moonless, but the stars were out in force in the clear desert air. I maxed the magnification on the binoculars and scanned the desert in front and to the right of Sid. Ned Harris and another man, both carrying handguns, slid around brush and rocks and over the rise that had blocked our view of the campfire. Behind them, several yards away in the gully, was an open white Jeep 4x4.

"It's Harris and another guy." Gasping, I slung my binoculars around my neck and started down the bluff. "I'm on my way."

"Stay put."

"But—"

"Damn it, stay put. Aah!"

My heart in my throat, I looked down at Sid. He recoiled, blinded by a bright, white, light. I could just barely make out Harris behind the flashlight.

"...that hand slowly out," said Ned Harris's voice. Sid had managed to turn up the transmitter so I could hear what was going on. "Now, Corporal, nice and easy, get those hands on your head."

I held my breath. On one hand, I wasn't sure what Sid would do if I disobeyed orders, but I knew it wouldn't be pleasant. On the other hand, it didn't look too good for him. On the other hand, he'd probably had a very good reason for telling me to stay put and it probably had a lot to do with my inexperience. [Yes and no – SEH]

"Get him frisked and cuffed," ordered Harris.

The second man did the honors quickly, pulling the gun from Sid's shoulder holster and another smaller handgun that Sid had strapped to his left shin. The man cussed when he found Sid's transmitter.

"He's wired!"

"Damn it." Harris scanned the sky. "I thought I heard a chopper."

I heard a ripping noise as the man pulled the transmitter off Sid's shirt, then a crunch, then silence. The man finished grinding the transmitter into the dirt, then grabbed Sid's ear for the receiver. A minute later, Sid's hands were cuffed behind his back. I couldn't just sit there and do nothing, but I didn't think I could plug the both of them quickly enough to keep them from killing Sid, not with a revolver from that height and with Harris either behind the light or right next to Sid. With a rifle, maybe, but not with a revolver.

Below me, Harris gestured and pointed to the other side of the hill. I strained for their voices. It was faint, but I made out Harris.

"It's got to be around here someplace," he said. "He didn't walk here."

So, they were looking for Sid's car. I reached out along the ledge to find a foothold that would take me towards the Mercedes. On the ground, Harris's companion had also gotten a flashlight and scrambled along the rocks around the other side of the hill from the car. Harris knocked Sid onto his seat and kicked him.

It was slow going on the bluff's face, but I wouldn't have thought Harris's friend could get around that hill faster than I could get up it. He did. I had just crested it when I heard the man holler that he'd found the car.

I heard scuffling behind and below me and guessed that Harris was having a hard time getting Sid to his feet. [I was out of the cuffs and jumped him. He lost the gun, and I kicked it away. Then it was just your basic fist fight. - SEH] Silently, I made my way down the hill, creeping behind the rocks. The man went through the car.

"Damn it," he yelped, dragging out the two blazers. I ducked behind a bush as he swept the light over the hill. The light passed over me, then returned and stayed. Drawing my gun, I blinked several times, trying to adjust to the new brightness. He was about twenty feet from me when I jumped out and aimed right at the source of the light.

The revolver cracked, and the man howled. I dove for the bush, my hand stinging with the kickback. All was darkness again. The flashlight rolled down the hill, somehow still on. It rested near the front tire of the Mercedes, lighting up the edge of the bluff. Still blinking, I listened.

The scuffle on the other side of the bluff had turned into a brawl if the sounds were any indication. [They were. – SEH] The man glanced that way, then back towards me, searching for me. Nearby, a rabbit scurried away. The man whirled at the noise and shot. Dirt flew where the rabbit had been.

Near the edge of the bluff, Harris staggered backward into the light. He dove forward, only to run into Sid, who beat him back. They wrestled for a moment, then Harris dove behind the bluff again. Sid dove with him.

The man looked anxiously around for me again, then back at the fight. Behind the bluff, a gun went off. Sid dashed around the hill right into the light. In a second, the man had his gun raised, but a split second before, I had squeezed the trigger. He howled as the bullet sparked against his gun. Sid shot at the spark and the man collapsed.

Just in case, I stayed put. Sid ran for the light. He swept it across the hill. Slowly, I stood up. He saw me and quickly jerked the light away. I hurried down the hill.

"I don't think there's any more," I hissed as I reached his side. "How'd you get out of those handcuffs?"

Sid gasped and leaned against the side of the car.

"You can always hide something," he said, wincing. "I had a piece of quarter inch spring steel in my hair. Got it out when they frisked me."

"Oh, my god, are you shot?"

"Nah. Just roughed up."

Harris's friend groaned.

"We'd better get over to that campfire," said Sid. "With all the shooting, they'll be wondering what's up. Did Harris have a car?"

"Yeah, a white Jeep over in the gully."

Sid stumbled over to the wounded man and checked him.

"He's not going anywhere any too soon," said Sid. "Let's go."

I pointed at the wounded man. "What about him?"

"He won't peg out before help gets here and dragging him around won't do him any good." Sid started off for the bluff.

"And Harris?" I scrambled after him, then stopped.

There in the glare of Harris's flashlight lay his corpse. The sob leaped from my throat as I stood transfixed.

Swearing, Sid trudged back. Gently, he covered my eyes and led me away from the grisly spectacle.

"Again," I whispered, trying not to weep.

"The gun went off while we were struggling with it," said Sid softly. "I couldn't even tell who pulled the trigger."

We found the keys still in the Jeep's ignition. As I started the engine, Sid opened the sole to his right shoe and signaled G-2 with the transmitter he pulled out. I drove because I'd driven offroad before and I didn't think Sid felt like it anyway. He was silent as we drove and had a hard look on his face as he sat with a rifle he'd found in the back of the Jeep on his lap. I had the lights on as we pulled out of the gully and towards the camp. Sid pulled one of those ski caps that covers the whole face out of his pocket and put it on.

"When I tell you to, turn on the brights and cover me. If you stay behind the lights, they won't be able to see you. But if you have to come out, try to keep your face hidden."

We were just on the edge of the ring of firelight when Sid told me to stop and turn on the brights.

"Police. Freeze," he yelled in that deep tone unique to cops. "We've got you covered."

The two men jumped up, startled. Both had rifles in their hands. Between them sat Lipplinger, bound and gagged. Sid had his seat belt off and his rifle trained on them but didn't move.

"Drop those rifles. Now," Sid bellowed. The men dropped them. "Kick them away." They did. "Face down on the ground. Move it. On your bellies."

Sid waited until they were completely down before moving. Handing me his rifle, he took a roll of duct tape from his jacket pocket. One of the men started crawling. I fired and the bullet glanced off a rock next to his head. The man froze.

"My partner only misses on purpose," Sid announced as he walked over to the men. "I wouldn't try anything else."

He gave each man a quick pat down search, then bound them with the tape.

"Sorry, gentlemen, but I lied," he said calmly. "I'm not the police."

I heard a helicopter approach. As Sid smoothed down the last bit of tape, he looked up and signaled. The chopper set down on the other side of the campfire. The noise drowned everything out, but I watched as Sid handed Lipplinger over to one of the two men who had come out of the chopper. Sid talked to the other man and motioned toward the hill. After a moment, Sid swung into the Jeep next to me.

"Okay, kiddo, let's make tracks," he said grimly buckling his seat belt.

"What about the wounded guy?" Slowly, I started the engine.

"We'll park the Jeep next to him, and they'll get to him as soon as we get out."

It didn't take long to get back to the Mercedes. As we drove past the face of the bluff, I sighed.

"In a way, he did get what was coming to him," said Sid.

I shrugged, keeping my eyes straight ahead. "I was just thinking about his wife and kids. She's pregnant, you know."

"I know."

I pulled up next to Harris's friend. We sat there silently for a moment. Then Sid undid his seat belt.

"Let's get back to L.A." He groaned as he got out of the Jeep.

"Sid, why don't you let me drive back. I don't think you're feeling up to it."

"No, I'm not. Thanks." He handed me the keys, then walked stiffly to the passenger seat. "Boy, am I going to be sore tomorrow."

"You'd better take a hot bath when we get home." I climbed in behind the wheel.

"Sounds like a good idea."

Daylight was just breaking when I pulled into the garage. We both yawned at the same time, too tired to move.

"You did a good job tonight, Lisa," Sid said quietly. "I was afraid after they knocked out my transmitter that you would stay put on that cliff, but you did exactly what I was going to tell you to do, and you did it smart."

"Thanks, Sid."

He opened the door and groaned as he tried to get out.

"Hold on, I'll help you." I ran around the car and helped him out and into the house.

We stumbled to his room in the semi darkness. Once there, I removed his arm from my shoulder.

"Sorry," I said. "This is as far as I go."

"It's far enough." Sid took off his ski jacket, laid it on the bed and started unbuttoning his shirt. "Don't worry about running this morning."

"Thanks. Don't forget your shoulder holster."

He looked down and chuckled. I left, shutting the door quietly.

[I was so glad you left just then, and at the same time, I wished I could tell you about the deep heaviness in my soul and the nightmares that would come that night. – SEH]

January 17, 1982

A week later, I finally got a chance to get the last word on Sid and I was taking it. I wasn't being completely fair. Sid was suffering the indignity of being in the dentist's chair and had the disadvantage of dental equipment and Neil's fingers in his mouth. But Sid had already had his chance at me and had made several snide comments about bad eating habits when Neil had found a cavity and filled it. Of course, Sid didn't have a cavity in his head, except the ones that belonged there.

Neil's got a full practice, although he does teach a couple classes at the nearby dental school. He had talked Sid into the appointment on Christmas Day when I'd mentioned it was time for me to get in. Neil won't touch Mae's or the children's teeth. But he doesn't mind working on me and he was quite happy to have another patient in Sid.

"Sid, have you been fighting lately?" Neil asked while he was poking around. "The inside of your cheeks are all chewed up."

"Probably one of his girlfriends," I said from where I was standing in the doorway. I slurred a little from the Novocaine.

Sid grunted.

"Uh oh," said Neil.

"Has he got one?" I asked, hopefully.

"Nope, just another crack. Looks like you need more sex, Sid."

"Huh?" Sid yelped as best he could with Neil's fingers in his mouth.

"You're chewing ice. You know what that means. And it's what's cracking your teeth."

I laughed. Mae came into the office and said hi to

the receptionist.

"Oh hi, Lisa," she said seeing me. "That's right, today was when you and Sid were coming in."

"Hi, honey," called Neil.

Mae went into the examination room and kissed Neil's forehead.

"Hello, sweetheart," she said. "How are you doing, Sid?"

Sid grunted.

"Good. You finding any guilty secrets, Neil?"

"Just that he chews ice."

Mae and I looked at each other and burst out laughing.

Neil snorted and put his probe down on the tray. After squirting some water into Sid's mouth, he fit the polishing bit onto his drill and slid the little pan of tooth polish onto his thumb. I chuckled maliciously. Neil's tooth polish was peppermint flavored, and Sid hates peppermint. Maybe I should have said something, but I decided to enjoy my revenge. [Thank you, Lisa. I'll remember that. – SEH]

"How was the funeral?" Neil asked Mae over the whine of the drill.

"Funeral?" I asked.

"Ned Harris's," Mae replied. "It was this morning."

"Yeah, I'd heard he got killed."

There had been a small piece in the paper a few days before about the mysterious desert auto accident of a prominent Fullerton businessman. According to the papers, the mystery was why he was out there and didn't say anything about how the accident occurred. Nor had it mentioned the raid on Harris's office. I wasn't surprised.

"It was a nice funeral," Mae continued. "Kind of sad, with his wife being pregnant and all. But she's doing real well. She's taking over the agency. I got a chance to talk to her and you know what she told me? She was kind of relieved about the accident. She was still sad about losing Ned, but she'd found out there was some funny business going on out of the agency, stuff the government was interested in, and if Ned had lived, he would have been in real trouble, but since he's dead, the government's overlooking it."

Which, of course, they were because the last thing the government wants is attention on any covert action, even if it's the good guys bringing in the bad guys.

"No kidding," said Neil. "You think Janey was right?"

"I'm beginning to think so, Neil."

"You two should know better than not to trust Janey," I said. "Sid told me he got busted for drugs in the army. Right, Sid?"

"Uh-huh."

"Well, I'll be," said Mae. "Did you get your article on the city council finished, Sid?"

"Just the outline," I answered for him. "He won't write it out until somebody says they want to look at it. We've got a query in to Ladies' Home Journal, I think." [Did that ever sell? – SEH]

"A query?"

"A letter asking an editor if he wants to look at a given manuscript."

"Oh," Mae looked a little puzzled. "I thought you just sent it in."

"Some magazines work that way. But most want to see if what you're writing about is something they're looking for first."

"Okay," Neil said to Sid, hanging up the drill and squirting water into his mouth. "Rinse and spit it out. You're done."

Sid did so, wiping his mouth on the napkin around his neck. Neil took it off and rolled back on his stool so Sid could get up.

"Well, that's that," Neil said.

Sid ran his tongue over his teeth.

"Thanks a lot, Neil." He got out of the chair and straightened his suit jacket. "Say hi to the kids for me."

"I will. Be seeing you two."

"Bye-bye," said Mae.

Neil and Mae stayed behind in the examination room. As Sid and I passed the receptionist, he winked at her and told her he'd see her Saturday. I waited until we were outside.

"You picked up on Neil's receptionist?" I glared at him.

"He isn't." Sid shrugged.

"That's beside the point. Have you no shame?"

"Absolutely none."

"You reprobate."

"Ice cube."

"Reprobate."

"Ice cube."

"Repro..."

THE NEXT OPERATION QUICKLINE STORY

Number Two in the Operation Quickline series is **Stopleak**.

Understanding is great - if they can stay alive long enough to appreciate it

There's been a leak in the courier system that is Operation Quickline, and Lisa Wycherly and Sid Hackbirn are sent to plug it. This is no straight up investigation. The two are being used as bait for a complex trap.

Lisa and Sid make their way around the country, starting in Washington, DC. Lisa eats her way through Manhattan, Sid puts up with rides at Disney World, Florida. But the tension really ratchets up in New Orleans, when Lisa is spotted by a pair of thugs determined to kill her.

The trail of dead bodies grows, but something else is happening. Sid and Lisa learn not just to accept each other, in spite of their very differing values. They try to understand each other, which means learning about their childhoods and how they became the people they are. And that understanding may be more critical than ever. Even if they manage to stay alive, there's a distinct possibility that they'll have to change their identities to a nice married couple and never return home again.

OTHER BOOKS BY ANNE LOUISE BANNON

I'm so glad you liked this book! Check out my other novels, available in print or ebook at your favorite retailer:

Freddie and Kathy Series:
Fascinating Rhythm
Bring Into Bondage
The Last Witnesses
Blood Red

Operation Quickline Series
That Old Cloak and Dagger Routine
Stopleak
Deceptive Appearances
Fugue in a Minor Key
Sad Lisa
These Hallowed Halls

Old Los Angeles
Death of the Zanjero
Death of the City Marshal
Death of the Chinese Field Hands

Daria Barnes
Rage Issues

Mrs. Sperling
A Nose for a Niedeman

Brenda Finnegan
Tyger, Tyger

Romantic Fiction
White House Rhapsody, Book One and Two

Fantasy and Science Fiction
A Ring for a Second Chance
But World Enough and Time

And I would be honored if you left a review for this and any of my books on GoodReads or any other retail site. It really helps.

CONNECT WITH ANNE LOUISE BANNON

Thank you for sticking it out this long! Please join my newsletter. It's the best way to stay up-to-date on my upcoming projects, blog posts and even games and giveaways.

Sign up here: http://eepurl.com/zH0Ab

Or connect with me on your favorite social media platforms:

Visit my website: http://annelouisebannon.com
Friend me on Facebook: http://facebook.com/RobinGoodfellowEnt
Follow me on Twitter: http://twitter.com/ALBannon
Favorite my Smashwords author page: https://www.smashwords.com/profile/view/MsBriscow
Connect on LinkedIn: http://www.linkedin.com/in/annelouisebannon
Follow me on Pinterest: http://pinterest.com/msbriscow

ABOUT ANNE LOUISE BANNON

Anne Louise Bannon is an author and journalist who wrote her first novel at age 15. Her journalistic work has appeared in Ladies' Home Journal, the Los Angeles Times, Wines and Vines, and in newspapers across the country. She was a TV critic for over 10 years, founded the YourFamilyViewer blog, and created the OddBallGrape.com wine education blog with her husband, Michael Holland. She is the co-author of Howdunit: Book of Poisons, with Serita Stevens, as well as author of the Freddie and Kathy mystery series, set in the 1920s, the Old Los Angeles series, set in 1870, and the Operation Quickline series, plus several stand alones. She and her husband live in Southern California with an assortment of critters.